PROOF OF LIFE

A BEYOND THE VEIL MYSTERY: BOOK 2

SHEILA LOWE

SUSPENSE PUBLISHING

PROOF OF LIFE
By
Sheila Lowe

PRINT EDITION

* * * * *

PUBLISHED BY:
Suspense Publishing

Copyright 2019 by Sheila Lowe

Cover Design: Shannon Raab
Cover Photographer: iStockphoto.com/ Rastan
Cover Photographer: MixPixBox

PUBLISHING HISTORY:
Suspense Publishing, Print and Digital Copy, May 2019

ISBN: 978-0578453156

DEDICATION

To my daughter, Jennifer Elizabeth Lowe, who has taught me so much about life after earth.

ACKNOWLEDGMENTS

I've only been studying the Afterlife seriously for a couple of years, but I've met many wonderful new friends through the Afterlife Research and Education Institute (AREI), where my beliefs about life after earth are continually re-affirmed. My grateful thanks go to Wendy Zammit, who, despite her incredibly busy schedule, read and corrected what I had written about the séance. To Lauren Mooney Bear for reading and commenting from a medium's point of view. To Tracey Bolton for the classes in mediumship that taught me how to open my mind, and for the friendship—you can't share this stuff with just anyone! To all the members of the Automatic Writing and Mediumship Zoom group—you know who you are—thanks for being so supportive. Another medium who deserves a Thank You is Christopher Meredith, for all the helpful readings over the years.

As always, my gratitude goes to Bob Joseph for being my first listener and never being afraid to tell me when I've got something wrong. After Bob, my manuscript goes to Ellen Larson, who has been my independent editor since 2007. Thank you, Ellen, for all the substantive guidance.

It's been a long time since I drove to Big Bear Lake in the snow, so I want to express appreciation for the Youtube videos and answers to my questions given by Nikkolas Amstadter of Big Bear Weather and More. To my beta readers, Rick Taylor, Nina Nelson, AJ Llewellyn, Becky Scott, Linda Green, SW Hubbard, and Pamela Asbury Smith. Apologies if I've left anyone out, it doesn't mean I appreciate you any less, I just have a sucky memory for where I wrote down your names. Last, but in no way least, thanks to Shannon Raab for the perfect cover, and to her and John Raab for publishing my books.

P.S. One of the characters in *Proof of Life* drives a Tesla. This was an homage to the scientist, Nicola Tesla, who, along with many other enthusiastic people in spirit, is working from the other side with Sonia Rinaldi at the North Station, helping to improve contact between those still on earth and those who have made the transition known as death.

PRAISE FOR SHEILA LOWE

"A wonderfully human voice, intense emotions, and a deep dive into the Afterlife. Lowe has created a brilliant backdrop in 'Proof of Life,' allowing readers to explore life-altering questions via the imminently likeable Jessica Mack."
   —K.J. Howe, International Bestselling Author of "Skyjack"

"The voices recovering amnesiac Jessica Mack hears compel her to search for a missing four-year-old boy, a quest that leads her to the doorway between life and the afterlife and challenges her beliefs on every level. This story rocks."
   —DP Lyle, Award-Winning Author of the *Jake Longly* and *Cain/Harper* Thriller Series

"A compassionate heroine bridges the divide between the spirit world and earthly evil in this well-paced thriller. 'Proof of Life' will keep readers flipping pages all night!"
   —S.W. Hubbard, Author of "Another Man's Treasure"

"Dealing with the expectations of dead crime victims takes a toll on Jessica Mack, until she encounters the one case where she must not fail. Highly recommended."
   —Barbara Petty, Author of the *Thea Browne Mystery* Series

"With 'Proof of Life,' Sheila Lowe continues her fascinating series that began with 'What She Saw,' where Jessica Mack's life was fractured in a terrible accident. Now, years later, she struggles to understand a gift she has been given, a gift that frightens her as she attempts to grasp its meaning in her life. 'Proof of Life'

is a heart-wrenching and heartwarming story that explores the universe beyond the veil, delving into the universal questions we all contemplate. I loved this book and couldn't put it down! I'm sure Jessica's story will take readers on a thrilling journey as she discovers new life and new love."
—Connie di Marco, Author of the *Zodiac Mysteries* and the *Soup Lovers' Mysteries*

"A delicious glimpse at what happens when the veil between the two worlds unexpectedly parts. I dare you to put this book down!"
—Suzanne Giesemann, Author of "Messages of Hope"
"AWESOME! I've already recommended it to friends."
—Joe Higgins, Amazon Bestselling Author, Medium, Spiritual Teacher and Intuitive Counselor

"Fiction can sometimes be a powerful and inspirational way to teach us about life and the afterlife. 'Proof of Life' celebrates this truth."
—Gary E. Schwartz, PhD, University of Arizona, Author of "The Afterlife Experiments"

"A brain injury, followed by a coma opens a door wide into the Spirit World. 'Proof of Life' will have you on the edge of your seat, late into the night as you discover we don't die."
—Sandra Champlain, Author of #1 International Bestseller "We Don't Die - A Skeptic's Discovery of Life After Death," and host of We Don't Die Radio

"As someone who is interested in the afterlife, NDEs and Mediums, I found that I wanted to find out what happens next, which lead me to read 'Proof of Life' in a day. Even without the spiritual elements, it is a great story with a fast moving plot and well-rounded characters. I highly recommend this book for anyone, if you already have an interest in spiritual matters, you will enjoy the portrayal of someone learning to be a Medium. If you currently don't have any interest in spiritual things, maybe this book will ignite a spark that will encourage you to learn more." (5 Stars)
—Andrew Rundle-Keswick, Soulful Books Blog

PROOF OF LIFE

SHEILA LOWE

Jessica Mack's head hit the windshield, killing her instantly.

Her spirit, detaching from her body, hovered above it for a short time before rising higher and higher above the cliff. High enough to see the driver of the eighteen-wheeler park his big rig on the shoulder of the highway and jump down from the cab, his yellow slicker a neon point of color in the night as he ran to the twisted guardrail and yelled down that help was coming.

The Camry had come to rest at the bottom of the steep canyon, a smoky plume drifting in defiance of the torrential rain over what was left of the engine compartment. The passenger side windshield where Jessica's head had connected was reduced to a spiderweb of glass mesh.

Through the moonless night, her eyes found her husband, full of alcohol and road rage, struggling up the steep cliff, clinging to the manzanita and scrub brush. Greg had been thrown clear when they hit the semi and the Camry went airborne, rolling over and over down the hillside.

Why wasn't he checking on her and Justin?

As her son's name entered her thoughts, a tunnel of brilliant white light opened in the heavens. His spirit, luminescent in the darkness, left the small body still strapped into its safety seat ten yards from the car and began to ascend.

Jessica tried to call out to him. *Wait for me.*

But like a dreamer whose voice fails to produce sound in the dream, her vocal cords were as unresponsive as the physical body she had left behind.

The tunnel grew and expanded, accepting her little boy into it, leaving his mother with a last glimpse of his face, radiant and beaming with joy.

As he disappeared from her sight, Jessica became aware of a shimmering presence, a majestic Being beside her, dressed in pure white robes and bathed in golden light as bright as the sun. Its features were indistinct, but she experienced the Being as masculine.

Are you an angel? Am I dead?

She sensed the Being smile with great tenderness as if her questions amused him. That he knew her completely, she had no doubt, and opened herself to the connection without reservation. No words were spoken. He touched her with his mind, impressing his thoughts upon her.

"You must go back."

But I don't want to. My baby is too young. He needs me.

"He will never leave you. At the proper time you will be together again."

She wanted to resist, to argue and insist that no one could care for her son the way she could. But within the deepest reaches of her soul, she knew that the Being spoke the truth, that her son would be protected and cherished, even though she was not there with him.

And so, for Justin's sake, Jessica made the most difficult decision of the thirty-two years she had existed upon the earth. She let her child go on without her.

In that moment, she felt herself enfolded in unconditional love more profound than anything she could have imagined. Glorious, incredible music entered her, permeating her very being. She *was* the music. She was the energy of every living thing: animals, plants, the elements.

There was nothing Jessica wanted more than to stay here, safe and infinitely cared for.

Without warning, as if she were cresting the tallest roller coaster on earth, then rocketing down the other side at breakneck speed, she found herself shocked back into her body. A body wracked with searing pain. A heart broken by the unspeakable loss of her son. And the utter wretchedness of being separated from the Light.

The whispers, quiet but incessant, started soon after Jessica awoke from a two-week coma.

For five years she had kept them at bay.

Now, they refused to be silenced any longer.

ONE

Ariel Anderson Arts on Main was one of several boutique galleries in downtown Ventura. Its high-ceilinged airiness and polished teak floor made it the one Jessica Mack loved best. She backed through the door, cradling a cardboard container the size of a cake box, and set it on the counter as carefully as if it contained the Crown Jewels.

Ariel's impatience to see what was inside was written in her body language. Without waiting for an invitation, she lifted the lid and removed the contents, beaming down at the miniature English garden cleverly housed in a vintage watch box.

"You've done it again," she said with a satisfied sigh. "It's *exquisite*. I already have a buyer who'll go crazy for this."

"I'm glad you like it," said Jessica, reminding herself that Ariel paid well, and the insurance money from the accident would not last forever. Still, the miniatures she created were infused with pieces of her soul. Relinquishing them always hurt like a bastard.

Sculpting the tangle of roses and hollyhocks that climbed the trellis arch had taken days. The wren perched on the rim of a sundial, hours more. Crocus, lavender, and heliotrope—each tiny flower was a work of art.

Ariel opened a drawer behind the counter and withdrew a large magnifying glass to inspect the miniature up close. "Look at that gown," she exclaimed.

The matchstick-sized Edwardian lady seated at a café table held a tea cup to her teeny-tiny lips. She was outfitted in a pink satin afternoon dress with a long, gold-colored lace jacket and wide-brimmed hat, an orange tabby at her slippered feet, begging for treats.

Each item had to be held with tweezers under the lens of a strong magnifier so Jessica could painstakingly paint the delicate roses and garlands around the edges of the tea service.

"How did you ever sew that lace?" asked Ariel.

Jessica smiled. "Very, very carefully."

"I adore the teapot. You painted it yourself, of course?"

"I did. And yes, I sculpted the cookies, too."

"They look so yummy. I can't imagine a more wonderful spot to sit and have tea than that garden. Jessica Mack, you are one talented artist. The check will be in the mail by Friday."

The sheer delight on Ariel's face made it the slightest bit less painful to leave the miniature behind. At least her art would be enjoyed by someone who appreciated it.

Jessica picked up her empty carry box. She started to say goodbye, but all at once her tongue was thick and sluggish, distorting the words that came out of her mouth.

Oh, no. Please not now.

"Jessica? Are you all right?" Ariel's voice came from miles away. "Hon? You're all pale; are you—"

Her hands were alien things attached to arms that refused to obey. The box clattered to the floor. A voice whispered in Jessica's head. *"My grandma. Tell her I'm here."*

Leave me alone.

Her vision was clouding over, growing rapidly darker. She knew Ariel was staring but there was no way she could explain…

The piercing whistle came next.

Leaving the box where it lay, Jessica whirled around and dashed across the gallery. She pushed past a startled customer entering the door. By the time she reached the Mini Cooper parked at the curb, the darkness that only she could see was almost complete. She fumbled the key fob from her jacket pocket and unlocked the driver door, collapsing into the seat.

Focus on the breath, Dr. Gold had taught her. Focus on the breath until the noise stops and vision returns.

Breathe in slowly to the count of four. Hold it. Out to the count of four.

Ninety seconds passed. She counted them, blessing silence when it fell, then checking in to make sure she still knew who she was.

The answer brought a flood of relief: *I'm Jessica Mack. I live in Ventura, California. I have an identical twin sister named Jenna Sparks. Breathe. In. Out.*

Two more minutes passed. Her body stopped its violent trembling. Her respirations slowed to normal. During those two minutes, Jessica could see Ariel and her customer, glancing repeatedly at the Mini through the gallery window. Probably talking about her weird behavior.

Before Arial could come out and ask what the problem was, Jessica fired up the engine and backed out of her parking space. The blackout episodes were a secret she had not shared with anyone, not even her twin. No way was she going to try and explain them to a client.

Dr. Gold called the episodes *syncope.* The word sounded almost romantic. But there was nothing romantic in blacking out at random. The blackouts used to happen rarely. Lately, it seemed to be exploding out of control.

Threading her way along busy Main Street, past the antique shops and thrift shops and restaurants, Jessica hooked a right at California, another at Harbor and turned left onto a quiet, tree-lined street. For once, parking at the beach was easy.

She was not ready to go home and face her fear of what was happening to her. Reaching over to the passenger seat, she snatched up the warm cable knit sweater she had brought and pulled it on.

The homeless folk who frequented the area were nowhere to be found on this cheerless day. *June gloom.* That's what Southern Californians called it when the hazy clouds formed a marine layer over the coast, hiding the sun until three o'clock in the afternoon. She had the promenade pretty much to herself.

Going north, she walked past the Crowne Plaza and the short row of condos beyond it. Along with the pier, the playground in the sand was closed today, no children swinging or climbing. Even the ground squirrels that acted like they owned the place were in hiding, waiting for better weather before they popped out of their burrows to forage among the boulders for peanuts and other treats.

Jessica began jogging toward Surfers Point. From time to time she paused for breath, leaning over the wall that separated the promenade from the beach. At high tide, the water rushed all the way up to the barrier, sending spray into the air. Lifting her face to meet the stinging drops that fell like rain, she took a perverse pleasure in the discomfort of the cold water on her hair and skin. Something to think about besides the whispers, and other thoughts she would sooner avoid.

Jenna—older by a mere ten minutes—was fond of chiding her: "I know there's nothing more painful, Jess. But you need to stop pretending it didn't happen. If only you could face the truth, I know it would get easier."

Face what truth? That it's been five years since my ex-husband's drunken road rage stole my son's life? Is that supposed to be some kind of milestone?

It was, in fact, a truth Jessica had been facing every day for one-thousand, eight-hundred and twenty-five of them. She wasn't pretending anything. What good did it do to memorialize the anniversary of the day Justin died—his birthday—when it was with her every minute of every day?

Jessica had emerged from a coma with questions that nobody wanted to answer. Of course, she knew. Impossible for a mother bereft of her child not to know that he was no longer breathing the same air; that the atoms and molecules that made up his physical form had ceased to exist.

Like too many drunks who cause fatal crashes, Justin's father, Gregory Mack, had suffered no significant injury. He was arrested on a DUI—not his first. In California, the maximum sentence for gross vehicular manslaughter while intoxicated was ten years. The trial judge, appalled by the reckless disregard for his family's lives, had brought down the gavel expressing her wish that she had the power to double it.

The day after she left the hospital, Jessica filed for divorce.

He wrote to her every few months even now, but nothing Greg

said could undo what he had done, give back the life he had taken with his rotten choices. If he expressed remorse or begged for her forgiveness, she did not know or care. She burned every jailhouse letter he sent, unopened.

The anniversaries were never easy, but this one was even more agonizing than the four that preceded it. *Five years.* Yes, it was a milestone. A milestone reflecting the misery that still lived in the cold, hard lump where her heart used to be.

She had given up trying to make Jenna understand, though it still galled her that her twin's compassion seemed to have limits. A few months after the accident, Jenna herself had survived a violent kidnapping. It was Jessica's belief that her sister was dead, compounded by the aftereffects of the head injury and coma, that had propelled Jessica into a terrifying period of retrograde amnesia. Over time, she regained most of her memory, but dying in the accident and coming back to life without her child had changed her fundamentally in ways that were beyond her ability to put into words.

And then, there were the whispers.

They had begun to plague her not long after she left the hospital. Brain scans and EEGs showed no abnormality, and until a few weeks ago, she had mostly succeeded in ignoring them. Millions of people with tinnitus heard strange noises day and night, she told herself. Maybe what she was hearing was a form of tinnitus. That the whispers were actual words and phrases, requests for help, which people with tinnitus did not hear, was beside the point.

The sporadic syncope episodes had also become an annoying fact of life, and usually happened when she was under stress. She had learned to accept that when her vision started to fade and her ears filled with a high-pitched, shrieky whine, if she waited it out, it would stop. The one at Arial's Gallery was different in quality and tone from what she was accustomed to. That shook her.

By the time she had jogged the mile to Surfer's Point, the tips of Jessica's ears were burning with cold and her face felt as though she had lain face down in a snowbank. Sinking onto one of the benches that lined the promenade, she pulled the neck of her sweater up over her nose and mouth, breathing into the wool.

Despite the foul weather, a dozen or so die-hard surfers were out riding their boards on the rough waves, looking like tasty shark snacks in their black wetsuits. The ocean, which on most days sparkled like diamonds on blue silk, was the color of a Brillo pad and matched Jessica's mood. She had slept poorly the night before, which was not unusual. Her dreams had been haunted by Justin. This should have been his seventh birthday.

She imagined him sitting beside her, bouncing up and down, excited by the surfers. She would have bought him a boogie board to get him started. He loved splashing in the ocean with her and Jen each taking a small hand and dangling him above the shoreline ripples, or paddling in a tide pool under their watchful eyes. She had been so careful to protect him from danger.

She should have protected him from the biggest danger of all—his father.

The perpetual self-recrimination was a bad habit. She knew it, but no one else was going to say that Justin's death was her fault, even if they secretly believed it. Reminding herself was a form of penance. For once, though, she did not want to hear it.

Jessica closed her eyes and listened to the soothing white noise of the ocean's steady roar, the whoosh of waves coming in to the shore and going out again. The soothing in and out, in and out. The tension began to melt from her shoulders...

...*The sun is a brilliant disk in a sky the same blue as Justin's eyes. Apart from one cottony puff that seems to follow two youngsters playing football, the day is cloudless. Shouting, kicking the ball to each other, having fun, they run down the field, coming closer. The taller of the two is an African American boy, the other is fair.*

The way the smaller boy moves, the way he laughs...She reaches out to him with her thoughts. Come over here. I need to see you.

The boy turns and runs toward her. His eyes, the same blue as the sky, are alight with mischief, his grin achingly familiar. But he's five years older now, growing up without her.

He calls out, "I'm fine, Mom, you don't have to worry about me," *then spins back around with a wave and kicks the ball to the other boy.*

Justin, come back.

Her son dissolves like sugar in water, leaving the other boy alone with her and her mangled heart.

She yearns for her child, but this other boy needs something from her. He drifts over and lifts his head for her to see…empty eye sockets, melting pink flesh, scarred and terrible like a creature from a horror film.

A strangled scream burst from her throat.

Jessica stared at the roiling ocean, dazed and confused. Where was the sunshine-drenched field? The two boys?

"Hey, hey, lady. You okay?"

She spun around. The man who had called out to her straddled his bicycle, untamed greying hair escaping from a short ponytail. No helmet. She noticed that. Despite the chilly temperature, he wore cargo shorts with a sweatshirt, and sandals. "Are you okay?" the man repeated.

What did he think she was going to do? Climb over the railing into the water and drown herself? Probably. To an onlooker, she must seem unhinged, standing there screaming at nothing anyone else could see. Mortified, Jessica tried to shake loose the horrific image of the boy in her vision, or whatever it was.

The man rested his bike on its kickstand and came around the bench to where she stood. "Want me to call 911?"

"Please don't. I'm fine," she lied. He did not need to know that her temples were throbbing, her stomach jumping summersaults.

He shook his head. "I hate to say it, lady, but you don't look fine. You ought to sit down, take it easy for a minute."

Wordlessly, Jessica followed his advice. Had she fallen asleep and had a nightmare? No. The boy with the melted face was real. He had died in a fire. Somehow, she knew it was true. Questions rolled like film credits:

Who was he?

Why was he with Justin?

Why did he show himself that way?

Will I see Justin again?

The man took a seat on the bench beside her. She was conscious of him speaking but her mind had room for nothing but the two boys. The shock of that ruined young face had launched her out of the vision before he could give the message he wanted her to hear.

How do you know there's a message?

I just do.

The snarky voice inside her was different from the whispers. This one had lived with her for most of her life, criticizing, nitpicking without mercy, always when she was at her most vulnerable.

Jessica turned to face the man whose kind, hazel eyes were worried.

"I'm fine," she assured him. "I just need to eat." As she said the words, she realized that they were true. She could not remember her last meal. Lunch, yesterday? Maybe. No wonder she was feeling spaced out.

"If you say so," the man said. He held out his hand. "I'm Jay,"

"Jessica."

His big paw closed around hers, soft and warm. "Nice to meet you, Jessica. Is there anything I can do to help?"

"No, nothing. But thank you for stopping. That was nice of you."

Jay gave her a friendly wink. "No problemo, senorita." He rose from the bench. "I suggest you get something warm inside you, the sooner the better."

Jessica got up, too. "I will. Thanks again."

Thus dismissed, Jay climbed back on his bicycle and pedaled away with a cheery wave.

Watching his broad back fade into the distance, tears welled in Jessica's eyes. Tears for the burned boy. Tears for Justin, who had taken her heart with him to the Afterlife. Tears for her own pitiful self, a young woman whose head was crowded with unwelcome voices and visions.

TWO

Dammit.

Jessica smacked the steering wheel with the side of her fist. She had forgotten the early morning text from Zach Smith, saying he would drop by after work. Now, fifteen minutes late, she was in no mood for company. Not that Zach exactly fit into that category.

The emotional exhaustion of the day dragged on her. It would be so easy to lay the seat back and just check out for a while. But if she didn't show up, he would come looking for her. She pulled around his silver Acura and parked on the driveway.

Her rented cottage stood behind a grey and white Victorian replica. There, she hid from the world and made art. Jessica pushed through the wooden gate, her mood lifting at the sight of the pocket-sized garden she had created. Pineapple sage, mint, rosemary, anemone, carnation, amaryllis, running riot along the path.

Therapy for the soul.

Zach, who had a talent for blending into the scenery when he had a mind to, materialized from the shadows of the jasmine arbor next to the front door. He was holding a pizza box and a grocery bag. The garlicky aroma made Jessica's stomach growl. Thanks to Zach, she was about to fulfill her promise to the man on the promenade and get something warm inside her. Maybe him coming over wasn't such a bad idea.

"I was gonna call out the cavalry," Zach said.

"You *are* the cavalry," she said, referring to his FBI Special Agent status. "Sorry I'm late."

"You forgot me again, didn't you?"

"I went for a walk at the beach."

"I guess you forgot your phone."

She dug for it in her pocket and checked the screen. Three text messages and a voicemail from Zach, two voicemails from her sister, Jenna. "Left it in the car," she said, unlocking the door.

He followed her inside. "How convenient."

Her workspace claimed a generous amount of space in the cottage. The worktable bore the tools of a miniaturist—dental tools for carving away the extra bits of clay and creating fine detail lines, loop tools for creating texture, a small rolling pin and cutting board, a strong magnifying lamp. Art supplies. Floor-to-ceiling shelves for sculpting clay, stacks of fabric squares, plastic bins filled with spools of thread, buttons, doll heads and limbs. Armatures that supported sculptures in progress—human and animal—in various stages of completion.

Zach unloaded a six-pack of Longboard Lager on the work top and flipped open the pizza box. "Extra cheese, olive and mushroom. No meat, the way you like it."

"Omigod, Zach, you are the best. Let me get some paper plates out."

"You look pretty wasted, little chick. You sit, I've got it handled."

Grateful to have him take over, Jessica plopped onto her favorite armchair, threw her legs over the side and watched him make himself at home. "You know what, Zach? You'd make some lucky woman a great wife."

He threw her the stink eye over his shoulder. "Why do I bother?" he said with feigned disgust.

"Because you're FBI Man to the rescue, and I'm starving."

He slapped a large slice of pizza on a paper plate and brought it over to her. "Here ya go."

She folded the slice in half and took a big bite, licking the melted cheese that dripped down with more enthusiasm than she had felt for food in weeks.

As soon as her mouth was full, Zach said, "We arrested Randy

Martin this morning."

Jessica froze mid-chew. For ten long seconds she did a fair imitation of a statue while the words hung between them like the smell of a rank piece of meat. She had relegated the Martin case to the back of her mind, not expecting it to come back and haunt her in a most literal way. The lump of pizza landed in her gut like a glutinous stone. She said nothing.

"You were right, Jess," Zach prompted. "It was the husband."

She didn't want to be right. Didn't want any part of it.

Two months earlier, twenty-five-year-old Hailey Martin had gone missing from Carpinteria, a small town forty miles north. Before the disappearance was made public, she had witnessed the young mother's death in a dream.

Except that in the dream, Jessica was the victim.

Jessica woke up choking and terrified. Like before, she was the passenger in a car, clinging to the armrest as they careened along a semi-rural road in the dark. This time, though, there were differences. No rain. No big rig ahead of them. And the car did not fly over the edge of a cliff.

This time, the man driving pulled over to the side of the road and strangled the life out of her.

For a while, Jessica convinced herself that she had conjured a nightmare about the accident; that her mind had constructed a symbol for what she had experienced five years ago. She dismissed the fact that the woman in the dream—younger, taller, round-faced, with short chestnut hair—looked nothing like her petite, slender, long blonde-haired self. That was the kind of thing that happened in dreams, she rationalized.

But the woman soon made it clear that she was no mere symbol.

She began to appear regularly, and with each appearance, showed more of her story and the brutal way it ended. Jessica would jerk awake, clutching her burning throat, gasping for air. And hovering near her bed, the apparition, not altogether material, a little hazy, would gaze at her, silently begging for justice.

It took five nights in a row of that treatment before Jessica was ready to acknowledge the fact that, unlike her own short visit to the Afterlife, the woman in the dream was *permanently* dead. No coming back to life on Earth for her.

After that, she did her best to stay awake and dodge the nightly visitations, sitting up, watching one TV show after another until darkness morphed into dawn when, exhausted, she could no longer distinguish between whether she was dreaming or awake.

On the sixth night, she was clicking through the channels, looking for a show that would keep her awake. She started to pass the flashing red and blue of a Breaking News Alert—they brought nothing but bad news—when something stopped her.

The news anchor in her neat pink suit was saying something about a missing woman. But Jessica could not hear past the *blah, blah, blah*. Splashed across the screen was the face of her spectral visitor and her name was Hailey Martin.

Jessica began to tremble. With every fiber of her being she wanted to be wrong. But more than simply believing that she was right, she *knew* she was.

A clear image of Zach popped into her head, and an insistent whisper that she had to let him know what she had seen.

No, I'm not going to call him.

"*Call him.*"

Zach was a pretty cool guy and a good friend, but he was an FBI agent. She could not count on him to take her seriously about something like this. Why should he? She had never had a predictive dream before. She wasn't psychic.

Was she?

The urging from Hailey Martin's spirit to call him went on and on until Jessica had no choice but to pick up the phone and tell him she could help locate the woman's body.

Zach laughed at her.

"You're screwing with me, right? When did you become psychic? Hey, how about giving me the winning lottery numbers?"

After all the sleepless nights and the anguish over what she had witnessed, his mocking tone infuriated her. "Do you want me to tell you where she is, or don't you?" she snapped.

"What's up with you, chick? I'm not going to use resources on some fool's errand because you're having nightmares. Are you okay?"

"Tell him again. My kids need to know."

Leave me alone, Hailey! Can't you see he won't listen?

"Tell him. Please. Tell him again."

No. I gave him the message. I'm done being your carrier pigeon. Find someone else.

Jessica, ignoring the woman in her head who was still begging for her help, spoke aloud. "Forget it, Zach. I've told you what she wanted you to know. Do what you want with the information."

"This is crazy, Jess. You never told me you saw ghosts."

"And I've never had a ghost make such a pest of herself that I needed to."

Days passed and no useful evidence developed, no clues to the missing woman's whereabouts. Eventually, when he ran out of investigative options, Zach showed up at the cottage, sheepishly asking about the woman who had visited her dreams.

The details Jessica delivered led to the discovery of Hailey Martin's decaying corpse. Her certainty that Hailey had been strangled and dumped on a deserted stretch of road between the towns of Ventura and Ojai never wavered. In fact, her information had been so specific and so accurate that had her brother-in-law, Roland Sparks, not been the supervising agent on the case, she might have been arrested as an accessory to murder.

"I know you want to hear what happened," Zach said again, draining his beer and going for another slice of pizza. "How we knew it was the grieving husband?"

Jessica got up, keeping her eyes averted from him, and dumped the rest of her food in the trash. He was wrong. She did not want to know.

"Jess?"

"Randy Martin," she said at last, knowing there was nothing she could do to stop him telling her anyway. "The husband."

Hailey had shown her the driver of the car she was riding in. The one piece of information she never shared was his name, or that the man, whose features Jessica had enumerated for Zach, was her husband.

"Randy's been banging one of the women who works at his car dealership," he said. "The minute we got her into the interview room, she started blabbing—and blubbering. She's just a dumbshit who made a stupid choice in boyfriends. She wasn't involved in the murder."

"Didn't this guy ever hear of divorce?"

"Millions at stake. Planned to keep all the money, greedy bastard. Now he'll have nothing. And get this—there was a life insurance policy that he claimed Hailey took out on herself six months before she was killed."

"And?"

"We had your handwriting expert friend take a look at it. Faster than the lab."

"You called Claudia?"

Zach nodded. "She says the signature on the policy is a forgery. She's prepared to testify that Hailey didn't write it, Randy did."

"Claudia's the best in the field."

"I'm sure you're right," he agreed, then snickered. "We won't be calling *you* to the witness stand. Think of how that would play—psychic chick leads FBI to—"

Jessica spun on him, her cheeks burning with indignation. "Not a joke, Zach. Do you think I wanted to watch her get strangled and not be able to do anything to help? Well, no, I didn't. And I definitely didn't want to *feel* it."

Zach raised his hands in defense. "Hey, chill. Nothing about this case is funny. Two kids got left without a mom and they're about to lose their dad, too. He's facing a nice long sentence, no parole. C'mon Jess, you know I'm grateful you helped us out. There's no way we would have found the body if it wasn't for you, but we can't let the public know. We'll call it an anonymous tip."

"Don't you get it, Zach? I don't *want* the public to know. You have no clue what Hailey went through. I do—his hands around her throat, squeezing the life out of that poor woman. I *never* want to experience that again. Ever."

Hearing her voice pitching higher, Jessica caught hold of herself. Zach would never understand if she told him that ever since the discovery of Hailey Martin's body, a portal had opened to another realm and she had been unable to close it.

Up until now, she had been able to pretty much ignore the whispers, but that had changed. As if her cooperating with

Hailey had given them permission, they crowded around her day and night, the spirit people—it seemed like dozens of them—whispering, whispering, whispering inside her head, chasing her wherever she went, wanting something from her. There were nights when she awoke to a shadowy presence hovering near her bed. Sometimes, she kept her eyes squeezed shut, just in case. And there were times, like now, when they were trying to get her attention, she could have clapped her hands over her ears and screamed at the top of her lungs to drown them out.

"Jess, you're shaking." Zach ambled over and folded her in his arms. For once, she let him. In this moment, all she wanted was to be taken care of and not listen to anonymous voices.

In her amnesia days, Zach had come close to losing his life, saving her and Jenna. The scar of a bullet wound on his throat was the permanent souvenir he carried of that time. For a short while, they had confused the emotion and drama for love. It was Jessica who had recognized that they made better friends than lovers, and ended the intimate relationship.

For the space of a few breaths, she leaned into his chest, allowing him to stroke her hair. His hands slid down her back, resting low on her hips. The next move would be to the futon bed.

"I'm pretty tired," she said, breaking the embrace. "Do you mind if we call it a night?"

She saw his disappointment, but she had worked hard to paint a strict line of demarcation separating what they'd had from the friendship that remained. She would have been a fool to believe they could return to where they once were. Not that she wanted to.

THREE

For once, Jessica was allowed to sleep uninterrupted. Or maybe she was so exhausted by the previous day's events that the spirits' entreaties did not reach deep enough to disturb her.

She awoke from the most vivid dream she had ever experienced. Justin, his seven-year-old self, was sitting cross-legged on the end of her bed, his face aglow as he chattered on about a friend named Mason. It was so real that her heart leapt with joy. Her eyes popped open, looking for him.

But there was no Justin. She would never see her boy in physical form again, bouncing happily on her bed.

After the beautiful dream, the gloomy early morning light depressed her. She wanted to bury her head under the pillow and throw herself a pity party, but self-indulgence of that kind was out of the question today. Jenna was picking her up in a half-hour.

Her sister had found two estate sales in Westlake Village. "No telling what treasures you might find if you get there early enough to beat the crowds," was Jenna's mantra. She was always on the lookout for bargain toys and little girl clothes—they outgrew them so fast, there was no point in buying expensive new ones. And most of the time there were bits and pieces for Jessica to use in her miniatures and shadowboxes.

With a wide yawn of resignation, she rolled out of bed. Her fee on the cold tile floor tempted her to dive back under the covers.

She pulled on a pair of thick socks and shuffled to the kitchenette hugging the comforter around her shoulders. Spooned coffee into the pot and waited, bleary-eyed, for the dark liquid to bubble into the carafe.

The dream image of Justin stayed with her, so intensely, undeniably real. Gazing out at the patio, she knew she would never stop longing for him, nor forgive herself for his death. Rain splattered against the window and rolled down the glass like tears.

Jessica moved around the small cottage, picking up clothes she had worn the day before, not much interested in what she wore to the estate sales. Since her preoccupation with the spirits, food had lost its appeal. The Levis she pulled on were loose enough that she had to buckle the belt in the last hole or risk them sliding right off her hips.

She picked at her neglected hair, which had grown wild and bushy. Dreadlocks could not be far away. Staring into the bathroom mirror, she thought of the kind man who had stopped his bike ride to offer help yesterday. Someone else with disorderly, "mad professor" hair. He had seemed truly worried about her. Strangers rarely took that much interest in someone they'd never met.

Taking care not to disturb Imelda in the Victorian, Jessica tiptoed past the front house at seven-thirty. Her peppery Castilian landlady would have plenty to say if her beauty sleep was interrupted by the toot of a horn before ten.

Jenna could always be counted on to be right on time. She was out front, idling in her Mazda when Jessica ran through the rain and climbed in.

"When did you get that coat?" she asked before Jessica had pulled the door shut.

Their teal blue hooded jackets were a perfect match, down to the gold-colored buttons.

"I bought it last weekend," said Jessica with a frown.

"Me, too. Shoot. I should have checked what you were wearing."

It was the twin thing. They were born mirror-images of each other. Despite growing up with personalities that were not at all alike, and having two widely divergent sets of opinions on most things, in some ways, they remained two halves of the same person. Coincidences, like buying the same jacket, were a commonplace occurrence.

You look anorexic," Jenna started in. "Have you been sick? Is that why you've been avoiding me for the past two months? Your face is so thin."

Jessica buckled herself in. "Good morning to you, too."

"You weren't all skinny like this at Christmas. What happened?"

Christmas. Before Hailey Martin and her entourage moved in.

"Nothing happened. I'm not sick. Weren't we going out to have fun?"

"We *are* going to have fun." Jenna kept her eyes on the road ahead, but Jessica sensed her probing like a scalpel-wielding surgeon slicing into her brain. While her twin prattled on, she was careful to keep her mind blank so there would be nothing for Jenna to pick up.

"You know how it is, Jess. You're my other half. If something's going on with you, I can't help but feel it."

"Of course I know, and everything's fine. I'd much rather hear what my nieces have been up to than have you give me the third degree."

Jenna huffed an exaggerated sigh of defeat. "Roland has the day off. It's father-daughter bonding day." At the stop sign on the corner, making sure there were no other drivers in sight, she plucked her phone from the dash and thumbed to a video of identical twin toddlers. They had inherited their father's rust-colored hair and green eyes, and their mother's pert nose and shy grin.

Jessica smiled at the screen. her heart swelling with love for her nieces. If she had a way to surround them with a big layer of protective padding, she would do it in a heartbeat. the sight of the two little girls perched on high kitchen stools side-by-side made her laugh. Wearing too-large aprons, sharing a mixing bowl, they mugged for the camera. One of them had chocolate cake batter smeared all over her face and held aloft a wooden spoon in a joyful salute.

"They still make Easy-Bake Ovens? Remember when we had one? Adventures in cooking."

Jenna grinned. "Omigod, did we make a mess. That's their favorite toy right now. Fritz the cat is getting tired of eating mini cupcakes."

"I bet Emma's the one with the chocolate mouth."

"Ha ha, how did you guess?"

"She's messy like me. Sophie's all prissy like you. She'd never let chocolate get on her face."

"You're such a mean girl." Jenna ended the video and returned the phone to its cradle.

"Were we that adorable when we were three?"

"We still are, doofus. Those two wear me out, but I wouldn't miss a minute. Well, maybe I would be okay with missing the cleanup after they bake."

"I miss them."

"You can come and see them anytime, Jess, you know that. Every time I've asked you over lately, you've been too busy."

Busy fending off dead people wanting my help.

It was time to stop letting the spirits push her around and arrange her life for her. "How about Sunday?" Jessica said with sudden inspiration. "I'll bring lunch."

Jenna's face brightened with anticipation. "It's been so long since Roland and I have gone anywhere. You could stay with the girls, we could go out for brunch. A win-win-win. I like it."

"You're gonna let me stay with them? You never let me babysit."

"I've been trying to protect you from those two little monsters."

"Duh. They can't be worse than we were. Remember the pranks you and I used to get up to?"

"Truth, sistah. Now, on to the first sale."

As they drove toward the 101, Jessica, after reciting the address, quoted from the Craigslist ad on her phone screen. "'Elderly woman, downsizing and moving to independent living facility. Collectible toys. Everything must go!' It's so pitiful, having to invite a pack of strangers over to paw through your mementoes and keepsakes. None of it *means* anything to anyone else. We're vultures, Jen."

"Except we almost always find stuff we can use, and whatever money we spend there will be helping the old lady. So, we're actually doing a good deed."

Thinking it over, Jessica grinned. "I like the way you think. The pragmatic twin."

The first sale took them to a World War II Craftsman house. A grandmother had passed on, leaving the kids to dispose of a wall covered in hand-painted plates, a cabinet that was more ornate than its collection of fake Fabergé eggs, an Encyclopedia Britannica set from the 1940s and 50s, a Lucille Ball figurine, and a kitchen filled with useless old pots and pans and mismatched dishes.

Grandma might have passed, but her annoying energy still loitered, nagging Jessica about the family's handling of her estate. With no intention of letting the heirs in on Grandma's disapproval, she hunted down Jenna, who was checking out Lucille Ball.

"There's nothing for us here," she said. "Let's go."

Jenna looked at her in surprise. "Can't you make a miniature out of some of those eggs?"

"No. They're junk. Can we leave now?"

"What's the big hurry, Jess? I think this Lucy is kinda cute, don't you? No? Okay, fine, let's go, then."

Jessica had been a little worried that Grandma would follow them, but to her relief, when they left the premises the spirit stayed behind. One less voice to add to the general background pandemonium.

The second sale, held in a five-thousand square foot mini-mansion, had more to interest them. Jenna wandered off on her own, leaving Jessica to pick through a basketful of sewing supplies and a pile of quilting squares that she could use for upholstery and clothing for her miniatures.

The rooms on the second floor were crammed with shelves and cabinets. It could have been turned into a Christmas store with its painted ceramic houses, reindeer and bears, little fir trees and snow globes. Jessica picked out some of the smallest trees, which she was visualizing in a winter scene.

Two of the six bedrooms were dedicated to dolls and their paraphernalia—hundreds of them—antique dolls, some dressed in national costumes from around the world. A Raggedy Ann and Andy sat together in a child-sized rocking chair. There were teddy bears of every size and type.

Jenna, a pair of gently-used Barbie dolls clutched to her chest, was in a room consumed by a village of dollhouses.

"Looks like Santa's workshop threw up," Jessica said, coming up behind her.

"I'd love to buy one of these old dollhouses but Roland would kill me if I came home with another one."

"Yeah, because your girls don't have enough toys, right?"

"I get the feeling those sly smiles are hiding some nasty secret vice," said Jenna at a shelf of vintage Kewpie dolls. "They're creeping me out. How about we pay up, then blow this joint?"

Jessica gave her a meaningful glance. "I thought you'd never ask."

They stopped for lunch at the local Mimi's Café.

The hostess at the lectern in the foyer did a double take when they walked in. The second looks and stares that followed them to their booth were nothing new. Both of them had answered the same questions countless times: What's it like to be around someone who looks exactly like you? Do you always know what the other person is thinking? Have you ever switched places? They had learned to overlook the glances, or give a pat comeback where one was warranted.

After the grey, drizzly day outside, the French restaurant was warm and redolent with the scent of freshly baked bread. They each ordered a bowl of corn chowder, then chatted about friends and movies and current events, nibbling on madeleines and buttered baguettes while waiting for their lunch to arrive.

There was no extended family to discuss. After graduating college, the twins had returned home long enough to pack up their belongings and say: "Thanks for raising us." Their adoptive parents' attitudes at the final farewell let them know that the relief to be done with each other was mutual. The girls were never abused. They viewed their upbringing as more a case of benign neglect. The last time they saw their parents was at Justin's funeral. Jessica was surprised they had showed up. Jenna must have let them know. To her great relief, they had begged off attending the reception afterwards. Some Very Important Function that was already scheduled blah blah blah.

Watching her sister talk animatedly about a bathroom

remodel that she and Roland were planning, her cheeks pink with contentment, Jessica was glad she had kept their date.

When it was time to pay, she pulled out some bills to cover the check. Jenna pushed them back and placed her debit card on the money tray. "This one's on me."

"But you drove."

"And you're bringing lunch and babysitting on Sunday. Remember?" Jenna's left eyebrow twitched. "Think you can handle those two imps on your own?"

A flood of unexpected resentment took Jessica's breath away. She knew that anger had flashed on her face, but it was better than shouting, *do you think I don't know how to handle children? I was a mother long before you were.*

As if reading her thoughts, Jenna gave a small gasp. She reached over and grabbed Jessica's hand. "I didn't mean it like that; you were a great mom. And I didn't forget Justin's birthday yesterday. I called, but you didn't pick up."

Jessica immediately forgave her. "I know. I got your messages. I went to the beach and then Zach came over with pizza."

"Oh, Zach. Is that it?" Jenna slid the plastic money tray to the edge of the table and signaled their waitress. "Are you two a 'thing' again?"

"No. We hang out once in a while. We're just friends."

"Really." Jenna managed to put a lot of skepticism into that one word. "C'mon, Jess, you aren't fooling me for a minute. I know something's up. You've canceled on me twice. You never call me anymore. You don't even return my calls half the time. Now, you know I'm gonna keep buggin' 'til you tell me the truth. If you're back with Zach, you can say so. I won't judge you for it."

Jessica stared down at her empty soup bowl. If only it was as simple as re-starting her relationship with Zach. That would have been easy to explain. The truth was anything but simple or easy.

Was unburdening herself to Jenna the wise course to take? They might share a physical appearance, but there the similarity ended. Jessica was the free-thinking liberal. Her twin was pragmatic and conservative in her ideals, her politics, and her religious views. What would she say about her sister talking to the dead?

Jessica busied herself stacking her bowl and utensils, brushing the breadcrumbs that had scattered on the table into a neat pile, all the while silently begging her twin not to push her. They had always joked about being womb-mates, an unbreakable bond. In her amnestic fugue state, Jessica had unwittingly assumed her sister's identity. Jenna was all she had.

She opened her mouth to speak, then closed it again, delaying the inevitable. A strong intuition told her that if she laid her cards on the table, a chasm would open between them as inevitably as if she did not. She was screwed either way. Her heart sank at what she read in her twin's unflinching gaze: they had reached a brink and it was time for her to make the leap.

"C'mon, Jess," Jenna prodded. "Are you gonna tell me what's going on, or not?"

After the weeks of holding her secret so close to her chest, bringing it into the open seemed impossible. Like prying open a tin can with her fingernails.

Jessica sucked in a breath, then lobbed the hand grenade onto the table between them.

"Does the name Hailey Martin mean anything to you?"

"Sounds familiar. Who—" Jenna broke off, a puzzled frown creasing her brow. "Wait, that's the woman who was killed by her husband?"

"Yes, that's her." Jessica hesitated. "Roland doesn't talk to you about his cases, does he?"

"No. He's always kept the gruesome stuff away from us. He doesn't want it contaminating his family. And tell me why we're talking about this?"

Jessica drew another deep breath and blew it out. "I helped them find her body."

"You *what*?" Jenna's mouth gaped open like a fish on the line. "I'm gonna need you to explain what the heck you're talking about."

So, Jessica let the story rush out, beginning with the first dream where Hailey appeared, going on to what the dead woman had gradually revealed about her murder. She told how she had contacted Zach with the information, and the involvement of Jenna's husband Roland Sparks, who was Zach's supervisor. When she came to the FBI's discovery of the body precisely where she had predicted, her sister stared back at her, her mouth slightly agape again.

Jessica paused to give her space to respond and when she did not, launched into her tale of spirit beings taking up residence in her head, topped off with an explanation of Justin growing into a seven-year-old in the other world.

"*Five years?*" Jenna's throat worked with emotion. She seemed more upset that Jessica had kept important information from her than the fact of the spirit communications. "You've been hearing voices for *five years* and you *never* told me?"

"I tried to in the beginning? Don't you remember? You never wanted to talk about it. You always changed the subject, so I stopped mentioning it."

"No, I don't remember that. You were so crushed about losing Justin, and then there was the amnesia—"

"As long as the voices stayed in the background, I could handle it. Everything changed with Hailey."

Jenna's mouth twisted into an angry pucker. "Dammit, Jess, I *knew* my head was messed up when it shouldn't be. I should have known it was *you.*"

"What the hell's that supposed to mean?"

"Think about it. If there's no good reason for me to be all buzzy, it's got to belong to you."

"That works both ways," Jessica retorted, stung. What she really wanted to say—the go-to excuse she gave her sister when she was being uncharacteristically nasty—was that the mood control chip that had been implanted in her brain when she was kidnapped, and which the doctors said could not be removed—was a more likely cause for her "buzzyness" than anything Jessica might have contributed.

Jenna glanced around the busy café. She stared at her twin as if she were a bug under a magnifying glass. A big, ugly, scary bug. "Are you hearing them now, the voices?" she asked, lowering her voice.

"They're quiet, but yeah, they're here."

They're always here.

"Do you *see* things, too? I mean, since that woman who was killed."

Jessica picked up her cup and gulped coffee, which had grown cold and bitter. Anything to distract from her sister's expression of distaste. Where was the waitress? She hadn't been by their table with a fresh pot in a while. She was nowhere to be seen. With a sigh, Jessica gave up.

"Sometimes I catch a glimpse of someone that I know isn't—well, isn't alive."

Now Jenna set her lips in a tight, disapproving line. Had she always used her mouth to express disapproval as she kept doing today? "How do you know?"

"How do I know they're spirit and not human? Uh—I can usually see through them."

Usually. But not always. To Jessica's chagrin, on two recent occasions, she had discovered that the person she was speaking with was visible to no one other than her. If she told her sister that those glimpses were growing more frequent, the shadowy figures becoming more distinct, more insistent, Jenna would have a fit.

Telling her had been a mistake. She should have kept her secret to herself.

"What are they saying?" Jenna pressed. Despite her promise not to judge, the tension in her body language shouted 'judgment' loud and clear.

"What do you mean?"

"You said they were here right now, didn't you? So, what are they saying?"

Jessica jerked her chin in the direction of their waitress, who was taking an order at the next table and ignoring her need for fresh coffee. "Don't look, but our waitress's mother wants me to get her attention."

"Why?"

Jessica closed her eyes and breathed deeply, tuning in to the mother in spirit whose voice was louder, more insistent than the rest. As she listened, the restaurant noise faded away. When she got the message, she opened her eyes. "She wants her daughter to know she's sorry she was a rotten mom."

Jenna made a scoffing *pfff* sound with her lips. "Are you sure? Sounds more like wishful thinking about *our* mother."

"*Yes,* I'm sure."

"So, are you going to tell her?"

"Tell the waitress? No frigging way am I walking up to a stranger like I'm the Long Island Medium and telling her that her dead mom is hanging around."

"Why not? Maybe she'd be happy to hear it."

"And maybe she wouldn't."

"You won't know unless you try."

"Why are you goading me, Jen? You don't know what you're talking about."

"No, I don't, thank God, and I don't want to."

"Look, I tried that once and got shot down. No way am I chancing that happening again."

Jenna's eyes widened. "What happened?"

Jessica felt her chest tighten with anxiety at the memory. "It was around the time it all started to ramp up, six or seven weeks ago. I was in the checkout line buying groceries at Sprouts. The father of the guy ahead of me started *begging* me to tell his son that he was there."

"His father?" Jenna looked confused.

"His father in spirit. I tried to brush it off, but he wouldn't stop nagging. So, finally, I did it."

"You did? What did you say to him?"

"I said something like, 'Excuse me. I realize this sounds kind of weird, but your father wants me to give you a message.'"

"And?" Jenna leaned toward her, avid, despite her earlier annoyance, eager to hear.

"His eyes got all bulgy. His face was so red I thought he was gonna have a stroke. The way he was looking at me—Oh. My. God. It was *so* scary. He didn't say anything, he just looked kinda crazy and stormed out of the store. He was waiting outside and he followed me all the way to my car, screaming at me the whole time. Everyone in the parking lot was watching. It was awful."

"Well, what was he screaming?"

"What was he screaming? 'Who the hell are you? What the fuck do you want from my life? My old man's dead and I pissed on his grave.'"

Jenna was giving her that dead fish gape again. "Omigod, he said that?"

"Every word is etched in my brain. I totally expected him to hit me." Jessica shrugged. "I guess he hated the guy so much he didn't want his apology. So, no, I'm not about to march up to that waitress and tell her that her dead mother is sorry."

"There must be a load of dead people who have something to say."

"Yeah, and half of them seem to be living in my brain."

At that moment, the waitress stopped by and picked up the money tray. She didn't offer a coffee refill, but she must have wondered why Jenna stared at her the way she did.

"You said you saw the doctor," Jenna said, once the woman was out of earshot. "Did you get checked out *thoroughly?*"

"Yes, thoroughly. I told you, the neurosurgeon ordered a brain scan. Everything was clear. No tumor; nothing."

"You should get a second opinion, maybe a third."

"Why? You didn't complain about my doctor when I was in a coma; or later, when I didn't remember who I was. You didn't think I needed a second opinion then."

"Coma and amnesia aren't the same as—as *this*. What about Dr. Gold? What does he say?"

Jessica faltered at the mention of her therapist. "I haven't told him yet."

The exasperated glare Jenna gave her was one she might turn on one of her misbehaving daughters. When she acted that way it made Jessica want to disappear. Or yell at her. Yelling in the restaurant was a bad idea but it would feel so good to let off some steam that way.

"Don't you think that's kind of important information you should be sharing with him?" said Jenna.

"I'll tell him, okay? I just haven't seen him in a while."

"Well, I think you should make an appointment. Like, right now."

"I'm not schizophrenic, if that's what you're thinking. I'm *not* crazy. It's not *those* kinds of voices."

"I'm not saying you're *crazy*." Jenna began tearing her paper napkin into long strips, measuring each against the other to make sure they were the same length. Then she tore each strip into a half-dozen more pieces. For at least half a minute, she studied the pile of confetti she had made before looking up. When she did, her gaze landed somewhere beyond Jessica's shoulder.

"It's just that—well, communing with the dead sounds to me like a really bad idea."

"*Communing?* Is that what you think I'm doing? What the hell are you saying?"

"It totally makes sense to me now, that you're looking so—so frail. You have dark circles under your eyes, too. I'm worried about you, Jess."

The temptation to start yelling was working its way to the front of the line. "There's *nothing* for you to worry about," Jessica said emphatically, again regretting having made this confession.

"You think you have dead people hounding you night and day, and there's nothing to worry about?"

"I *think* I have…?"

"Whatever. I think—"

"I'll *deal* with it, Jen."

"You can't *deal* with evil spirits."

"What the—? There's nothing evil about them. They're not scary, they're annoying."

Jenna swept her pile of napkin shreds onto a plate and avoided Jessica's eyes. "Still. About Sunday. I think you'd better 'deal with it' before I let you stay with my girls."

Jessica blinked at the gut punch her twin had just delivered. "Did you really just say that?"

"Wait, Jess. It's—"

"Wait for what? You're afraid to leave your kids with me? That's all I need to know."

It was not merely her twin's attitude that cut Jessica to the quick. The worst part was the fear in Jenna's eyes when she looked at her—the belief that her children needed to be protected from their aunt. She was acutely aware of the words that her sister left unspoken: the belief that she was possessed.

Jessica slid out of the booth. "Take me home."

"Wait, Jess, stop!"

With the faint hope that Jenna had thought better of what she'd said, Jessica turned around. "What?"

"Why can't you at least try to understand—"

Of course, she hadn't thought better of it. She was digging in.

"No," Jessica said. "*You* try to understand. I'm the same person I've always been."

"No, you're not."

Without another word, Jessica turned on her heel and strode out of the restaurant.

FOUR

Jenna jacked up the car radio too loud for conversation, leaving a stony silence between them on the way back to the cottage.

Jessica spent the time erecting a mental barrier, a force field designed to prevent her twin from accessing her thoughts. They had perfected the skill as teens, when identical twinhood had made the need for privacy an all-important issue.

Almost before the vehicle came to a stop, she jumped out and slammed the car door without a goodbye. She let herself inside the cottage, still fuming, and changed into sweats, turned on the oven for heat, and zapped the leftover coffee from this morning. If Jenna didn't have such a big stick up her ass, maybe she could open her eyes long enough to see that Jessica had not asked to be plagued by spirits lining up with their whispers, wanting her to do their bidding.

She did some stomping and throwing things around until she ran out of steam and realized that the tantrum had not made her feel any better. Throwing herself into an art project was the better solution.

Some of Jessica's earliest memories involved finger painting and Play-Doh. The olfactory memory of the musky odor from those cans still had the power to make her smile. It was Jenna who had been most interested in their family of baby dolls, dressing and arranging them in their carriage, explaining that she was their mother and she loved them very much. Not much had changed since then.

Her anger over her sister's judgments about the spirit voices was a waste of time and energy. Jessica perched on the stool at her worktable determined not to spend another minute on them and switched on the desk lamp.

She plucked the dust cover from the life-sized bust of a German Shepherd she had been working on and brought the armature closer to her, inspecting it to see what more needed to be done. The sculpture, commissioned by her friends, Claudia Rose and her LAPD detective husband, Joel Jovanic, was an extra-special project. The couple had played a vital role in helping Jessica recover her lost past when she'd had too few places to turn. She gave her all to every piece of art she created, but she wanted this sculpture to be perfect for them. Plus, completing it would keep her mind occupied long enough to cool off her anger at Jenna.

Jessica ran a critical eye over the life-sized head of the handsome German Shepherd. She spent a few minutes gazing at the photo Claudia had sent of the real-life dog, Flare. The ears were not quite right yet. Softening her focus, she waited for the creative side of her brain to take over and tell her what was needed.

When she was ready, she set about tweaking and adjusting, making minute corrections. She could practically feel Flare's wet muzzle pushing her hand, making sure she got it right. Once she was satisfied that the head was cocked to the perfect angle, the ears pricked up as if listening for a command, she painted the golden-brown eyes.

Hunched over the sculpture absorbed in what she was doing, Jessica worked straight through to mid-evening. Ignoring the ache in her neck and shoulders, she kept going until she was confident that the same intelligent curiosity radiated from the sculpture as the dog in the photograph. Even the voices faded into the background. Finally, she released a long breath of satisfaction.

Climbing off her work stool, she stretched, surprised to realize that aside from the pool of light on her worktable, the cottage was dark. Her phone showed the time at just past eight o'clock.

Was she imagining a soft whine for attention?

"Why not a spirit dog?" Jessica said to the Shepherd bust. "Join the crowd. But I'm not telling Claudia. She'd think I've totally lost it for sure."

The phone rang right then, startling her. As if speaking the name had summoned her, Claudia was calling.

"Great timing," said Jessica. "Flare is just about ready to go."

"That's awesome. I must be psychic."

"You must be. I'm sure the fact that I promised to have it by this weekend doesn't have anything to do with it."

"Of course not," Claudia chuckled. "I'm gonna love it."

"You haven't seen it yet."

"I know your work, silly girl. I have zero doubt that it looks *exactly* like the photo I sent you."

Flushing with pleasure at the compliment, Jessica said, "Please tell your neighbor that I'm sorry for her loss. I get the impression you loved Flare as much as she did, even though it was her dog."

"Thanks, Jess, you're right. Flare was a sweet, old dog." Claudia's voice was wistful. "In her younger days there was no fiercer protector. That's why I want this sculpture. She saved my life a few years ago."

"Seriously? What happened?"

"It's kind of a long story. I'll tell you about it sometime."

"I can't wait to hear it. For now, how would you like me to send it to you? FedEx?"

"As it happens, I have a friend driving down here from Ojai on Saturday afternoon. If it's okay with you, I'll have him drop by and pick it up. You're not all that far out of his way."

"Of course. What time?"

"How's three o'clock?"

"I'll be here."

"Great. His name is Sage Boles."

Jessica scribbled the name on her calendar. "I'll have it packed up and ready for him."

"I'm so excited to see it!"

They ended the call. Jessica found a box and packed up the bust. With Claudia's friend picking it up, there was no need for a label. With the task out of the way, she realized she was famished and zapped a slice of leftover pizza from the refrigerator. While she waited for the ding, she guzzled half a Longboard. The beer hit her empty stomach fast and hard, making the thought of pizza less appealing.

What do you expect? You never eat right.

The one positive thing Jessica had to say about that snarky voice was that it did not come from the dead people. It had resided within her mind for as far back as she could remember, relentlessly nagging and complaining, reliably showing up to carp at her when she was tired or vulnerable.

There was one less voice from the spirit world knocking at the door of her mind with their ceaseless requests. Ever since Hailey Martin's body had been recovered, she no longer showed up to badger her. Hopefully, she had gone on to the light, or whatever she was supposed to do next.

Jessica stretched out on the futon bed and wrapped herself in the warm comforter, ready for a break after the long hours of work. Within seconds she had fallen into a sound sleep.

She awoke close to midnight. Rain pelting the roof again. Even in her sleep, the argument with Jenna had been looping in her brain. How could identical twins be such different people? She had asked herself that question many times. They shared the same DNA. They had shared the same uterus for nine months, they had come from the same egg, for crying out loud.

Of course they'd had spats that sometimes got physical when they were younger, but they had always made up and laughed about it later. She could not remember any argument that had left her as miserable as this one. *Seriously?* Her sister believed she was *possessed*?

Why couldn't Jenna be on her side? She had asked for the facts with a closed mind and judged Jessica without hearing her.

If only she could retreat back into sleep instead of lying in her dark little cottage. Lying there, listening to the wind whistling eerily through unseen cracks, trying to tune out the furious thoughts, the images rushing through her brain, the more awake Jessica became.

Then the whispers turned up the volume. As usual, they were pleading for her help and there was nothing she knew to do to help them. Hailey Martin had made very clear what she needed. These other voices were like a radio station fading in and out.

Even if she had been inclined to do their bidding, not enough information came through for her to follow up. Hailey must have been an unusually strong spirit to communicate the way she had.

The constant noise was driving her crazy, but there was no place to go. She pulled up a Queen album on her phone and tapped the sound up as high as it would go, then put her pillow over her head. Still, the low whispers persisted. Was it her imagination or were the voices extra-loud tonight? A discordant symphony that made her wonder whether she *was* crazy. Or possessed.

Thanks, Jenna.

After an hour of fighting it, Jessica gave up on sleep. She got up and brewed a fresh pot of coffee. Her stomach was growling but the fridge was as empty as it had been when she went to bed. A trip to the grocery store was definitely on the horizon. In the meantime, she resorted to re-heating the slice of pizza she had left in the microwave earlier. The chewy cardboard crust and gummy cheese were hard to stomach. She told herself that she needed a new project for distraction.

She washed the grease off her fingers and logged into her Etsy account, glad to find a new order waiting in her in-box. It came from a mother who wanted her to make a custom shadowbox for her eight-year-old daughter. She had described down to the tiniest detail what she wanted done: the model for "a perfect fantasy princess bedroom."

Obviously, the fantasy was the mother's own and she was foisting it on her daughter, Jessica concluded grumpily with no basis. Then she reminded herself that just because *she* would never choose that icky marshmallowy pinkiness, it didn't mean that the child wouldn't love it. In fact, she decided defiantly, she would create the best damn shadowbox in the whole world and make sure the little girl was happy with it.

Still, she thought as she sketched out the room, if she had a daughter, this was not what she would choose for her. Not even Jenna would put her twins in a room this sweety-sweet.

Sour grapes, Jess.

You can't replace love with a stupid room.

She should know. When they were eight years old, the room she and Jenna shared could have been a children's TV show set.

Their mother, Lorraine, knew all the "right people." she created the perfect place to display her adorable twins and impress her café society friends. The girls were never allowed to make a mess, so it wasn't much fun to play there.

Despite the noise in her head, the cottage was too quiet. Shaking off the unhappy memories, Jessica scrolled through the music on her laptop for a UB40 album. The staccato off-beats of Reggae seemed to do a better job of muffling the whispers than some other genres.

With *Red Red Wine* playing in the background, she rummaged through her supplies and decided on a 12 x 12 wooden frame for the display case. The bed and café table and chair she would cut from small rectangles of hard foam. Striped sateen pink and white rectangles would be turned into the bed cover.

She added other items she would need, a lump of modeling clay and her sculpting tools, then made notes based on the email: *Tufted canopy bed, pillows, bedspread. Shabby chic night stand, café table and chairs. Loveseat. Pink shaggy rug. Plush animals. Bookshelf, books.* Anything else, she would add along the way.

Starting with the itsy-bitsy bed, she carved the Styrofoam with an X-acto knife into a neat rectangle. Next, she formed a length of thin wire to make the canopy frame. Soon, she was engrossed in the task, singing along with Gregory Isaacs. *Night Nurse.*

Oh, the pain it's getting worse…I don't wanna see no doc. I need attendance from my nurse around the clock…

Threading a fine needle, she sewed a tiny pink pillowcase with what had to be the smallest stitches in the world, and stuffed it with tufts of cotton from a swab. She thought of her nieces with a thrum of renewed anger at her sister. She would have loved to show them what she was making, but Jenna had decided she was demon-possessed, so she didn't get to. It infuriated her. Most little girls would be enthralled to see the sateen bedspread she had just hemmed, and the tablecloth for the little round table.

Jessica sewed until the music ran out, concentrating on keeping the stitches in a straight row and tamping her emotions back down where her sister's comments could no longer hurt her. She had been at it for a couple of hours when her vision began to blur. She reached up to rub her eyes. Her hands and feet began to tingle.

Was she having an episode? If so, it was unlike any of the others. She looked around for her phone, then remembered that she could not call Jenna. Who, then? Zach? Dr. Gold? Claudia? And disturb them in the middle of the night, for what? She would never ask them to come and take care of her.

Something was happening to her vision. Wavy lines hovered at the edges of her line of sight, bending the light oddly, so that it seemed as if she was under water.

Then the lamp flickered. Off/on. Off/on. Off/on. The pace of her breathing picked up. What was happening?

Was it the wind, wreaking havoc with the electricity? Jessica shivered. She should climb back into bed and hide under the warmth of the comforter, pretend that her head wasn't humming with dead people's thoughts.

An ice-cold breeze blew straight through her. She leapt up, poised to run.

But Jessica did not run. She found herself paralyzed by a loud shriek that swelled to an agonized scream.

HELP ME!

FIVE

The ear-piercing chorus of birds whooping it up roused her to consciousness. Jessica stared at her surroundings, struggling for meaning. Why was she standing in waterlogged grass in a cold, silvery dawn, shivering violently, hair and clothing soaked through?

Omigod. How long have I been here?

In her experience, finding herself in a strange place and not knowing how she got there equated with amnesia. The realization that *this* time she was in her own backyard came with a small burst of relief. She stumbled to the back door of the cottage and opened it with a whimper of gratitude. It would have been awful to find it locked and have to find some way to explain, cold and wet, to Imelda that she needed a spare key.

Jessica ducked inside, skating on the thin edge of hysteria. She locked the deadbolt on the back door, then double-checked it to make sure it was secure. Then she hurried to check the front door, too, her sodden socks leaving a trail like snail slime on the tile as she struggled to remember how she had come to be outside.

As though a thick black curtain had dropped down over her brain, nothing seemed to penetrate but the cold, hard fact that she had been out there, rather than snug inside the cottage.

Am I losing my memory again?

As if to protect herself from that terrifying thought, Jessica locked herself in the bathroom. Her teeth were chattering, partly due to standing outside in the cold and rain, partly from her tangled nerves. She turned on the hot water full blast and peeled out of her wet clothes, dropping them to the floor in a heap.

She stepped under the shower head, and as she turned around and around, letting hot water soak every part of her until her skin stung, a Joyce Kilmer poem drifted into her head.

A tree that may in Summer wear a nest of robins in her hair;
Upon whose bosom snow has lain, who intimately lives with rain.

She almost smiled. Left matted and tangled by the rain—with which she had become intimately familiar—her hair was pretty much a bird's nest.

She was so tired. The simplest act of reaching for the shampoo bottle seemed an impossible task.

Why was I on the patio?

Squeeze a dab into your palms. Massage it into your hair. Come on, just do it.

The black curtain opened a crack.

It had been well past midnight; she remembered that much. She was at her desk, working on the shadowbox. That icky sweet miniature bedroom. Stitching the bedspread for the miniature. She'd felt strange. The light had flickered on and off. After that, nothing.

Why was I outside? What's happening to me?

Amnesia had long ago acquainted her with that frustrating condition of questions with no answers.

Even after the tank was empty, the water running cool, the shivers would not stop. Fear had seeped into her marrow, settled in her soul and left her chilled to the bone. Jessica wrapped herself in a plush, terry cloth bath sheet and dried her hair, an awful suspicion taking hold that she might never feel warm again.

The voices were whispering:

"Tell my kids I'm okay."

"Let my dad know I'm with his mom."

"Grandma wants Josie to have her ring."

On and on, an endless thread.

How can I help any of you when I can't help myself? She wanted to scream. But what good would screaming do when the voices lived inside her mind? Bitter tears spilled over and wet her cheeks. Ever since the accident, her entire life had spun out of her control.

Goddamn you, Greg Mack.

Goddamn me.

The temptation to crawl into bed and pull the covers over her head was getting stronger by the minute.

Oh, poor baby, throw yourself a pity party, why don't you?

Why don't you shut the hell up?

Spirit voices, judgy voices, she was sick of them all.

Wearing her heaviest fleece sweats, a sweater coat and two pairs of socks, Jessica curled up in her armchair under a blanket with a mug of strong black coffee.

Until now, the episodes had taken no more than a minute or two to complete and she had always retained *some* understanding of what was happening to her. Never, since getting her memory back after amnesia, had she lost so much time in one episode. What was causing the change?

She thought long and hard about her situation. By the time the mug was empty she had reached a decision. She had lived through worse. Whatever was happening, it was not going to defeat her.

And with that, she began to feel almost human again.

A sudden loud knocking on the front door vibrated along her nerves like a broken violin string. It came again, insistent, urgent, before she managed to cross the room. Who would be knocking at seven a.m.? It was unlikely to be someone selling the *Watchtower*.

"Who is it?" she called out, unwilling to face whoever was on the other side of the door.

"Open the door, Jess, it's me."

Zach Smith.

Jessica opened the door with a scowl darkening her face. She did not want to see Zach. Didn't want to talk to anyone until she got her head sorted out. "Why are you here?" she asked bluntly.

Ignoring her curt tone, he strode past her. He wore a heavy Pendleton jacket and a watch cap pulled low. The scruffy stubble darkening the lower half of his face had not seen a razor in a day or two. He looked more like a burglar than a special agent for the FBI.

"You're okay?" he asked.

Jessica shut the door and faced him with her arms folded

across her chest. "I'm fine," she snapped. "Why?"

"Jenna's freaking out. She thinks something happened to you."

Jenna. Her anti-twin shields had not held up well enough. The last thing she needed was for her nighttime excursion to the patio to get back to her twin's ears. If Jenna was freaking now, how would she react to hearing about the latest episode?

Jessica gave an elaborate yawn to give Zach the impression that he had woken her. "Why would she say that?"

"You're asking the wrong person. Call your sister."

"Shouldn't have drunk that beer on an empty stomach last night. I've been sleeping it off."

Zach took off his jacket and draped it over a kitchen chair. "Why is it so hot in here?"

"I was cold. I turned the heater up. Do you mind?"

His suspicious FBI eyes darted around as if he suspected someone of hiding in the cottage.

"You really oughta answer your phone, Jess."

"Forgot to charge it. You look beat. Go home."

"I *am* beat. And I was *on* my way home, but when my boss's wife calls and wants a welfare check on her twin—"

"As you can see, I don't need a welfare check." He looked so tired, she felt bad for being harsh. Resigning herself to the fact that he wasn't going anywhere until he had convinced himself that she was telling the truth, Jessica relented. "I made some coffee. Want some?"

"Sure; I'll get it."

"No, let me. It's the least I can do. Why don't you take it easy?"

The thing was, Zach did not know *how* to take it easy. He had told her once that he'd had ADD as a kid. She thought he still did. While she set about washing a mug and filling it, he prowled restlessly, his long, slender limbs like a daddy long legs, always on the move.

When Jessica turned with the mug in hand, Zach was standing at her worktable, his attention was on the shadowbox she had been working on before last night's episode. Since her early morning foray onto the patio, she had avoided her worktable as if *it* was the cause of her problems. What had happened was too weird and frightening.

"That's not exactly the décor *I* would have chosen," she said. "It's what the client—" The look he turned on her stunned her into silence. Shock and anger seemed to be at war on his face.

"What the *fuck*, Jess?"

"What's wrong?"

"I don't even know what to say." His gaze roamed back and forth between her and the shadowbox on her worktable as if seeing her through new eyes. "How the *fuck* did you know—"

"I don't know what you you're talking about. What the hell is wrong?"

He flicked an angry hand at her creation. "Are you fucking kidding me?"

Jessica couldn't help staring at him. Zach was the most laid-back person she knew, but the energy bristling off him now was making her nervous. It reminded her of her ex-husband. A sour feeling in the pit of her stomach told her that whatever had set off his anger was going to hurt her. She set the mug back on the kitchen counter and joined him at the worktable.

And saw it…

Vomit rushed into her throat.

"Well? How do you explain it?" Zach's FBI special agent voice was one Jessica was not accustomed to hearing directed at her.

All of a sudden, her nighttime outing to the patio was about as consequential as a single flame in a forest fire. She stared at the abomination on her worktable, desperate to work out how it had come into being. Gone was the sugary pink and white little girl's room she had constructed in the shadowbox. In its place was a house of horrors.

The charming dollhouse-sized furniture she had meticulously constructed and arranged in the wooden frame was now broken and turned on its sides as if a violent struggle had taken place in the miniature room. Rivulets of crimson paint had dried on the wallpapered walls, splattered the satin pillow and bedspread.

Hogtied on its side was a nude female figure, shocking in its realism. A tiny butcher knife protruded from the sculpted clay back.

Jessica would have torn herself away from the cruelty of the scene, but her feet seemed to be nailed to the floor. What unseen force had compelled her to create this monstrosity? And why? Forcing the bitter bile back down, she looked up at Zach, then away.

"I don't understand. What—this isn't—I didn't do this."

"You didn't? Has someone else been here?"

"No." She said it as if she knew it to be true. But the fact was, she did not know for sure. *Something*, or someone, had driven her outside into the dark and the rain. *Something*, or someone had destroyed her work.

Zach raised his palms in a question. "So, if you didn't do it, who did?"

"I—I don't—"

"You said you have a client who wanted this?"

"What? No! Not *this*. Are you crazy? You think I would take a client who wanted something like this?"

Zach's expression was as deadly serious as she had ever seen it. "Jessica, I don't know what's going on here. You need to tell me how you knew about this crime scene. We just got the case yesterday. How the hell did you—"

"I didn't. I *don't* know what this means. What case?"

"Stop it, Jess. No one outside the homicide team knew about that symbol on the victim's back. How did you know?"

"What symbol?"

Zach jabbed his forefinger at the figure, not touching it. In her shock, Jessica had overlooked the tattoo-like image a mere millimeter or so below the knife. A five-pointed star.

"It's an upside-down pentagram," Zach said. "Look, the two points on top symbolize the horns of a goat, the two on the side are the ears, the beard is the point on the bottom. Don't tell me you can't see it." He paused, either to catch his breath or to give her a chance to respond.

When she had no answer, he went back to railing at her. "C'mon Jess, you had another Hailey Martin 'visitation,' or whatever it is you call it. *Didn't* you?" He grabbed her upper arms in a tight grip and shook her. "Snap out of it, Jessica. Tell me the goddamn truth."

She pulled away from him, shaking her head. Shaking it until she was dizzy. But whether or not she was willing to admit it, as unpalatable as it was, the indisputable evidence made a fool of her denial. The truth Zach demanded was staring her in the face.

She forced the words out. "You're telling me this actually happened? It's a *real* crime scene?"

"That's exactly what I'm telling you. This is *my* crime scene. We don't even have an ID on the vic yet. The evidence—the upside-down pentagram—points toward a satanic cult killing. That's why we got called in. It's tied to some other cases we're working. So, you gotta tell me, Jess, how did you know about this scene?"

"I didn't, Zach, I truly didn't. Don't." An inkling began working at her brain, a worm burrowing deep into a hole. A flash of memory.

"I heard someone screaming, 'help me.' I heard it. Not out loud—in my head. That's all I remember. The next thing I knew, it was hours later. It must have been your victim I heard. Maybe she didn't know she was dead."

"Do you know how weird that sounds?"

"Of course I do, but you asked."

"Can you get hold of her again? Ask her name? Who killed her?"

"No, Zach, I can't. That's not how it works." She struggled for a way to explain a phenomenon that must be impossible to comprehend for someone who had not encountered it themselves. "They come to me when they want to. I can't pick up the phone and 'dial the dead.' One thing I have learned, though, if I did hear your victim and she caused me to make this horrible thing while I was having an episode, she'll be back."

Zach got out his phone and started tapping on the screen.

"What are you doing?" Jessica asked.

"I'm gonna take some photos."

"Why?"

"Because I want a record of it, that's why. Don't worry, I won't show anyone else." He snapped pictures from every angle. Then, having gotten what he wanted, Zach collected his jacket and jammed his hat on. "This is getting to be a bad habit, Jess."

The look of displeasure he turned on her made her blood boil. "I suppose you think spontaneously going into a trance and destroying my own work is my idea of a fun time? What the hell, Zach?"

He shrugged. "If you get anything, call me, okay?"

"What's that supposed to mean, 'get anything'?"

"If you get another 'Hailey Martin' out of this. That's what I'm saying."

"Oh, so first you're pissed that I made your frigging crime scene, and now you want me to 'get another Hailey Martin'? What's wrong with that picture?"

"Like I said, we don't have an ID on the victim yet. I'll take any leads I can get."

"Help me."

The memory of that terrified scream made Jessica painfully aware that a woman had been brutally murdered. Her anger deflated. "I would anyway, Zach. But listen, don't tell Jenna, okay? She already thinks something's wrong with me."

"Lucky she thought so this morning, chickie, or we wouldn't have known about this—*thing* you made. That twin connection you've got—also pretty weird."

"Yeah," Jessica said. "Weird."

She saw him out to his car, then went back inside and locked the door. As if deadbolts offered any real protection. They had not protected her from the shock of finding herself outside and unconscious, for what may have been hours. Nor from unwittingly turning an innocuous piece of art into a bloody crime scene. Questions poured into her brain:

How could I have made that thing while I was unconscious?

How long was I outside?

When did I—

"Stop." Jessica gave herself the command out loud.

For five years, her will to rebuff the voices and deny their existence had been stronger than the need to investigate what she was experiencing. This new episode made it crystal clear that there had been a major shift in her universe. If these events were going to be a regular occurrence, the best protection was to arm herself with information—anything that would help her learn to manage them better—assuming that was possible. She intended to find out.

Formulating the biggest question was easy, one she could

answer right now: where to start?

When Jessica told her sister that her auditory and visual hallucinations were not symptoms of schizophrenia, she had said it with absolute certainty. That was the one thing she *had* researched. Her investigation into mental illness showed that there were important differences between the auditory hallucinations of schizophrenic patients and what Jessica was hearing.

Booting up the laptop, she opened a browser and searched on the phrase "spirit voices." Google produced a long list of sites for a Paul Simon song of that name, which was of no use. She tried again, using the search term "spirit communications," and turned up a number of companies by that name, none related to the unseen spirit world.

"Spirits talking to me" improved the results. One of the top hits was "10 signs a spirit is trying to communicate." The list included phenomena like lights flickering, seeing butterflies or feathers; finding pennies everywhere.

Jessica was experiencing far more in-your-face contacts than butterflies or pennies. She clicked from one site to the next, taken aback by the number of people who reported contact with someone who had passed on from this life. She was not alone, there were thousands of them. The difference was, most were writing about dead relatives who visited them in dreams.

The websites cheered her up, but on their own, they were not enough. What she needed was to find someone who could appreciate what it was like to be at the mercy of dozens of voices not shackled to a human body, lining up to ask for help.

If Claudia had not mentioned to Jessica that a friend from Ojai would pick up the sculpture on Saturday, she would have overlooked a less-than-impressive website. But the town's name was in her mind. When the Ojai Valley Spiritualist Association came up, she followed the link.

It was pronounced "oh-hi," a name the Chumash Indians had given the moon. Jessica lived twenty-five miles south of the artsy town, whose population hovered around seven thousand. The Little Mermaid Gallery displayed her mermaid paintings. She sometimes strolled the small strip of shops on the main drag, known as The Arcade. Rain's department store was a favorite browse. Sometimes she ate at Hip Vegan, known for California Cuisine—a euphemism for dishes that included ingredients like sun-dried tomatoes and avocados—or at Azu when she had a yen for Mediterranean.

Before the birth of Jenna's girls, the twins had given themselves pampering weekends at their favorite Ojai spa. They shopped at the quirky open-air bookshop, Bart's Books, later treating themselves to a healthy lunch at Agave Maria Mexican Restaurant.

Yet, for everything she knew about the place, Jessica had never contemplated seeking help there for her "dead people problem," as she thought of it.

Whoever had thrown together The Ojai Valley Spiritualist Association's website was not a web design pro. She liked that it was not slick and commercial. The plain-wrap site offered a ton of material. A lengthy list of events and services had been uploaded into an old-fashioned template. Links to members who performed crystal healing, Reiki, chakra meditations, energy cord cutting, Akashic records readings, past life regression, soul retrieval. It all sounded exciting, exotic and foreign to Jessica. When she got to the "mediumship" link, her brain was ready to explode.

She had never guessed there were so many ways for spirit to contact people still in human form. Under the general heading of Mediumship were sub-categories: spiritual mediums, physical mediums, evidential mediums, mental mediums, channeling mediums, each one claiming to be in contact with people who had crossed into the next world.

That's what's happening to me. Is that what I am—a medium?

She was ready to test whether she would receive an answer to that question. Despite what she had said to Zach about waiting for the murder victim to return to her, she intended to do some proactive work and attempt to make contact.

After some of the reading she had done on the Ojai website, she knew that she needed to slow down her thoughts. She already knew how to do that. Following what Dr. Gold had taught her, she began a purposeful breathing exercise. Listening to her heartbeat, she focused on the breaths.

Once her mind was relaxed, she reached out, silently speaking to the murder victim. *Come back, please. I want to help you. Tell me who you are. I'll do anything I can.*

Now that she *wanted* the voices to speak to her, they had turned down the volume. Jessica listened, hearing nothing, seeing nothing. Keeping her mind focused was hard when other questions were eating at her.

How did I know what the crime scene looked like?

The answer was obvious. Jessica did not know, but the victim did.

Starting over, she relaxed her mind again and visualized the mayhem on her worktable: the pieces of miniature furniture destroyed, the bloody-looking paint saturating every surface. The clay figurine, the knife plunged into its back. The pentagram tattoo.

Her thoughts skidded to a halt.

The pentagram.

What was it about the five-pointed star that her subconscious was trying to tell her? It nagged like a splinter just under the skin, so close but can't grab hold of it.

Jessica jumped up and threw a dishrag over the ruined shadowbox. The smart thing would have been to ask Zach to take it with him and trash it somewhere far away. Maybe if she couldn't see the abomination she had evidently made, she could convince herself that it had never existed. She started to walk away from the worktable, weighing whether it would be too wimpy to ask him to do the deed for her.

The splinter worked its way into her awareness.

Moving on autopilot, Jessica turned back. Moving on autopilot, she gathered up her tools in a bundle and set them aside. Shoved pieces of fabric out of the way, picked around the modeling clay and the bag of cotton swabs she'd used to stuff the pillow.

And there it was, half-hidden under a square of denim cloth, the *something* she had failed to perceive with her eyes, but which her subconscious had spotted.

A *something* that did not belong there. A *something* she had not laid eyes on in more than ten years.

A memory came slamming back as intense and powerful as the reality.

In her sophomore year of high school, Jessica went through a Goth phase. She dyed her blonde hair jet black. Wore black lipstick, and enough black eyeliner for her mother to complain in disgust that she looked like a raccoon. Her jeans and tees were stylishly torn. Even in the heat of midsummer, she wore boots. And invariably, pentagram pendant—the pendant that had been hiding on her worktable. Even after the Goth phase passed, the pendant had remained a constant throughout high school.

She had come by it one summer vacation. With nothing better to do, the sixteen-year-old twins took the bus to Venice. Jessica in her standard black gear, intended to check out the dudes working out at the Muscle Beach, the open-air gym. Jenna, already the more conservative twin, in a gauzy handkerchief hem dress and boots à la Taylor Swift.

It did not take long for the narcissism of near-naked men showing off their oiled-up muscles to bore them both. They soon left the gym and strolled the boardwalk, stopping at T-shirt shops and poster shops. Eating ice cream cones, they strolled on, coming to a blackboard-style sandwich board outside a store called The Black Mirror.

Written in chalk on the board were the words "palm reading, tarot cards, jewelry."

Jessica, excited at the prospect of prowling through an occult store, urged Jenna to go inside. Her twin's answer was a self-righteous sniff. "No way am I going in there. The whole place is probably full of demons."

Jessica rolled her eyes. "Omigod, Jen, you've been listening to Lorraine too long."

"If you ever went within a mile of a church you'd know the Bible says you're not supposed to look into the future or do witchcraft or talk to dead people. Father Steadman said so. It's wrong."

"You'd better learn to think for yourself," said Jessica, wrinkling her nose in scorn. "How's some moldy old priest gonna tell you what you should be interested in? How do you know if he's telling the truth?"

Jenna might as well have said "Harrumph." She marched toward a bench across the boardwalk on the beach side, speaking over her shoulder. "I'm not going in that place. I'll wait out here.

Just don't bring back any demons."

Jessica gave her a one-shoulder shrug. No way was she about to miss the chance to find a cool gothic piece of jewelry for her secret stash; maybe some black candles. Tossing the squishy end of her ice cream into a trash can, she wiped her sticky fingers on a napkin and entered the store.

After the vivid sunshine, it was dark and deliciously creepy inside. Shelves and cabinets jammed with candles and incense, Egyptian figurines and mermaids, crystal balls, skulls, dragons.

Drawn by a life-size painting that hung on the back wall, Jessica wandered over. Her hands were already itching to get to her paints and create her own version. Against the black velvet background, the painfully thin girl was as pale as death, dressed in a virginal white dress. Garlands of wilting gardenias wove through her long hair. The flesh around her smoky eyes was smudged. She seemed to gaze back at the viewer with an expression of such suffering that Jessica decided it had been caused by the death of her one true love. The painted girl would never get over the loss, and like Ophelia, would drown herself.

Satisfied with her solution to the painting's imagined troubles, she moved around the store, lingering at display cases filled with rings and earrings. Some were plain but most of the jewelry was embellished with cool symbols—moons and ravens and skulls. She wanted to scoop them all up and take them home.

Of course, anything she purchased would have to be hidden from Jen, who would be smugly disapproving. And that would be nothing compared to their mother's reaction if she knew Jessica had brought home anything from a place like this. It was a sure thing that if she did, Lorraine would drag her to a lecture with Father Steadman, who would accuse her of consorting with the devil. Luckily, she could count on Jen not to rat her out, disapproving or not.

A chill touched the back of Jessica's neck, the feeling of someone staring at her. She swung around. One other customer was visible, on the other side of the store and faced away from her. She shivered. Damn Jenna and her stupid dire warning. Despite her best efforts, it had gotten under her skin.

She pushed the feeling away and made her way to a rack of

pendants atop a display case. The pendants were made of silver, gold, other metals—Jessica had no idea what some of them were—and stone. Each one had the same basic design of a star, some within a circle. Some bore a semi-precious gem at the center, yet each appeared to be unique.

On some of the pendants, the tips of each of the five points of the star glittered with a different color stone. On others, the circle that enclosed the star was etched with mystical-looking designs.

Jessica reached out and took one of the pendants off the rack. It was larger than the others—about the size of a silver dollar. At the center of a burnished alloy background was the horned head of a goat. She gazed at it, fascinated by the brilliant citrine yellow eyes, and the flaming torch that sprang from the goat's forehead. The unusual orange stone from which it was fashioned was one she had never seen.

"That one is not for you," said a soft voice behind her.

Turning around, Jessica came face-to-face with a woman whose long, wavy, gray hair and full-length, flowing, plum-colored dress gave her the look of a Renaissance crone. No taller than Jessica herself—which was to say, petite—her arresting green eyes seemed to pierce her soul.

"Why isn't it for me?" asked Jessica, thinking it was kind of weird for someone to try and talk a customer out of making a purchase. The woman took the pendant from her hand and rehung it on the rack. "The goat is Baphomet, Satan's symbol."

"So? What if I *like* Satan?"

Despite the fact that she did not, in fact, like Satan, Jessica, like many girls her age, tended to want the opposite of what others insisted was good for her, or at least act like it.

The woman, paying no attention to the retort, asked her, "What do you know about the pentagram?"

"Penta—what?"

"These pendants that you're looking at are all pentagrams—the five-pointed star. Sometimes it's enclosed in a circle, in which case it may be called a pentacle. One point of the star is always upward, which represents spirit. The number five is symbolic to the human being. You have five fingers on each hand and five toes on each foot. You have five senses—sight, hearing, smell, touch, taste."

She paused to make sure her student was paying attention. "So, the first point is spirit and the other four are the elements—earth, air, fire, water. In the pentagram that you picked, the pentagram is inverted. It has one downward point, which symbolizes the subversion of spirit, of Man being ruled by his carnal desires. In this form, it is associated with devil worship."

"So why do you sell it if it's so bad?" Jessica retorted.

"We have many kinds of customers." The woman gestured to the rack. "I see this one calls to you." She picked out a pendant that had caught Jessica's eye while she was speaking. It hung from a woven black cord and was made of a dull greenish-blue metal. The outside ring was encircled by a band etched with nine symbols.

"What makes you think I was looking at that one?"

"The symbols on the circle represent the planets," said the gray-haired woman as if Jessica had not spoken. "This pentacle is the one for you."

She took Jessica's hand and turned it palm up, gazing at it for several seconds. When she raised her face, the green eyes had acquired a faraway expression. "You have an intriguing destiny," the woman said in a dreamy voice. "But first, tragedy comes before you find your path."

An icy finger traced its way along Jessica's spine. "Tragedy?" she echoed.

The woman laid the pendant on her open palm, then closed her hand around it and held it for a long moment. "Take it," she said at length, letting go. "It's yours."

"But I—"

"It chose you. It's not often I give away my creations, but you need to wear this. It will protect you."

The chill again. "Protect me from what?"

Sadness entered the woman's green eyes. She squeezed Jessica's hand tighter, then let go.

"Nothing to be concerned about for many years to come. Just be sure to always keep it somewhere on your person."

And Jessica had worn the pendant faithfully. Until, in the excitement of leaving home for college, it had gone into a velvet bag, stowed in a box of keepsakes, forgotten until this very moment.

She picked it up from her worktable and closed her hand around it the way the green-eyed woman had done all those years ago. The green-blue metal felt warm, pulsing with a heart of its own. What if she had followed that woman's advice to keep wearing it? Would she have married Gregory Mack? Would she have had the accident that led to her memory loss and the spirit voices?

Would Justin be alive?

The cord slipped easily over her head. The pendant fell between her breasts under her sweater. Feeling safer now that it lay against her skin, Jessica removed the cloth she had thrown over the shadowbox and switched on her magnifying lamp. She took the sculpted figure of the hog-tied woman and laid it on the tabletop, positioning it under the magnifier. Looking at the magnified figure, she drew a sharp breath.

Zach had pointed out that the pentagram on the spine of the figure was inverted. Under the powerful lens, it was easy make out what his naked eye had missed: the head of the goat, Baphomet, at its center. More evidence of a satanic cult killing.

The inclusion of the symbol associated with the devil left Jessica uneasy, knowing she had been used to create it. The victim had used her to destroy the child's bedroom she had created and change it into a brutal crime scene.

That's one powerful spirit. Now, how can I get her to come back?

When she was in treatment for the brain injury and aftereffects of the coma, the physical therapist she worked with had trained Jessica that when her brain went into overload and started to fry, taking notes and writing down what was happening in her life would help organize her thoughts. It had proved true on more than one occasion when confusion and frustration began to take over.

She wanted so much to help solve the murder, and to help the victim in the afterlife if there was a way. Getting a pad and pen, she started setting out a timeline:

— Voices (background until Hailey showed up)
— Occasional episodes, no regular times
— Hailey M. shows up, all hell breaks loose
— Voices, Voices, Voices
— Episode at Ariel's Gallery

— Episode at beach—Justin and burned boy

— Burned boy in car

— Justin in dream

— Episode—Sh

As she started to write the word "Shadowbox," the temperature in the room dropped at least ten degrees, the way it had just seconds before the last episode.

She was alone in the cottage, yet somehow, her shoulders were being roughly wrenched behind her. Her wrists and ankles, too. Jessica cried out in pain. The pen dropped from her fingers and rolled on the floor.

Agonizing pain seared her back, spread along her spine. Her back arched and she cried out again. What was happening to her? Was there a way to stop it? She turned her head left and right, trying to see whoever, or whatever, was causing the pain.

A few feet from the chair where she sat, trussed with invisible bindings, a filmy white mist hovered close to the floor.

The apparition was not the first Jessica had ever seen, but it was the first she had encountered while being helpless, hogtied by invisible bindings and about to lose it.

The mist began to rise and take a human shape.

The only defense she had was her voice. She yelled as loud and strong as she could.

"What do you want? Leave me alone!"

She sucked in a breath and opened her mouth wide. Before she could scream for help, the mist disappeared. And with it went the sickening pains in her joints and her back. The room temperature returned to normal.

Jessica let out a shaky sigh. She rubbed her wrists, her ankles, which seemed to be none the worse for her experience. With blinding clarity, she understood that in the same way the burned boy in her vision at the beach had showed her his scarred face, the satanic cult murder victim had just made her spirit presence known. Like the clay figure in the crime scene she had created, she had been subjected to how it felt to be hogtied and helpless. The pain in her spine was the victim's pain from the knife embedded in her back.

Now that she had sent the spirit away, she regretted it.

A voice spoke in her head as if she had made the remark out loud. *"You did ask for it."*

Dude, could you do it a little less dramatically?

Jessica's gaze fell on the notepad, which she was surprised to see was still on her lap.

Under the last line, written in a handwriting not her own, were the words *"retribution,"* and a signature: *"Finley Hunter."*

SIX

Jessica drove the sixty-five miles to Venice Beach, where Zebediah Gold saw patients in his home office. Like her, he lived in a studio behind a larger house. His was behind an Asian-style home enclosed behind a high wall.

In the amnesia days when she believed *she* was Jenna, the first time she met him she had arrived at his door for what the doctor expected to be a *second* visit. He was as unaware as Jessica that he was treating the wrong twin.

Ever since then, Dr. Gold had been a constant in her life, the rock she had clung to through the years since amnesia. Whenever the weight of the past threatened to crush her; when the void left by the death of her child wanted to swallow her whole, she would call him. He never insisted she see him on a regular schedule. Knowing he was there when she needed him was as comforting to Jessica as she imagined a loving mother's hug might be.

Every time she strolled through the Japanese garden between the two dwellings, she made it a point to pause at the miniature bridge that spanned a koi pond. Stopping beneath the Japanese Black Pine, she patted the head of the laughing Buddha statue and said a prayer for the Buddha to help Dr. Gold fix her problem with Jen.

Today, Zebediah Gold wore his standard casual linen shirt, shorts and sandals. He ushered her inside with a brief hug. "I'm happy to see you, Jess."

"I know, it's been a while."

"That wasn't a reproach. I hear from you when the time is right."

She grinned. "That's very Zen of you."

"A paradox, my dear?" He grinned back. "How many Zen masters does it take to change a light bulb?"

"Tell me, Dr. Gold, how many Zen masters *does* it take to change a light bulb?"

"Three. One to change it, one not to change it, and one to do neither."

She gave the expected chuckle and they settled into their respective chairs at either end of a low table. Even after all this time, Jessica felt more comfortable with that barrier between them.

"How's everything going?" asked Dr. Gold after pouring, as he always did, green tea from the iron pot that stood on a trivet.

"I guess if it was going well, I wouldn't be here, right?"

"Sad, but true." He handed her a cup of tea and sat back, ready to listen after his standard opening of 'How can I help'? Then waited patiently until she was ready to unburden herself.

Accepting the cup, Jessica set it on a coaster on the table. Over most of the drive down to Venice she had worked out how best to explain what had been happening to her. Their many conversations had taught her that he was all compassion and empathy. There would be no judgment from Doctor Gold.

She sat back, crossed her legs and got herself ready for the big reveal. "I'd like to get your opinion, okay?"

"Of course."

"What do you believe happens when we die?"

Both his brows went up. "I must say, you've surprised me, Jessica. That's not a question I would have predicted. I need a moment to think about it." He stroked his beard, as he was apt to do while pondering a philosophical question. His answer, when it came, was as philosophical as the question.

"What is the sound of one hand clapping? Since no one has come back to report on it, there is no answer. So, I believe that we die and that's the end of it. We do what we've come here to do, and then we disappear into nothingness until the next life—I do believe in reincarnation."

"What do you think of people who say they've seen the spirits of their dead relatives, or they've gone to heaven and been sent back with a mission to complete?"

He smiled. "Wishful thinking, I suspect. Strong emotions can make us imagine all sorts of things."

His words disappointed her more than she would have expected. "I thought you would be the kind of person who would *believe* in the sound of one hand clapping."

As she was speaking, a woman materialized behind him and looked at her in a meaningful way. Surprised, Jessica asked her telepathically to identify herself, and was further surprised when the woman began impressing thoughts on her mind.

"I take it you disagree?" asked Dr. Gold. "I'm sure you have a good reason for—" He interrupted himself and turned his head to look over his shoulder. "What are you looking at, Jess?"

The spirit woman was being quite insistent, talking so fast that Jessica had to struggle to keep up. She spoke to her therapist. "This might be a strange question, but who is the lady you knew with the M name—M-Mad—Madison, Maddy—Oh, *Madeleine*? Is that it?"

Dr. Gold startled as if she had poked him with a branding iron. "What? What did you just say, Jessica? How do you—?"

Jessica raised her hand, signaling him to wait while she listened to the spirit. "Okay, I get it," she said, then brought her eyes back to him again. "She was your wife? Not for very long. But you always stayed friends. For a long time. Obviously, she's on the other side now. I'm so sorry."

Dr. Gold's expression was a mix of astonishment and bewilderment. "Who told you—" Then, "Claudia? She told you about Madeleine?"

"No, not a word. Maddy is standing behind you on your left side. She's *beautiful*, Doctor Gold." The spirit woman drew her attention again, continuing to transmit thoughts. "She says she knows she wasn't the right one for you, but she wants me to tell you that she never stopped loving you and…what? Oh. She wants to say thank you for finishing the book. She's very happy with the way it turned out, even though there were some serious problems with—I'm not sure what. Do you understand that? She doesn't say what the problems were."

Refocusing her gaze on her therapist, she saw that his eyes were shining with unshed tears, which he covered by blowing his nose. "I'm so sorry, Dr. Gold," she said, at once contrite. "This must seem super-intrusive to you, but the spirit people can get very insistent. *This* is what I've come to talk to you about. Some pretty strange things have been happening to me."

"Jess, I—I'm speechless. How in the…?" She had never seen him at a loss for words before, but he was staring at her as if she were an alien trying to talk him onto her spaceship, bound for the outer reaches of the universe.

"I'm like that little boy in the movie, Doc. I see dead people. Until recently, I only heard them, but now—"

Dr. Gold, still looking shell-shocked, collected his wits and sat forward in his chair, elbows on knees. All engaged interest, he was back in therapist mode. "How long has all this been going on, Jess?"

"It started not long after I came out of the coma, these quiet voices in my head. I was afraid to admit I was hearing voices and have everyone think I was crazy, so I pretty much turned a deaf ear and tuned them out as best I could. When I first met you, when I had amnesia, there were no voices. After I got my life back, they started up and I went back to ignoring them. Then, one night a few weeks ago, a woman who was murdered came to me in a dream and gave me clues that helped Zach solve the case. Since then, it's escalated. I started having these blackout episodes and the voices got louder and nonstop. Now they line up, trying to get my attention."

"Why don't you tell me about the blackouts."

"It starts with this whistly-shrieky noise in my head and then my vision fades to black. I don't fall down or, like, faint. When it first happened, I couldn't see anything at all, but within a couple of minutes, everything was back to normal. But now, it's different. A couple of days ago I saw my son, Justin, and another spirit boy playing ball. We spoke to each other and it was as real as you and me sitting here now." Pausing for breath, Jessica looked at Doctor Gold to see if he had anything to say. He gave an encouraging nod to continue.

"The next time it happened, I was out of it for hours. I made a shadowbox and have no memory of doing it—it was horrible, a crime scene. When I woke up, I was standing out on my patio in the rain. And in case you're wondering, when all this started, I went to see my neurosurgeon. The tests showed nothing physically wrong with me. Maybe I'm just crazy, but I don't think so." The telling of it for the second time left her drained.

Doctor Gold looked at her, his face neutral. "It sounds to me as if you entered a brief fugue state, similar to when you had amnesia, although of course, that was for a far longer period." He tipped his head to one side, considering her. "Do you have any thoughts on what these spirits want from you, Jess?"

"There's no mystery. They want me to give messages to people, like I just did to you, and I'm okay with that. The problem is, there are so many of them; it's overwhelming when they want to reach people that I don't know how, which is most of the time. It's different with Maddy because I know you. Of course, I had no inkling that she was going to show up here, but when I sat down, there she was. I think maybe it's because she wanted you to believe me. She gave some evidence so that you would."

"It's hard to disregard. You're *sure* Claudia has never mentioned her?"

"Absolutely one-hundred-percent sure. Besides, she's still standing there. I can see her as plain as day. Not in the flesh, but semi-transparent. She's saying she wants you to tell her nephew how proud she is of him for what he's accomplished."

Dr. Gold blew a breath through puffed cheeks. Now he was the one to raise a hand to stop her. "Okay, okay, I believe you. And yes, tell her I will pass along the message."

"You can tell her yourself if you hurry. Her energy is starting to fade."

"Okay." He turned around in his seat and spoke to the woman who was invisible to him. "Thank you, Madeleine. I will definitely tell him." Turning back, he shook his head in apparent amazement. "Well, that came out of left field, to say the least. Now, let's focus on you. How can I help you?"

"I told Jen everything I told you. Let's just say it didn't go well."

"You hadn't told her before now?"

"No, she's way too judgy. And the way she reacted proves I was right. We'd just arranged for me to babysit the twins. Then, after I told her about the spirits—and I only told her because she *insisted* I tell her what was going on with me—she changed her mind. Now we're not talking.

"Look, Doctor Gold, I'm here because I need to convince her that she doesn't have any reason to be afraid of me. I'm not possessed by demons, which is what she thinks. She should let me see my nieces without her hovering over us. I need you to help me." Jessica picked up her cup and drank the bitter green tea, wishing he would keep some sweetener on the table. Why did it have to taste nasty to be healthy?

"I understand you've waited quite a while to babysit your nieces. You've mentioned it before and I know how much it means to you. They're what—two now? *Three?* Time does fly. Have you thought about the situation if it was reversed? Wait—I'm not judging, I'm just asking."

"No, I haven't thought about it. I just know she has nothing to worry about."

"Wait, Jess. Take a second, please, and let yourself go into neutral. I want you to imagine her telling you that she's been hearing and seeing ghosts, and talking to murder victims. If that wouldn't disturb you at all, it's fine. I'm asking you to be honest with yourself."

The mere suggestion made her uncomfortable, but since she had asked for his help, Jessica did as he asked, visualizing a situation where Jenna was the one who was getting these visits from the spirit world. Would she have left a three-year-old Justin alone with her sister under those circumstances? She wished she could say "yes," but the truth was, she knew better.

With a sigh of resignation, she said, "Fine. I get it. But look, I can't help that these spirits are bugging me. Does that mean I'll never get to spend time alone with my nieces?"

Dr. Gold favored her with his best avuncular smile. "I'm pretty sure it doesn't. Maybe you need to give Jenna some time to adjust to the idea. She might be afraid that you'll talk to the girls about it and scare them. You can reassure her about that, right? How about starting by spending more time with the whole family?

Once Jenna sees that you're the same Aunt Jessica you always have been, she'll relax."

Jessica cast a skeptical glance. "You do remember who we're talking about, right? You used to be her therapist, too. My sister the perfectionist doesn't do 'relax' very well. She has one way of doing things. Her way."

"What's the alternative?"

"Okay, good point. But I'm still mad at her. I'm not ready to grovel."

"Groveling isn't necessary, Jess. But giving her time to miss you won't hurt." He chuckled. "Besides, you have that twin thing going on. She must *know* how you feel."

"Yeah, she sent Zach over to check on me right after I blacked out and woke up outside. She told Roland—her husband—that she felt something had happened to me."

"See, Jess, she loves you. And you love her."

"I know, but she sure doesn't make it easy."

SEVEN

Claudia's friend, Sage Boles, arrived precisely at three o'clock to pick up the sculpture.

Gazing up at him standing in her doorway, Jessica wished that Claudia had given her a warning. He was nothing short of drop-dead gorgeous. Short-cropped, curly black hair, a straight white smile and startling sapphire eyes fringed by long, thick lashes. Bronze skin that came, not from the sun, but from mixed heritage. Jessica, whose skin was always pale regardless of how much time she spent on the beach, decided that he had gotten the best of both parents.

As they introduced themselves, her artist's eye caught a shadow behind his penetrating gaze, a certain sadness around his mouth that made her want to sculpt him. The two women in spirit who stood together on his left were pretty interesting, too. Especially since one of them was Madeleine, Dr. Gold's former wife. Jessica had already delivered her message. What was she doing here, and who was the woman with her? She couldn't ask Sage.

She invited him in, silently requesting the ladies not to bother her for the next ten minutes, floored that they complied. The pair of them faded away so fast, she wondered whether she had dreamed them up.

Sage was a tall man—though most people were tall next to Jessica, who might just reach five-four if she stood on tippy-toes.

His presence radiated, making the cottage shrink in a way that Zach never had. When she took the hand he extended, a spark of electricity ran through her that took her breath away.

For a second or two, the unexpected rekindling of emotions left her unable to speak. She had packed those emotions into a neat box and buried them deep long ago. Now, when she least expected it, here they were, thrusting their way back into her life.

"Uh, the sculpture is all ready for you," she stammered, moving over to her worktable and indicating the large cardboard box, which was sealed with packing tape.

Sage towered over her, not in an intimidating way but—Jessica smiled inwardly—protective was the word that came to mind. How bat-shit crazy was that, when she had never laid eyes on him until ten seconds ago?

"How do you know Claudia?" she asked a little breathlessly.

"She authenticated my aunt's will. Ironically, we met last year in Maine."

"Maine?"

"My aunt lived there. We found out we both lived on the West Coast, not all that far from each other."

"I'm a big fan of Claudia's," said Jessica. "She's such a good person."

He smiled. "You won't get any argument from me. How about you? How did you meet her?"

"She analyzed my handwriting several years ago," she said. "When I also had a—" she hesitated, "a legal matter."

If she told Sage that the legal matter was having Detective Jovanic check her name in police records to determine whether she had a record, or anyone had filed a missing person's report on her, he would, of course, want to know why, and that would get too complicated.

She saw the curiosity in the extraordinary blue eyes, but he was too polite to ask the question.

He had the box in hand but was not making a move to leave. Nor did she did want him to. Should she offer him coffee or a beer? Her cheeks were fever-hot. She cleared her throat. "What do you do in Ojai?" she asked, her voice sounding higher than usual.

It was ridiculous to think that something might start between them. As soon as he knew she heard voices, it would be over before it began.

Dating had been rough once the voices got in the way. She had tried a few times since the divorce. The trouble was, when the men she met realized that Jessica did not live wholly in the same world they did, they tended to disappear in a hurry. Her last date—it must have been six months ago—had fled with some flimsy excuse during dinner at a cozy bistro. She had decided right then that her art was enough. She could get along fine without a man in her life. Sex was a distant memory.

But Sage Boles made her want to try again, and it was not just his super-hot looks. Her spidey senses were tingling; the attraction went both ways.

He was looking at her with a question. She had missed his answer to hers. "Oh, sorry?"

"I paint murals, sculpt with iron, draw. Stuff like that."

Another frisson of wonder ran through her. "You're an artist, too? Claudia didn't tell me that."

Sage smiled like the Cheshire cat, as if he knew something he was not going to share with her. "I have a feeling there's a lot she didn't tell either of us."

"I'm sure you're right about that."

"Maybe we can get together and share."

Her heart did a somersault. "Maybe we could." This was not like picking a date from an internet site. Claudia was the connection point. She must have thought there was a good reason to introduce them.

She doesn't know about the whispers. Would she have introduced us if she did?

Jessica got a strong sense that something important was happening. Maybe she could head off potential heartbreak if she tested him now. If he had no interest in spirituality there would be no point in starting anything with him.

"Have you ever heard of The Ojai Valley Spiritualist Association?" she asked.

His eyebrows rose in surprise. "Sure. I know it well. Why do you ask?"

"Does it have a good reputation?"

"Yeah, it does. I attend services there sometimes."

"Oh, it's a church?" Jessica said, disappointed and hopeful at the same time. "I don't do religion."

Sage shook his head. "It's not a regular church. It's more like a group of free thinkers who get together and for some pretty good talks about universal love and spiritualism."

"That definitely doesn't *sound* like church. I've read a little online about spiritualism, but I want to learn more about it."

"Why don't you go with me tomorrow?"

Sage's confidence impressed her, like he was comfortable in his own skin the way she had always wished to be. "Tomorrow? Well, okay, yeah, I could do that."

There was that smile again, full of charm and intrigue. Should she trust it?

"I'll introduce you to Bella Bingham," he said. "She's the pastor. She also leads some of the groups that meet there."

"Thank you. That would be awesome."

Sage said, "If you'd like to meet me at the Center at ten-thirty, we can walk over for the eleven o'clock service. It's not far."

"What Center?"

His smile spread. "I guess you were serious when you said Claudia didn't tell you anything. The Regina Boles Center for Traumatized Children. It's named for my mother."

As he spoke the name, a thunderbolt slammed through Jessica's body, and a message.

"*Go.*"

Something was happening here, and it was more than physical attraction.

Wasn't it just yesterday when she had decided to look into spiritualism? Now, here was Sage to take her hand and lead the way. Had the spirits heard her and sent him?

She couldn't help feeling a bit like a pawn being moved around a chessboard by an unseen presence. It was not an entirely unpleasant sensation.

"Are you okay, Jessica?" Sage asked.

She smiled up at him. "Your mother must have been an incredible person."

"Yes, she was."

"What's the address of the Center?"

He took out his own pen to write the information in the sketchbook she handed him. Jessica took a quick glance, wondering what Claudia thought of his handwriting, which to her untrained eye looked bold and black, artistic and just a little on the wild side.

Sage tapped the box under his arm. "I can't wait to see your work. Your reputation precedes you."

"Now you're making me nervous. Give Claudia a hug from me."

With another of those killer smiles, he promised he would.

Jessica walked him out to an expensive-looking Tesla. He started to lean toward her as if he intended to kiss her cheek, but then thought better of it, leaving her with mixed feelings.

They said goodbye and she watched him drive away, for once, allowing herself to dream just a little.

EIGHT

Zach called while she was clearing away the remnants of the salad she'd had for dinner.

"Jess, you are incredible. You did it again."

"Did what?"

"The cult case is practically solved. The vic's name was indeed Finley Hunter. You were dead on, if you'll excuse the pun."

"What did you tell Roland about how you found out her name?"

"Confidential informant. I can't let him know the truth this time."

How convenient that he had already forgotten how pissed he had been about the shadowbox crime scene. He had his information, all was well.

"Thanks for letting me know."

"I've already been reassigned. Got a more urgent case."

"More urgent than a satanic murder?"

"We've handed the murder over to the local field office. They have all the dope on cult activity out there—and there's a ton of it. The new one is a parental abduction. Can I run it by you?"

"Sure, go ahead," Jessica said, her suspicions raised. Hadn't he been skeptical of how she got her information?

"It's a marriage gone bad—cliché, right? The mom is an associate at a law firm, Dad's a realtor and the kid's primary caregiver. She's miserable, makes secret plans to take the kid and run. She comes home from work ready to hit the road, but Dad beat her to it. He's gone and so is the kid."

At that point Jessica stopped listening. The final argument with Greg was ringing in her ears. They had been getting ready for a road trip to San Francisco. He was screaming at her over some minor transgression, the cause so small, she had forgotten what had set him off. It was no different from all the other times he had gone ballistic on her. One moment he was the captivating Prince Charming; the next, the rug was pulled out from under her. Jekyll and Hyde had nothing on Gregory Mack.

That night, he had backed her against a wall, spewing hateful vitriol, his face thrust close enough to hers that a spray of spit landed on her lip. Justin was on her hip, wailing. She could feel his face pressed into her neck, his little arms holding on as tight as two-year-old muscles could manage. The memory of his fear would never, ever be erased from her mind.

Jessica would always remember it as her saturation point—the moment she ran out of excuses. No longer could she lie to herself that he would treat her better if she just didn't make him mad—not that there was ever any rhyme or reason to his anger. It all depended on how drunk he was at the time.

Jenna, who had not liked Greg from the first time they met, urged her to leave. Now that Jessica had found the courage, they worked out a plan. After settling in their hotel in the city, Greg would drink himself to sleep. He always did. He would sleep through Jessica taking Justin and their luggage to meet up with Jenna in the lobby. Jenna was going to take them to a safe place. Jessica and her son would hide out until she could file for divorce and custody.

Then fate got involved. Now Justin was dead and Greg was in prison.

"Jess, are you still there?" Zach's question bumped her out of the memories.

"Yeah, I'm here. Sorry, could you repeat what you said?"

"Are you busy? Should I call you back?"

"No, I just got distracted. Go ahead. What happened?"

"The husband texts Abby, the wife, that he's taken the kid to

Disneyland, sends photos of him having a ball on the Small World ride—the one with the song that can drive you nuts?"

Jessica started singing, "It's a small world after all; it's a small world after all—"

"Shit, Jess," Zach interrupted in protest. "Now that stupid song is gonna be stuck in my brain."

"Okay, I'll stop. Tell the rest of the story; it'll get rid of the earworm."

"Thanks, thanks a lot. Ugh."

Picturing him shaking the song out of his head like a dog shedding water, she laughed. "Anytime, Zach. Anytime."

"Okay. The dad tells her they're fine and to quit bugging him. Mom relaxes a bit, starts packing up her stuff and the kid's stuff so she'll be ready to go when they get back. Problem is, he doesn't come back. Two days later, he still isn't back and now he's not responding to texts and calls. So, she calls the cops."

"Did they do anything?"

"There's no divorce, both are custodial parents. The cops have no jurisdiction. There would have to be a court-ordered custody agreement that was violated for them to pursue it. There's no custody order, so their hands were pretty much tied."

While she listened, Jessica rinsed and dried dishes, put leftovers in the refrigerator. The automatic action helped her concentrate on what he was saying. "What if he took the kid out of state? That's a federal violation, isn't it?"

"Again, only when a parent defies a custodial agreement. After the mom—her name's Abby—got nowhere with the police, she waited two more days. Then she calls them back, freaking out. Says her husband called, tells her she's never going to see her son again. And he has a weapon—she checked where he kept it and it's gone."

"Has he threatened the son's safety?"

"Not in so many words, but the threat is implicit."

"Where do you start looking?"

"According to the file, Abby already called his parents, in case he took the boy to Arizona, where they live. They claim they haven't heard from him, and they don't want to, either. Nice family, huh? After some initial investigation, the local cops ended up referring her to our field office. We step in and help local agencies when an abduction might take a child far away."

"That poor mother," said Jess. "I feel for her—that is, I'm assuming she's the good guy and the dad wasn't rescuing the child from a bad situation."

"I'm getting up to speed on the case. She seems like a pretty devoted mother. Besides, she claims that her husband has a history of minor violence against her, but not the boy."

"'*Minor* violence'? What's that supposed to mean?"

"Bruises where they don't show, mainly."

"Police reports?"

"Nope, so far we have to take her word for it. She says she has photos in her safe deposit box at the bank. Plus, she has a confidant at work who she says will corroborate. She's forwarded the photos her husband took at Disneyland."

"Proof of life," Jessica said. "Like when someone's kidnapped and they photograph them with the current newspaper so you know they haven't been killed."

"Except in this case, all we know is the kid was alive a few days ago. The father used a debit card to pay for food and gas and a hotel near the park. He's since checked out of the hotel and hasn't used the card again, except to get enough cash to keep going for at least a week without being traced."

"What about his phone?"

"We haven't been able to pick it up. If he's smart, he's gotten rid of it and picked up a burner. Which may not bode well for the kid."

"You think he'll hurt his son?"

"It isn't uncommon, Jess. We're taking it seriously."

"But couldn't he get fake passports and leave the country?"

"Anything is possible. We've got BOLOs at all the points of entry."

"How old is the boy?"

"Four. Ethan."

A year older than Justin. She couldn't help making the comparison. There were times when Greg had been wonderful with him. And then there were the other times. She sent a quick prayer that Ethan's father was treating him well.

"That's so young," she said. "I hope the little guy is okay."

"According to Abby, Trey was a good father—he's been the

primary caretaker since Ethan was an infant. Now he's using the kid to get back at her for threatening to leave him, and she believes he's capable of following through."

"She must be frantic. I sure would be."

"She is. I was wondering whether maybe you could help."

"Me? How can *I* help?"

"You could tune in to Ethan and help us figure out where he is, like you did with Hailey."

"Zach, I told you it doesn't work that way," said Jessica, exasperated all over again. "Anyway, the people who show up are dead." Her stomach tightened. "Do you think Ethan is dead?"

"Not necessarily. I just thought—you were so good with the Martin case—maybe you could get some information we could use."

"That was different. Hailey came to me as a spirit. She wouldn't let me sleep, remember? She hounded me for days until I called you. And her voice was the strongest out of all the voices I was hearing. Besides, she was dead. I don't think a little boy would be loud enough to—" She broke off, picturing her own frightened boy crying for his mother. "I can't promise anything."

"Thanks, Jess. Look, I hesitate to ask—in fact, I feel kinda stupid. But since it's a kid's life at stake…"

"You didn't feel stupid asking about Finley Hunter."

"Yeah, that box thing you made—that was extreme." He gave a sheepish chuckle. "Maybe I'm getting used to the idea of you being psychic or something."

"Or something."

"Hey, wanna get together for breakfast tomorrow? My treat. We can kick around some ideas, and take a ride out to Benedict Canyon. There's a vacant house I have to look at. We think Starkey may have taken the kid there to hide out. He's a realtor, and—"

"Can't tomorrow. I've got a thing in Ojai."

"Ojai? What's up there?"

"I'm going to a talk on spiritualism."

"No joke? I never knew you were into that stuff. Is it because of the voices?"

"Yeah, the voices. I'm hoping to meet some people who can answer a few questions."

"Want some company? We can go to Benedict Canyon later."

"Not this time, but thanks."

"Maybe we can get together later for a beer."

"We'll see."

Why couldn't she shut him down and refuse? Oh, yeah. There was that "he saved me and my sister" thing.

It was an open secret that Zach would be happy to reignite the relationship they once had. Knowing he was bummed at her rejection gave her a twinge of regret, but not a big enough twinge to tell him about Sage Boles.

"Can you ask if there's some way to reach out to someone who's alive?" Zach asked.

"I said I would try, Zach. If I get anything, I'll let you know, *okay?*"

Her goodbye bordered on snappish. Zach had some nerve, asking her to do this for him after he had been so angry about the shadowbox crime scene.

Jessica went over to the wastebasket where she had dumped the evil thing. Being near it made her feel ill. Apart from the red paint, the wooden box itself was intact. It was the furnishings and torn bits of fabric that were destroyed. For half a millisecond she considered painting over the bloody-looking mess and re-using it. The thought made her shudder. She didn't want to even touch it. Using a rag to pick it up, she carried the wastebasket out to the bin in the back alley behind the cottage and emptied its contents inside. The lid dropped shut with a satisfying bang.

Many more episodes and nights of fending off the voices and she might go over the edge, she was *that* close. She let out a sigh. The rain had petered to a sprinkle. At least if another episode came on and she woke up outside again, she would not get wet this time.

Then, reality hit her over the head with the weight of an anvil. She was dealing with murder victims and the safety of a missing child. Zach seemed to think she was his personal hotline to heaven.

What the hell am I getting myself into?

Please, let me find what I need in Ojai.

NINE

The Regina Boles Center for Traumatized Children was encircled by a six-foot high fieldstone wall with no signs proclaiming the semi-rural property as the location. But there was Sage, standing outside the wrought iron gates, waiting for her. In black Levis and a turtleneck sweater, he was as stunning as she remembered.

Jessica left the Mini on the street and headed up the long driveway. A quarter mile back from the gates, visible beyond massive oak trees was a sprawling ranch house. Under the watchful eye of a young woman in purple overalls, a half-dozen children crawled and climbed and swung on a jungle gym on the vast lawn.

"I gave your hug to Claudia," Sage said, coming down to meet her. "She sent one back." He leaned down and wrapped her in an embrace, then let go.

"Uh…oh…okay…thanks."

What's wrong with me? He's not the first good-looking guy to hug me.

But none of them made me feel like I stuck my finger in a light socket.

"You're an extraordinary artist," he went on, acting as though he had not noticed that Jessica was struggling for words. "Claudia couldn't have been happier with the piece. Her neighbor who owned the dog full-on cried real tears."

"It's so cool that it went over well," she murmured, flushing.

"It was incredibly lifelike. I see why Claudia is such a big admirer of your work."

"Thank you. I hope you show me yours sometime. I mean, your art. I'd love to see your art. Artwork." *Omigod, did I really say that?* She could feel the blush deepen.

"I'll be happy to show you mine," said Sage with a definite twinkle in his eye.

Jessica turned away, regarding the tall gates guarding the property behind them, where children needed to be hidden behind that kind of security. "Are the gates always locked?" she asked.

"Always," Sage said. "We're very careful. There are motion sensors around the walls. We give the kids every protection possible. Some of them are here under court order. Nobody gets in without proper credentials. I'll show you around later."

He told her that The Ojai Spiritualist Association was a half-mile away and asked whether she minded walking. She didn't.

They set out on the tree-lined street, where rain-washed sidewalks were dappled with shadows and the sun beamed down on them like a good omen.

"You're a tiny person, aren't you?" said Sage.

"And you're a very tall person. I'm 5'3."

"I'll have to mince my steps so I don't get ahead of you," he said, doing a ridiculous little prance to demonstrate.

Laughing, Jessica tried to match his gait. "I know I'm short. Just pretend I'm one of the kids at your Center."

"Not short. Diminutive. And adorable. And I definitely can't pretend you're one of the kids. I'd go to jail for what I'm thinking."

"Stop it, you're embarrassing me. Tell me about the kids. Where do they come from?"

Sage got serious. "Some of them were removed from their parents 'care'. A couple were brought over from countries that are at war—you can imagine how traumatized they are. And there are other situations. We have a seven-year-old boy who was rescued from a human trafficking operation in L.A. They were selling him for sex up to nine times a day. The Feds found nineteen children in that one house."

Seven years old. Justin's age, had he lived. The age he had shown himself to be in the spirit world. Everything came back to Justin.

"What kind of person would—" Jessica stopped herself. "Never mind, it's pretty clear what kind. Do the kids live on site?"

"We have space for twenty full-time residents, the toughest cases that need extra-special full-time attention. Some kids come for day therapy. If everything goes as planned, once we're up to speed, I intend to add a wing."

The decision to take on such a project and the dedication it must have taken to see it through kindled Jessica's admiration and respect, as well as just plain liking him. Everything she had seen and heard heightened her interest in the program and, if she would admit it, in Sage. She was curious to understand what had motivated him, but her intuition told her it was too soon to ask.

"How long has the Center been here?" she asked.

"We've been operational for three months. Our grand opening was the week before last Thanksgiving. I bought the house and land back in March but renovations took longer than expected—isn't that always the way with construction?"

Thinking of her rental cottage Jessica grinned. "Can't say; I've never had anything built."

"Take my word for it. On top of everything else, City and County building permits, all the licensing requirements—it's a nightmare to get through. Long before we were ready to open, we had a waiting list of kids needing a place. I wish we were able to handle every one of them, but there are so many. We had to accept the ones with the most urgent needs."

His use of the singular pronoun when he spoke of purchasing the place, rather than referring to a board or a group, aroused Jessica's curiosity. She would love to know where the money had come from to buy an estate of this size and renovate it. Property in California was far from inexpensive. His murals would have to bring in a lot of money if his art had paid for it.

"I hope this isn't a rude question, but does insurance cover the treatment?"

Sage shrugged. "In some cases, but it doesn't matter, we won't turn anyone in need away."

"That's—I don't even have a word for how great that is," said Jessica. "I can't begin to imagine how hard it must be for a child to recover from the kind of abuse they've had to suffer. From what I saw back there, it looks like a wonderful place for the little ones to recover."

"Recovery takes time and tons of care and attention. We use anything and everything that emphasizes creativity and helps them express their emotions—art, music, dance. Graphotherapy, too. Claudia comes up to work with the therapists once a month."

"Graphotherapy? She teaches them to write?"

"No, it's a system of special drawing exercises they do to music. She says it makes changes in the brain to help them release trauma. I'm amazed at how well it works. Claudia teaches the therapists and they teach it to the kids, then she checks their work to make sure they're doing it right." Sage warmed to his topic. "We have a totally awesome team of doctors and therapists. Plus, there are volunteers, amateurs like me."

"Can anyone volunteer?"

"Sure, as long as they can pass a very strict background check. Plus, Claudia analyzes the handwriting of every successful applicant, regardless of whether they're a paid employee or a volunteer. If there's one red flag, they're toast. What I care about most is that the kids know they're safe. The best way to do that is to bring in the right people."

"It must be a huge amount of work," Jessica said, throwing caution out the window and deciding to get personal. "What made you do this, Sage?"

When he hesitated, she regretted not following her instincts. She should have waited to raise the subject.

"Let's talk about that another time," he said.

Why did he look so uncomfortable? He had named the Center after his mother. That made her think he must have had a good childhood. But what had sparked his interest in traumatized children? With her own secrets to protect, she could hardly blame him for his reticence.

"Okay, sure. What kind of work do you do here as a volunteer?"

"Art projects. I'm working with the kids on a jungle mural we're painting on the dining room wall. I've painted several murals, but none with kids." Sage grinned broadly. "I'm having a blast learning how to work with them."

"Sounds like a lot of fun."

"It is." He paused on the sidewalk, turning to her with a look that was hard to interpret. "How about you, Jessica?"

"What about me?"

"We can always use more volunteers. Have you got any experience with kids?"

Now it was her turn to hesitate. How do you tell a virtual stranger—one that you have a strong desire to get to know—that you have a dead child, without making him feel awkward for asking? She decided on the short version. "I have three-year-old twin nieces."

"Wow, twins. Do they look alike?"

"*Exactly* alike." Thinking of Sophie and Emma made Jessica smile. "Of course, they're the most adorable little girls that ever lived. Take it from their aunt."

"I bet you're right," said Sage, stopping at a two-story office building. "This is it."

A sign on the unpretentious front door stated that The Ojai Valley Spiritualist Association met in a suite on the first floor.

Inside, the sanctuary wasn't a whole lot larger than Jessica's cottage. In lieu of church pews were rows of folding chairs. At the front of the room was a podium on a small riser, fronted by a beautiful flower arrangement: pink roses, lilies and baby's breath.

"There's coffee at the back," Sage said, indicating a table at the rear of the sanctuary, where a white-haired woman was arranging a basket of cookies and coffee paraphernalia. He leaned close to Jessica and said in an undertone, "You might want to decline. They use instant."

She grinned. "Thanks for the warning."

"Let me show you the gift shop. You said you wanted to learn about spiritualism, and they have some excellent books."

The gift shop was no bigger than a walk-in closet. A sweet-faced woman with tight grey curls and a pleasant smile stood behind a counter, ringing up a packet of incense.

Jessica perused the shelves, which held crystals, candles, bundles of sage and bottles of essential oil—wild rose, patchouli, sweet orange, white jasmine. And books.

The ones Jessica was looking for dealt with talking to the

dead—an entire shelf was devoted to the topic. She read the spines: John Edward, James Van Praagh, Suzanne Giesemann, Sandra Champlain. Names unknown to Jessica that excited her, made her impatient to dive in and immerse herself in their knowledge.

Sage, who had been chatting with the woman behind the counter while Jessica browsed, turned to her. "Found anything that looks interesting?"

The truth was, she would like to scoop up every book on the shelf and buy them all. But for now, limiting herself to three, she laid her choices on the counter.

"These sound pretty interesting: "Journey of Souls" and "One Last Time" and "We Don't Die.""

A big smile lit up Sage's face. "Three of my favorites."

"That's a great recommendation."

"You're gonna love them." He pushed a credit card across the counter to the woman who was already ringing up the books. "A gift from me."

"You don't need to do that," said Jessica, flustered for reasons she couldn't begin to explore.

"True, but I'd like to. Is it okay?"

The warm glow that suffused her as she thanked him was either an affirmation from spirit that she had selected the right books, or a sign of her growing attraction. Maybe both. It crossed her mind that Greg would have scoffed at her interest in an afterlife. He would have told her she was stupid to believe in 'that crap.' Sage could not be more different than her ex-husband.

They left the gift shop and returned to the sanctuary. They were not the only millennials among the boomers milling in small groups, but close. Most of the members filtering in showed signs of being on the far side of sixty.

Everyone who stopped to speak with Sage gave Jessica knowing smiles as he introduced her. They liked him, it was pretty obvious. And it was equally obvious that they were curious about the small woman with the blonde, almost-dreadlocks at his side. Had he brought other women here for them to check out? Jessica wondered as he led her to seats front and center, near the podium.

The woman who hurried up the aisle and took the stage was dressed in a tailored rose-pink jacket over a fitted, black skirt whose oversized magnolia flowers accentuated what Jessica thought of as a 'fluffy' body.

"That's Bella," Sage whispered.

Bella Bingham took a brass bowl from behind the podium and held it aloft in the palm of her left hand. When she tapped the side with a small mallet, a chime rang out and the chitchat meandered to a halt. The bell tones died away, leaving a hush.

With a warm smile, she introduced herself in an unpretentious British accent as Reverend Bella and welcomed them all.

"You said this wasn't a religion," Jessica said, *sotto voce.* "Reverend" said *religion* to her.

Sage leaned close and whispered, "It's not. You'll see."

Mimicking the movement of stirring a pot, Reverend Bella began to slowly run the mallet around the rim of the bowl, gradually increasing the speed. The soft sounds that emanated from the bowl grew to a haunting frequency until the vibrations enveloped Jessica and surrounded her heart, stirring emotions that were buried as deep as the grave.

"What is that?" she whispered.

Sage's breath was warm against her ear. "A Tibetan singing bowl."

"It's beautiful."

"Yes."

"I hope you will all join me in a nondenominational prayer and song," said Bella. Serenity shone from her face and radiated across the assembled crowd. "Len is handing out copies, so everyone who wants to can follow along."

A thin man in a golf shirt went from row to row, joking with members as he left small stacks of photocopied sheets to be passed out. When they all had a copy, a chorus of enthusiastic voices joined in with Reverend Bella's recitation of the prayer:

"Let my light shine with the spirit of All That Is, so others may know that I am becoming pure of heart. Let us live always in Love and Light. Allow only the highest and purest energies to touch us. Help us to understand the purpose of our lives and guide us to work through the lessons we have come here to learn. So be it."

Jessica chanted the words along with them all, an unaccustomed warmth spreading through her. Her head felt strangely empty of the murmuring spirit voices. She had become so accustomed to their chatter that she missed them. Sort of.

The prayer ended and a young man who looked a lot like Mr. Rogers in a cardigan and chinos took a seat at the piano. He began to play and they all sang:

> Let there be peace on earth.
> And let it begin with me.
> Let There Be Peace on Earth.
> The peace that was meant to be...

As Jessica began to sing, an unexpected lump clogged her throat and choked off the words. She sneaked a hand up to wipe away a stray tear, hoping no one noticed. But someone had. Sage leaned in with a gentle nudge. She glanced up into his face and was struck that somehow, he understood. The knowledge both comforted and rattled her at the same time.

"For the soul to grow," Bella began, "you must listen to what others are thinking and feeling. Do you butt into conversations? If you do, you will end up not listening to spirit any more than you listen to other people in a human body. Be aware of what is going on in the world so we can send our thoughts out to help those affected by tragedy. Send out a healing, send out soothing balm. Light a candle, say a prayer..."

The spellbinding gentleness of her voice set Jessica's mind adrift. The room faded away and the image of a small boy came to her. His pale face shone through a heavy darkness that Jessica understood was symbolic, not real.

Ethan. Where are you? Ethan...

Her ears, latching onto what Bella was saying, jerking her back to the sermon.

"...if you are receiving a name from spirit, let yourself go into the name. Register it on all levels. Allow yourself to know who it is and how it relates to a person who is here in the physical realm. Relate to the name..." Bella's gaze turned on Jessica. A slight smile curved her lips as their eyes met and the pastor appeared to deliver the message directly to her.

Closing her eyes, Jessica concentrated on the name, *Ethan.*

An impression of impishness in his eyes reminded her of Justin. Was she confusing the two boys? She dragged her attention back to the reverend.

"What has your soul made you aware of in the last few months? Have you been moving through a time that felt empty and cold? Go inside yourself, investigate the experience. Every tragedy or trauma holds a lesson. You wouldn't be where you are today if you had not first been there. What is your soul telling you? What is unfolding in the next chapter of your life?" Bella's gaze had been traveling around the room. Once more, it rested on Jessica.

"Have you lost a child? Remember, love can never die. Life never ends. Mediumship is about proving the connection between this world and the next. There is no death; only life after earth."

The words overwhelmed her, leaving her emotions stripped raw and exposed. Tears filled her eyes and spilled over, trickling down her cheeks and onto the hands tightly clasped in her lap. She was aware of Sage at her side, digging into his pockets, searching. He slipped a clean handkerchief into her hand.

In the years since Justin's death, the events that triggered her emotions were unpredictable. At times, his short life seemed unreal, nothing more than a beautiful dream. At other times, it was as if the accident had happened five minutes ago. Grief was an unreliable foe, always at hand, rearing its ugly head at its own amusement.

What if she disappeared without having to explain herself? Sage would never have to know about the crazy that lived inside her. How would he react when the information came out, as surely it would if they started seeing each other?

We're already seeing each other.

The group sang more songs, a woman in the audience made announcements about an upcoming potluck luncheon, then Bella uttered a closing prayer and stepped off the stage to greet the church members who hurried to huddle around her. Soon, the room was awash with the hum of conversation.

"It won't take long for the herd to thin and I can introduce you," said Sage. Then, apparently reading the truth in Jessica's eyes, "Or would you prefer to meet her some other time?"

She managed a weak smile. "Another time, I think. I enjoyed

the service, but I'd better get home. Headache."

His handsome face fell. "I was hoping to take you to lunch, show you around the Center. I bet we have some ibuprofen there."

"Could I get a rain check? Please? I'd love a tour, but I'm not up to it right now."

"Of course."

Retracing their steps to the Center where her Mini was parked, their talk stayed impersonal. The trees and plants, the local restaurants.

For Jessica, some of the pleasure had gone out of the morning.

TEN

Jessica was walking up the path to the cottage when she felt a vibration, like the wings of a bee near her face. It came and went in a blink. Then a soft, high voice spoke next to her ear.

"*Momma.*"

"Justin?" She hurried inside, listening with all her might. Again, as clear and recognizable as if her boy was standing right beside her, she heard him.

"*Mom. Please help my friend.*"

Now that he had her attention, the voice had moved inside Jessica's head. She answered him the same way, telepathically, reaching for names and faces of children Justin might have played with during his short life. "Which friend, sweetheart? Can you tell me a name?"

"*My new friend. You know, Mom.*"

An image flashed and took her breath away. Right in front of her was the face of the boy from her trance. Before she had time to react, the image of his melted face switched to skin as soft and clear as a newborn's, a face shining with a beautiful smile.

Is this the friend you want me to help?

As she framed the question to Justin, the truth of it pinged throughout Jessica's entire being. Yes. The next question was, what did he need help with and was it within her power to do what he needed? She would do anything for her son and if that meant helping his friend, she would be glad to comply with the request.

Who is he, baby?

"Mason. My friend. He needs you."

The words were not as clearly formed as they were an impression. The urgency in them made her listen. "What can I do for him, sweetheart?"

"Tell his mom he's okay."

How do I find her?

Another picture flashed. Mickey Mouse ears.

I don't understand. Mickey Mouse—Disneyland?

She waited for an answer, wondering how Mickey Mouse tied in with Mason. What would a seven-year-old boy use mouse ears to symbolize? When nothing happened, she asked another question.

Is it his mom's name—is it Micki?

No. The mouse ears flashed again. And again, and again with each guess. Jessica plopped onto the armchair and racked her brain for the meaning of the mouse ears. Reverend Bella's sermon came back to her. She'd said to focus on the name.

Visualizing the name Mason, and the boy's healthy face, she focused her attention on it.

Sleeping Beauty's castle popped into her head. Disneyland again.

Spirit shows me a picture and I'm supposed to guess what it means? This is like playing charades. Why don't they just tell me what they want me to know?

Sleeping Beauty. Disneyland? This isn't making sense.

Mickey Mouse hat with mouse ears.

A memory of Jen and her taking Justin to the Magic Kingdom came into her mind. The echoes of his delighted squeals made her smile even now. Having his picture taken hugging Mickey Mouse was the highlight of his day. Justin neither knew nor cared that the cartoon mouse suit was inhabited by an actor.

Jenna had insisted on buying him a mouse ears hat from one of the insanely expensive gift shops in the park, just like the one he was showing her now. She'd spent half as much again having her nephew's name embroidered on it in a premium font. Justin wore that hat everywhere, even to bed. For the next week, Jessica had to wait until he fell asleep before removing it and placing it close by so he could see it when he woke up.

Why was he showing her that hat now?

A huge letter "A" appeared in the air in front of her. Then the scent of orange blossoms. That was new; she'd never had olfactory visions before.

The puzzle was starting to come together. Oranges—Orange County—Sleeping Beauty's castle—Disneyland. Disneyland is in Anaheim.

Justin, does Mason's mom live in Anaheim?

The hat stopped flashing. Sweet relief. But how in God's name was she supposed to find some random mother in the tenth largest city in the state of California?

Even as the question formed in her mind, a holographic image appeared that made her laugh. A long-haired, black and white guinea pig that Greg had brought home for Justin during one of their better periods. Justin had named it Piglet.

What's Piglet have to do with it, Jus'?

The image switched to a brown, short-haired guinea pig. She heard, *"Binky."*

Binky? Okay, we're playing a guessing game. Is Binky like Piglet? He's a guinea pig, too?

"Tell Mason's mom. Binky is with him."

Okay, baby, I will. But I need more than that.

Next, she got the image of a house on fire. Of course. Mason had died in a fire and he lived in Anaheim. Jessica sighed.

Couldn't you just give me the address and phone number?

Apparently not. She booted up her laptop and launched a browser. Mason was not a common first name. If Justin was able to impress upon her the information he already had, it must be possible to find his friend's mother. She Googled the few facts she had, "Mason, child, fire, Anaheim."

An article from the *OC Register* popped up from a year ago, detailing the story of a deadly house fire.

> *Franklin Carpenter of West Anaheim arrived home late Thursday afternoon to find black smoke and flames billowing from his home. Roneisha Carpenter was in the front yard with their infant daughter in*

a hysterical state. Their son, Mason, was inside the home. The fire department was not yet on scene.

Mr. Carpenter was able to carry his eight-year-old son from the house, but sustained serious injuries to his hands. Unfortunately, Mason Carpenter succumbed to second- and third-degree burns and smoke inhalation two days later.

The articles left Jessica wracked with sadness for the family. In a very real sense, she was one of them. A member of the club no one wanted to join.

Now that she knew their name and location, her next task was to find a way to pass along their son's message.

The face of the horrible man at the grocery store popped into her mind. His reaction to her attempt to deliver the message from his father had given her a very real scare. That was one experience she was eager not to repeat.

The thought came to her, if someone wanted to give her a message from Justin, there was nothing she would not do to get it.

She had to find Mason's mother.

Once again, Jessica felt her life taken over by another world, one shrouded in mystery.

As she thought how to go about the task, the words of Bella Bingham's sermon came back to her again. "…go into the name. Register it on all levels. Allow yourself to know who it is and how it relates to a person who is here in the physical realm. Relate to the name…"

Mason Carpenter.

It took time, but the images came. Flashes of scenes from the child's life. A sweet boy who loved to help his mother in the kitchen, wearing an oversized apron, a floppy chef's toque, and a happy grin as he slathered mayonnaise on bread and constructed a bologna sandwich.

Mason's father, Franklin Carpenter of Anaheim, had a Facebook page. His profile picture showed a good-looking African American couple in their late thirties, a small baby on the mother's lap. Mason stood beside his father, wearing a grin. Another photo, dated a month ago, showed the baby grown into a cute toddler. The too-recent tragedy was written on the parents' fixed smiles.

Jessica hesitated. As she was not their Facebook friend, they might not receive a private message. Considering what had happened with Grocery Store Guy, a phone call might be safer than an in-person visit. The family was listed on a White Pages site. She wrote out the phone number and let it sit while she pondered over whether to make the call.

How would these people accept the news Justin wanted her to give them?

"Tell her, Mom," Justin said, flashing alternating images of Mickey Mouse ears and Piglet and Binky. *"Tell her. Mason. Binky."*

Okay, Justin, I will, but please, baby, stop the pictures. You're making me dizzy.

She spent a few minutes deciding what to say, then reached for the phone.

A pleasant female voice answered on the second ring. Jessica's mouth went dry. Everything she had planned was suddenly erased from her mind.

"Hello? Can I help you? Hello?"

Jessica cleared her throat and forced herself to speak, stumbling over her words. "Is this Mrs. Carpenter? Hi, um, my name is Jessica. This is going to sound kind of strange but, I, um…you don't know me."

"Who did you say this is? What is it you want?" The woman's voice had turned suspicious.

"My name is Jessica Mack, and I had a son who died." Even without seeing the woman at the other end of the line, Jessica felt her stiffen.

"What? What did you say?"

"Please, let me—lately, I've experienced some—um, unusual things. I have a message to give you. Does the name 'Binky' mean anything to you?"

After a long silence on the line, Jessica heard a faint, "Oh, my Lord. Who told you—? What is it you want? *Who are you?*"

"I'm just a person. I—I'm not a professional medium or anything, but my boy brought your son to me. Mason wants you to trust that he's fine and that he has Binky with him."

Roneisha Carpenter began to sob, which made Jessica want to cry, too. Holding back her own tears, she gave Mason's mother time to regain her composure before she continued. "I'm so sorry to burst out with it that way, but I didn't know how to—"

"What is it you want?" she asked for the third time. "Money?"

"No, no, I don't want anything, just to give you the message."

"How do you know about little Binky?" Roneisha Carpenter demanded, her tone heavy with suspicion.

"My son in spirit, Justin, showed me a picture of a brown guinea pig he used to have."

"That poor little creature died in the fire."

"I'm sorry about your boy, and I expect this must sound crazy to you..."

"Wh-what did you say your name is?"

"It's Jessica."

"Jessica," Roneisha Carpenter echoed. "Praise the Lord. My Mason loved his Binky. I'm so happy to know his pet made it to heaven with my child. God is good."

Mason's face appeared to Jessica, who was limp with relief that his mother had accepted the message. "He's smiling. He has such a beautiful smile."

"Yes, he did indeed."

"He still does."

"That makes me so happy, I can't even tell you. What else did my Mason say?"

"He wants you to know how much he loves you and his dad, and—" Jessica listened to the boy in spirit. "He says it wasn't your fault. He wants you to stop blaming yourself."

A wail burst from Roneisha Carpenter. It tore at Jessica's emotions but she was convinced she had done the right thing in making the call.

"He liked to cook, didn't he?" she said, when Mason's mother was calmer. "He shows himself wearing a chef outfit."

"Oh, my good God, he did love to help me. If only I..." Roneisha Carpenter excused herself and went to blow her nose. When she returned, she said, "I left him alone in the kitchen and went outside to talk to the neighbor, just for a couple of minutes. I'd told him to watch the soup I had on the range. The firemen think maybe it boiled over; that he was trying to move the pot and a dishcloth caught fire." She wept some more. "I'm always so careful not to keep those dishcloths near the flame. If I only..."

"It doesn't help to say I'm sorry, but I am," said Jessica, wanting to spare the mother from more self-recrimination. She knew all too well how easy it was to lapse into hating oneself for an unintentional act that could never be undone.

"Why can't I hear him myself?" Roneisha wailed. "Why does he have to go through you?"

"I can't answer that." Jessica searched for the right words. "Hearing from people on the other side this way is very new to me. From the little bit I've learned, I'd guess that your grief is so strong it's made it hard for him to get through to you. There's nothing wrong with that; I totally get it. But maybe now that you know he's around you, even though you can't see him, it will help. I know he'll find ways to say hello if you look for them. The most important thing I've learned is, there's no such thing as death."

"Thank you, Jessica," said Mrs. Carpenter through her tears. "Thank you, thank you. If it means I can feel him near me, I'll never cry again."

"I'm sure that's not necessary," Jessica smiled. "Talk to him like you did while he was here. He'll hear you, and he'll show you that he's with you."

"How can he do that?"

"It might be lights flickering or a song on the radio that brings him into your mind, or maybe a certain smell, or a butterfly," Jessica said, recalling what she had read on some of the spiritualist websites.

"I *will* talk to him," Roneisha Carpenter said fervently. "You better know I will. And I will listen for him, every minute of every day. Did you say you lost a child, too, Jessica?"

"Yes, in a car accident. He would have been three the next month."

"Oh, my dear, I'm so sorry for you, too. How long has it been?"

"Five years."

"Five years," Roneisha echoed. "Tell me, does it get any easier?"

Jessica blew out a sigh. "Honestly? In my experience, the pain doesn't away. You just learn to live with it. *Knowing* that my child is alive, though he's growing up in another place, helps me."

They chatted for a few minutes longer, then Mason's mother

said she couldn't wait to share her son's messages with his father. She asked for Jessica's phone number and thanked her a dozen more times before ending the call.

Jessica clicked off, thinking how much better that experience was than the one with Grocery Store Guy. She was thanking Justin and Mason for connecting her with Roneisha Carpenter when a brilliant beam of sunshine came through the kitchen window and brightened the entire cottage. Bathed in its warmth, Jessica felt something rare. Pure happiness.

That evening, Sage phoned, asking if she was feeling better. Jessica caught herself smiling into the phone. Greg had never expressed concern over her well-being. From the perspective of five years distance from her ex-husband, she was disgusted with herself for having stayed with him for so long.

Until now, the one caring man in her life was Dr. Gold, and he was her therapist, so he *had* to care. It's what he was paid for. Her father had humored his wife in adopting the twins but showed virtually no interest in them during the rare times he spent at home. The men she had dated had not stuck around long enough for her to get to know them. As for Zach, he was a good guy, but the relationship was short-lived.

It struck her that she had not allowed anyone to get within emotional touching distance in a very long time. Maybe ever.

Recognizing the bad choices she had made in the past made Jessica question her attraction to Sage. Instinctively, she knew there was much to be explored there. Yet, with her lousy track record, she worried there must be something wrong with him that she had yet to discover. He was the best-looking dude she had ever met but it was not his looks that had captivated her. She had only to look at her failed marriage to appreciate that on its own, physical attractiveness had a limited shelf life.

"Bella can't wait to meet you," Sage said, bringing her attention back. "She noticed you this morning."

"Yeah, I bet she did," Jessica muttered. "Look, I'm sorry I ran out on you. I enjoyed her talk, I really did, but—it was all a bit overwhelming."

"It's fine. How about tomorrow? Bella's in the office after nine."

"I would love that, thank you."

"I can pick you up."

"You're going to drive all the way down here, pick me up and go back to Ojai, then reverse the whole trip? Thanks, but it's not necessary."

"I don't mind, I like to drive."

"I know where the place is now. Can we meet up after I see Bella? If you're not too busy. I mean, if you're still willing to give me a tour—" Jessica trailed off, half-expecting Sage to be annoyed at her refusal to go along with his plan. Greg would have pitched a fit.

It was important to nip the impulse to make that comparison in the bud. The two men were nothing alike.

Sage did not hesitate, nor did he argue with her decision. "Text me when you're finished with Bella," he said. "I'll collect on that lunch rain check."

She could not help smiling. "I'll be there by nine-thirty."

ELEVEN

The Reverend Bella Bingham had traded her Sunday finery for a green, floral-print, maxi dress. Her white, candy-floss hair stood out in a halo around her head, like a motherly angel.

"Come along and sit down, darling," she said, in her down-to-earth Northern English accent, guiding Jessica through the sanctuary to a door at the back. "We'll have our little talk in my office."

The office was a small room crammed with file cabinets and bookshelves. The desktop was invisible, hidden under stacks of paper and books. Bella took the seat at the desk and offered her guest a folding chair.

Jessica, having been hit by a fit of anxiety as she left her car, seemed to have lost her voice.

Praying that an episode was not on the horizon, she took her seat and forced the words out. "Reverend Bella—"

"Oh, please luv," Bella interrupted, pronouncing the word "loov." "It's just plain Bella. We don't stand on ceremony here. C'n I get you a cup of tea?"

"No, thanks. I'm fine."

"All right then. Now, before we begin and you tell me what's on your mind, I have to say to you, I've got a little boy here. He's been pestering me all morning." She leaned forward and took both of Jessica's hands in her own. "He's a dear little thing, isn't he? He says he wants you to know that he's going to help you."

Nothing had prepared Jessica for Bella's announcement. The shock made her stammer. "My—I—"

"It's all right, darling. You're on the right path. Now, what can I do for you?"

"Wait—you can see him? Is he saying anything else?"

"Mmm, give me a minute, luv." Bella looked past her, letting her eyes droop to half-mast. "He's showing me the letter 'J'. Of course, your name is Jessica, but it's not you. It's another 'J' name connected with you. Does that mean anything to you, darling? Just say yes or no."

"Yes. Yes."

Bella tipped her head to the side, seeming to listen to the spirit that Jessica was not able to see.

"What's that? Oh, okay. J—Judah? No, wait a minute." With her eyes closed, Bella started talking very fast, as if she couldn't keep up with what was being shown to her. "The spirits are drawing the letter 'J' over the little boy's head. It must be his name. Come on then, give me a clue—no, not you, dear. I want *him* to tell me. *Oh,* I see. It's Justin, is it?"

"Yes."

"He's crossed at a very young age, hasn't he? Not an infant, but—more like a toddler. This is your child? I feel like I'm going very fast, flying through the air. I'm strapped in, like an airplane, but it's not a plane. Ohhhh, it's a car accident, is it? Just yes or no."

"Yes."

"Well, darling, you're not to worry about him at all. He's not alone. There's an older lady in spirit who's taking care of him. She's standing beside you on your right."

Reflexively, Jessica turned her head to look but saw nothing.

"Is there a grandmother for you in spirit?" asked Bella.

"I don't know. I was adopted as a baby, so it's possible."

"It's all right, darling. This lady in spirit is named Elizabeth and she says she's your grandmother. She's on your right, and that's my symbol for being your father's side. She says she was there to meet little Justin when he crossed and she's taking care of him for you." With her eyes still closed, Bella took a box of tissues from her desk and handed it to Jessica, who was wiping away tears with the back of her hand. "Now, who is—Jen—Jennifer?"

"Jenna."

"All right, I'll take that. Jenna."

"My sister."

"She's the spitting image of you, isn't she? Like a mirror reflection. Are you twins, then?"

"Yes, we are. We're identical twins"

"I thought you must be. Your grandmother is showing herself sitting in a rocking chair with two little baby girls in her lap. She looks so pleased."

"I don't remember her at all."

"No, you wouldn't, would you at that age? I'm losing the connection now, but granny Elizabeth and Justin are sending you waves of love. Oh, my darling girl, I can't tell you how much love is surrounding you. You must never feel that you're alone."

Every agony from the past five years welled up, an immense balloon, filling her up and bursting. Jessica gave up trying to control her emotions. Bella gave her tissues and she wept them sodden. The pastor let her go until she was drained, then handed her a bottle of water.

"The loss of a child is like no other," said Bella. "It goes against nature, doesn't it, luv. Now, tell me what I can do to help."

Jessica drew a shuddering breath and gulped down the water. She scrubbed a fresh tissue across her face. "I've been hearing voices since I had a head injury in a car accident—the accident where my son was killed five years ago. I've tried not to listen, but lately, it's been impossible. They line up, the dead people. There's even a red velvet rope they stand behind, like they're going to an event. And they all have messages they want me to give, day and night. I'm barely getting any sleep."

A benevolent smile warmed Bella's face. "Never mind, luv, you've got to set office hours."

"*Office* hours?" Jessica echoed.

"Well, yeah. You can't be open all the time, can you?" Bella reached over and patted Jessica's hand. "It's a bit like this: let's say you open a bakery. You bake the most delicious cakes and pies and donuts. Word spreads. Soon, everybody's heard how fabulous this bakery is. What would happen then?"

"People show up to buy the goods?"

"That's right. And if you don't post your hours on the front door, you'd have hungry people showing up all hours, expecting you to always have cakes in the display case.

"It's the same with the world of spirit. It's hard for them to get messages to the people on earth who they love, so once they know someone can hear or see them, word gets around fast. They don't mean any harm by it, but time isn't the same over there. What you've got to do is put a nice little sign by your bed, telling them you keep office hours—let them when you're available to help them. Or if you'd rather not help at all, you can say that, too."

Jessica shook her head. "It's not that I don't want to help. My son brought me another little boy and I got hold of his mother, gave her his message, which I was happy to do. I've had one bad experience, too. So, I can't go around looking for people and telling them I've got messages from their dead relatives."

Bella grinned. "Well, not unless you want to become a career medium."

"Um, no, I already have a career in art."

Bella wagged her finger like a teacher to a student. "Spirit might have other plans for you, darling, you'll have to wait and see. Which of the clairs do you have?"

"Excuse me? I don't—"

"The clairs, darling. There are five main ones. Clairvoyance is clear seeing—that means you see images, or the actual person in spirit. Claircognizance is clear knowing. It means you have well-developed intuition, you just know. Then there's clairaudience, clear hearing—in other words, you *hear* messages from spirit. And there's clairgustance, clear tasting. If you have that ability, spirit might give you the taste of a flavor that's meaningful to the sitter—that's the person you're giving the message to. And clairsalience, which is clear smelling—you might smell a flower or a perfume that the sitter identifies with. Some mediums have all the clairs, but most just have one or two."

Struggling to grasp the mass of information, Jessica deliberately slowed her breathing, keeping herself bound to the present instead of going off into a syncope episode. "I think I must have clairaudience because I hear the voices. I've started seeing images and sometimes whole people, so that was clair—?"

"Clairvoyance. Well, dear, others may come along as you develop."

"Develop? This is all so new to me—how do I know—"

"Don't upset yourself. It will unfold as you learn to sit in the power." At Jessica's questioning look, Bella continued. "Find a quiet place where you won't be disturbed. Close your eyes if you like, and imagine yourself surrounded by a column of white light that goes up into the heavens and down into the earth. Ask spirit for only the best and highest energies to protect you. Remember how we asked that in the prayer yesterday? You see, luv, not all energies have your best interests in mind. Open your chakras—you know about chakras?"

"A little. They're different energy centers through the body, right?"

"That's right," said Bella, beaming as though Jessica was her star pupil. "Open your chakras and concentrate on your breathing. Don't try to make anything happen, just let it happen naturally. It might take some practice. Or, since you're already in touch with spirit, you might start getting messages straight away.

"You might meet a spirit guide or an angel, or maybe your grandmother Elizabeth. If that happens, you can ask questions and see what answers you get. While you're in the light, nothing can hurt you."

"I will do that, thank you, Bella. But I have a question. Is it possible to—I'm not sure how to ask this—to connect with someone who's missing?"

"Someone who is still on the earth plane, you mean?"

"Yes. At least, I think so. It's a young child. He may be in danger. I'm hoping to locate him."

Bella's forehead wrinkled into a slight frown as she considered the question. "It's quite possible, but there's no guaranty, you see, dear. The process would be the same, but that's more on a psychic level. Here's what I would do if I were you. Put on some nice meditation music and sit in the power, ask spirit to step into your energy and merge with you. Focus on the name of the person you want to locate. Ask your guides for help."

"I have guides?"

"We all have guides, darling, we just have to introduce ourselves. Now, I've got to go. I've got someone else coming in, but let's talk again soon."

They rose and as Bella walked her to the exit, Jessica decided to create a miniature fairy garden for her as a thank you. "I appreciate everything you've done for me today. Thank you so much, Bella."

"Don't you think another thing about it, luv. You'd do well to come to one of the mediumship classes we hold here. And as I think of it, there's a well-known medium in Los Angeles who has a development circle. His name is Russell Levine. It's a bit of a drive, but you might want to sit in some time and see what they're doing. He's listed on our website. People come from all over to see him. He's one of the very few successful physical mediums in the world."

"I read about physical mediums on your website. I'm not sure I understand how that's different from the other kind."

"Mental or evidential mediums deliver regular messages that spirit wants to get through—like what you and I do. Real physical mediumship is quite rare these days. The spirit team that works with the medium from the other side decides in advance who is going to materialize."

"Someone actually materializes?"

"Oh, yes, dear. Mind you, there has to be a very good reason for them to do so. Like stopping someone from committing suicide or giving a warning or wanting to express regret. Things like that. It's not something light, done for fun."

"Sounds incredible. I'll definitely check it out."

Bella put her arms around Jessica and gave her a warm hug. "I can't tell you how pleased I am to see Sage looking happy again. It's been too long."

"He seems very nice."

'Nice' was inadequate, considering the emotions he stirred in her. They arrived at the exit.

"He's such a dear soul. He's gone through so much. I was *that* relieved when they dropped the charges."

Jessica jerked around. "What charges?"

Bright red blotches bloomed on the medium's cheeks. "Oh, dear, I must be speaking out of turn. Never mind, luv. Forget I said anything. He'll tell you all about it when he's ready."

TWELVE

Dropped the charges? Charged with what?

It had to be major or why would Bella have mentioned it at all? And why had she then refused to elaborate? Maybe it was something that would stop Jessica from wanting to continue seeing him.

It would have to be pretty bad to do that.

Claudia would know. And if Claudia was matchmaking—as Jessica was quite certain she was—it would not be like her to bring them together if she knew anything awful about him. But if it wasn't bad, why did Bella say—

"Hey, Jessica, where are you?" Sage's appearance at the Center's gate brought her back to earth with a thump. He must be wondering if she always walked around with her head in the clouds.

"Oh, sorry, I was thinking of what Bella said."

"Was she helpful?"

"She was sensational. I got way more from that visit than I expected."

"I had a sneaky feeling you two would get along well."

"Yes, I think we did."

"Let's go up to the house," he said. "I'll show you around."

Today, the jungle gym and lawn were deserted.

"Where are children?" Jessica asked.

"They're in class." He exchanged waves with a gardener on a

riding mower cutting the vast swath of grass around the house. "Thinking about lunch, I bet."

The foyer of Regina Boles Center for Traumatized Children brought the outdoors inside. Airy, light-filled, flourishing green plants everywhere, which seemed symbolic—the traumatized children growing strong and healthy. The entire back wall was an arched window that looked out onto a field bordered by woods. The architectural details had turned the ranch house into a therapeutic school.

"This is wonderful," Jessica exclaimed. "It must take a big staff to keep up a place of this size."

"You're right, it does."

"How old are the kids?"

"Four to twelve. At this point we're not planning to take teenagers. Can't mix older kids with the little ones. With the kind of trauma they've endured, they each need a specialized environment."

They peeked into two classrooms. More plants, bright colors, modular furniture. The youngest children filled the first classroom. They were seated at low round tables, bent over coloring projects. Their teacher, a fiftyish woman, strolled around, enthusiastically praising them. She looked up and waved at Sage and Jessica with a smile. He waved back.

"We felt that having an older teacher, like a grandma person, would be comforting to the little ones. For the older kids, the teacher is younger, relatable on a different level," said Sage.

In the second classroom, the tables were empty. The older students sat cross-legged on mats in a semi-circle, their faces rapt as their teacher read to them. She was holding the book so the cover was visible: "The Girl Who Drank the Moon."

"How long do they typically stay with you?" Jessica asked.

"It's a basic eight-week program. Intensive therapy helps stabilize them. They have their art therapy classes and playtime, plus two hours of regular schoolwork to keep them up to date and help get them ready to go back into regular school or into a longer-term therapeutic situation. A few stay on if they need to—the most difficult cases. This group is in their last week. If you'd seen them when they arrived compared to now, you wouldn't believe they were the same kids."

In the kitchen he introduced her to the chef, Leon Small, who was anything but. Leon was busy putting the garnishes on lunch.

"Nutritious *and* delicious," he said, flashing a smile that gleamed against mahogany skin. Viewing the array of sliced turkey, fruit, and salad vegetables set out on a long table beside loaves of steaming bread fresh from the oven, Jessica was inclined to believe him. Leon told them his helper, his granddaughter, Akilah, was setting tables in the dining room and they left him to his preparations.

"What about the mural you told me you're painting in the dining room?" Jessica asked as they left the kitchen.

"Some of the kids and me. I'll show it to you when it's done."

"Okay."

He showed her the nurse's office and the six bedrooms, each with four beds—half for the younger kids, half for the older ones. There were two additional bedrooms for the psychologist in residence and an aide. Student artwork decorated the walls in all the hallways.

"This seems like the kind of place where a kid could thrive," said Jessica.

"We have a consulting psychologist and two others on staff full-time, plus three clinical social workers—one is a registered nurse who also teaches. And currently we have three volunteers." Something caught his attention past Jessica's shoulder. He beckoned. "Hey, look who's here. Hey, Annabelle, c'mon over."

Turning, Jessica saw a petite teen who did not look much older than some of the students. She wore her long hair in a sleek, black ponytail that swung behind her as she approached. A dark fringe fell over her eyebrows. She did a slight chin jerk in greeting and gazed at Jessica with frank curiosity. "Hey, Sage. What's up?"

"You and Jessica know each other, don't you?"

"Jessica?" the girl echoed. "Claudia's friend?"

"You know Claudia?" Jessica said. Then it clicked. The name was not all that common. "Oh, wait, you're Claudia's Annabelle?"

"Yep, that's me."

Sage seemed amused by their reactions. "You two have never met?"

Jessica shook her head. "In all the time I've known Claudia, this is the first time Annabelle and I have come face-to-face."

"I know, huh? Kinda crazy," said Annabelle.

"So, you're a volunteer here?"

The dark head bobbed up and down. "I started last month and I love it. I come once a week and I get work credit at school, too."

Jessica calculated her age. "You must be a senior, right?"

"Yep. I graduate in June."

"Wow, that's great. So, you're killing two birds with one stone. Not that I throw stones at birds, of course." As she was speaking, a soft voice entered Jessica's head.

*"For the moon never beams, without bringing me dreams;
Of the beautiful Annabelle Lee."*

A woman in spirit was now standing at Annabelle's left side, hazy but definitely present.

While Annabelle rolled her eyes at the inane comment about bird killing, Jessica spoke telepathically to the woman.

The poem by Poe? Who are you?

*"And this maiden she lived with no other thought;
Than to love and be loved by me."*

"I gotta go help Akilah," said Annabelle, twirling with a finger wave. "Nice meeting you, Jessica."

"Nice meeting you, too. Say hi to Claudia for me."

"I will."

As the teen started to turn away, the woman in spirit reached out to caress her hair. The girl jerked as if feeling the touch. Looking puzzled, she reached up and scratched her head. She then shrugged and continued along the hallway and out of sight.

The spirit woman was a true beauty. She looked young—late twenties—and wore modern clothing. Who was she and why did she want to talk about Annabelle? Remembering Bella's advice, Jessica asked the spirit to leave. This was not the time nor the place to blab to the girl that a dead lady was here and wanted to contact her. To her relief, the spirit obeyed and faded back into the ether, or wherever she had come from.

"This is my office," Sage said, showing her inside. "If there's anyone who can relate to these kids on their own level, it's Annabelle. Her mom was killed in a car accident when she was six years old."

Her mom. Cha ching.

"I remember Claudia told me she was raised by a rotten stepfather and attempted suicide more than once before she was fourteen," said Jessica. Should she try to call the spirit woman back? "She was kidnapped, then went to live with Claudia until her dad was able to take her. That's a load of trauma for a kid her age."

"Yes, and she's had loads of therapy," Sage said. "Annabelle is the youngest volunteer and came to us through Claudia." He grinned. "She would like us to think that she doesn't care too much, but if you ever watch her with the kids, it's obvious that she loves working with them. It's going to be hard on her when this group graduates. The younger ones fall all over themselves to get her attention."

"I guess the best person for the job is someone who's been there."

"I think so, too."

Would Annabelle welcome hearing from her dead mother?

Duh. Who wouldn't want to hear from the mother you'd lost as a kid?

Sage was giving her that quizzical look. Wondering where her mind was, she guessed. Again. Maybe he was already questioning her sanity. And then she thought of Bella's parting words. *What charges?*

"Oh, Sage, I'm so sorry. I just remembered a call I've got to make. Would you mind if—"

He put up his hands to cut short her apology. "Take your time. Come find me in the foyer when you're ready."

The moment he stepped out into the hallway and closed the door, Jessica sent an urgent message to Annabelle's mother in spirit. Not knowing her name, she concentrated on Annabelle and the apparition she had seen.

Come now. Connect with me, please. Tell me what you want her to know.

Seconds later, her hand started tingling, like pins and needles. As if someone else had taken control of her hand, she fished her phone from her purse and began tapping on the keyboard, faster than she had typed in her entire life. As soon as she pressed send, she regained control of her hand.

She looked at the screen. She had sent a text to Claudia:

Tell Annabelle: check left rear tire before driving.
Urgent. Will explain later.

Jessica spoke telepathically to Annabelle's mother.

What's wrong with her tire?

"Don't let her drive until it's fixed. My beautiful Annabelle Lee."

With that, the young mother faded again. Jessica went out to the foyer to meet Sage. Annabelle was entering through the front doors from the outside, a worried frown on her face.

"One of my front tires is way low," she said to Sage. "I've gotta call AAA to come and change it. Is it okay to let them through the gate?"

"If you have a spare I can change it for you."

"My dad always takes care of stuff like that," she frowned, looking baffled. "It's so weird. I just got a text from Claudia. She said to check my tires right away. I wonder what made her do that."

Sage sent a suspicious glance at Jessica, who was doing her best to look innocent. She said, "Wow, I guess she must be psychic. Thank goodness. You wouldn't want to get a flat tire on the way home."

"Right, huh? Especially at that curvy section of PCH right next to the ocean? It'd be so scary to have a problem there. You could go right off the road." Annabelle gave a little shudder. "That's what happened to my mom."

Jessica, who was not a touchy-feely person, reached over and gave her a quick hug. "She's watching over you. I bet she gave Claudia the idea to send you that text."

Annabelle looked at her strangely. "You really think so?"

"I really do."

"If you've got a decent spare, it won't take long," Sage said. "Jessica, you can hang out in here, if you like, and kid-watch."

"Sounds good."

They walked off together. Annabelle looked back at her with a huge smile and Jessica sent a silent thank you to the woman in spirit, who she was now certain was the girl's mother. It made perfect sense for someone who had died in a car accident to watch out for her daughter's safety on the road.

Following her phone call to Roneisha Carpenter about her little boy, Mason, it felt good to deliver another well-received message. It canceled out Mean Grocery Store Guy, Jessica decided, feeling pleased with herself.

A gong sounded and the classroom doors opened. Children spilled out into the hallway.

"Remember, walk, don't run," the older teacher called after them.

Jessica watched them hurry to the dining room, walking in pairs, some chattering to a companion, others head-down, shy or perhaps avoiding eye contact.

If only Justin—she cut off the thought. Her wistful yearning would not bring him back. She reminded herself to be grateful that he had come to her in spirit. Most grieving mothers lived without the knowledge that their children were safe and alive in another world. It made her want to become a spiritual evangelist and tell them all the truth.

The kids at the Center were here because they had suffered terrible harm. Instead of spending energy on the impossible dream of cuddling her own child, she could use it to send out waves of love to these children, the way Bella had said that her grandmother was sending love to her. So, that's what she did.

Osteria Monte Grappa in Downtown Ojai billed itself as an ItalAgriGastroBar.

Their table was under an umbrella among the trees on the patio. The sun was pale in a bright blue sky, the temperature cool. Space heaters kept them comfortable.

Sage made his choice and laid down the menu. His hands were slim and well-shaped with long fingers. On his right hand he wore a gold ring with a green stone.

"That's a beautiful ring," Jessica said.

He thanked her and slipped it off, passed it across the table. Seeing it up close, she was intrigued. On each side was a carved design that resembled a cross, but whose top arm was instead a loop.

"That's an ankh. It's the Egyptian symbol of life."

"I've never seen a stone quite like that."

"It's called green copper turquoise. It has healing properties. It's supposed to get rid of negative energy and instill calm. I'm not sure whether it works, but I like to think so."

"You do have a serene sort of air about you," said Jessica, liking the fact that he was secure enough to let her know he was interested in things like Egyptian symbols and healing.

He grinned. "You haven't seen me in traffic."

Once they had ordered and the waiter left them alone, he sat back and said nothing, just looked at her.

"How long have you lived in Ojai?" Jessica asked, feeling pushed to fill the silence.

"Since I was a young kid. How long have you been a medium?" When she gasped, he smiled. "Bella told me she got a strong message about you."

Jessica quirked an eyebrow at him, relieved that he knew her secret and was still here with her, and annoyed with Bella for telling him, all at the same time. "And here I thought you were psychic. The fact is, I'm just beginning to learn what a medium is. That's why I asked about Bella's Association."

The sapphire eyes bored into hers, sparking with interest. "You mean you've just started getting messages?"

She had gone through her explanation with Jenna and Dr. Gold. The third time, it was getting easier. "I've heard spirit for several years but until recently, I ignored them."

Right at that moment, Dr. Gold's dead wife, Madeleine, chose to appear. This time she brought with her the same female spirit that had showed up when Sage came to collect the German Shepherd sculpture.

The two women stood together, arms linked, a good-looking pair who resembled each other, dressed in a style of clothing that Jessica guessed was from the 1950s. The woman with Madeleine was pointing at Sage.

"You look distracted," said Sage. "Are you seeing something now?"

"Yes, and I'm confused. There's a woman I've seen twice before. She showed up the day you came to my house. Now she's brought another woman with her but they're not telling me what they want. Normally I would think they belong to you because they're standing on your left, which is the mother's side, according to Bella. What's confusing me is, they showed up at my therapist's office, too. One of them is his ex-wife and she wanted me to give him a message. Why are they here with you?"

Sage was gazing at her with an intensity that made his eyes spark. "Do you mind if I ask who your therapist is?"

"His name is Zebediah Gold, why?"

He nodded as if expecting her answer. "He's our consulting psychologist."

"I guess that makes sense, with you knowing Claudia. So why is his ex and this other lady—she keeps pointing at you—"

"The other lady is my mother."

Jessica's mouth dropped. "Your mother?"

"Zebediah's ex-wife is my Aunt Maddy—Madeleine Maynard. She's the one who left me the money I used to fund the Center and…another project. My mother, Regina Boles, and Aunt Maddy, were sisters. They both died within a few months of each other, not very long ago—less than two years."

The shadow that crossed his face reached right inside her and twisted her heart as if his pain were her own. "Oh, Sage, you've had two huge losses so close together. I'm so sorry. I had no idea it was your aunt who gave me a message for Dr. Gold to give to you—that she is proud of what you've done. Now it all makes sense. You've created a wonderful legacy in her name."

"She deserves it," he said. "When Zebediah gave me the message, he just told me it came through a client. Jessica, this is huge."

"True, that." Her eyes focused on the space to his right, where the two women in spirit were standing. She said, "Your mom has a big grin. She's making her hands into a heart. That's so sweet. Oh, they're fading away. I think they just wanted you to know they're here and that they love you, and they're still in your life since they crossed to the other side."

Sage's eyes were glistening. He swallowed hard. "I'm happy they're together again."

"Me, too." Jessica gave him a long look. "So, knowing what you know about me now, you don't think I'm a total weirdo?"

"I wouldn't go that far." He grinned. "The truth is, I think you're amazing and I'd like the chance to get to know you better."

Annoyed with herself blushing in front of him yet again, Jessica said, "I think you're pretty amazing yourself, using your inheritance to help these kids."

He shrugged as if the money meant nothing to him. "Maddy was obscenely wealthy and had no kids of her own, so she made me her heir. My grandfather disinherited my mother when she ran away from home. He was a big muckety-muck attorney with tons of family money. Maddy got it all when he died—my grandmother had already passed. Then, a few years later, Maddy's second husband was killed in a plane crash. He owned a bank and was loaded. So…you get the picture."

"You didn't have to use it that way. You're a good guy, Sage."

"Do you always make such quick judgments?"

Jessica, who had been stirring sweetener into her iced tea, looked up. "What?"

"We've barely met. What makes you think I'm a good guy?"

"Well—I can only judge by what I've seen, and…"

"You should be more careful," he said. Then he smiled again, slow and easy. "Ah, I'm just yankin' your chain. You've got all those spirits to warn you if there's a problem."

All those spirits. Jessica reached up and touched the pentacle necklace that she wore under her clothing. She thought again of Bella's words, and wondered.

What charges against Sage?

THIRTEEN

"No new information today in the *desperate* search for four-year-old Ethan Starkey."

News anchor Jeanine Riley was known to get emotional in cases involving children. With her wavy blonde hair and large eyes, it played well for the camera. Shuffling papers on her desk, pouting her botoxed lips, she looked earnestly into the camera.

"The Thousand Oaks child was reported missing after his father failed to return him home from a trip to Disneyland last Thursday. What kind of father takes a boy away from his mother like that? She's been pleading for his safe return ever since. Police have released surveillance footage from the hotel where the pair was staying. Our own Keith Lewis is outside the Federal Office Building in West L.A. Keith, tell us what's happening."

The screen had been displaying grainy black and white security video of Trey Starkey walking out of a hotel, Ethan beside him. Over and over, the station replayed the scene. A man and his son, walking over to Disneyland from their hotel. To any onlooker, nothing was out of the ordinary.

The screen switched to a reporter on the sidewalk in front of the Federal Building sign in Los Angeles. Mid-thirties, short hair brushed straight up, his face arranged in a serious expression. He brought the microphone up to his face. "Unfortunately, Jeanine, there are apparently no new leads in this investigation. As we've just seen in the security cam images released earlier today by the FBI, the boy's father, Trey Starkey, and his young son Ethan entered their hotel. They left around six o'clock last Thursday evening and haven't been seen since. The boy was last spotted wearing denim jeans, a medium-blue, hooded sweatshirt with characters from the *Despicable Me* movie on the front, and black high-top sneakers. The FBI called this press conference and we're waiting for Ethan's mother, Abby Starkey, to speak to us." He turned to check behind him. "I think she's ready, Jeanine. Here we go."

The camera cut past a gaggle of reporters to a grim-visaged group stepping up to a portable podium fronted by a bank of microphones. Flanked by Jessica's brother-in-law, Special Agent in Charge Roland Sparks, and Special Agent Zach Smith, was Ethan's mother.

Dwarfed by the two tall men, Abby Starkey was average height, trim in a grey jacket and pencil skirt, light brown hair combed back and held in a clip. Zach had said she was an attorney. She looked ready for court, except for her trembling lip and tight grip on the edges of the podium.

Standing behind Abby was a heavyset older woman in a sweatshirt and jeans. The way she was hovering, Jessica guessed the woman might be Abby's mother.

Large, square sunglasses hid Abby's eyes, but Jessica had gazed in the mirror at her own swollen, red-rimmed eyes enough times to picture what they looked like.

Abby leaned toward the microphones, speaking in a shaky voice. "Trey, I know the kind of father you are. You've always taken care of our—our son." She halted, her face twisting in anguish, and stood there, breathing heavily.

The older woman pushed a tissue into her hand and Abby dabbed at the tears rolling down her face. "Please bring him home, Trey. Don't hurt him. I'll do anything you want. Bring Ethan home safe." Every word seemed to be an effort. She turned away from the podium, swaying like a palm tree in the breeze.

Jessica knew from painful experience what came next.

Zach, looking uncharacteristically neat in his FBI regulation dark suit and tie, caught hold of Abby just as her knees gave out. Roland leapt in and helped him grab her as she crumpled. Half-carrying her between them, they hustled her along the walkway and inside the seventeen-story structure that housed the FBI offices.

Jessica well acquainted with the sensation of having her heart ripped open, of being left defenseless and exposed. She figured she knew much of what Abby Starkey was going through. The toll of endless days of worrying and sleepless nights she must have endured, praying in vain for her son to come home safe. The stress of facing the cameras to beg for his life, had caught up with her.

The reporter, Keith Lewis, had his hand up to his earpiece, listening for input from his producer. "As you just saw, Mrs. Starkey was understandably overcome. 911 has been called for medical assistance. The FBI asks that anyone with information or tips of any kind regarding the location of Trey and/or Ethan Starkey contact their local field office. The information will be held confidential and forwarded to the proper resources. Meanwhile, an Amber Alert continues in force. We will continue to provide updates as they become available. Now, Jeanine, back to you in the studio."

"Thank you, Keith," said Jeanine Riley. "Do we know whether there's any history of violence? Is the father considered dangerous?"

Jessica shut off the television. Zach had already given her the answer to the reporter's question. A sick sense of helplessness spread over her. Any mother in these circumstances deserved empathy, but this case was personal. Ethan Starkey was the child Zach had asked her to help locate.

According to Bella Bingham, it might be possible to reach the little boy if he was still alive.

She started with the books Sage had bought for her, skimming the tables of contents, flipping to pages that seemed most relevant. She read as fast as she could, sponging up knowledge.

"Sit in the power," Bella had said, "and ask for help."

YouTube offered a staggering array of choices in meditation music. Jessica had never heard of an Archangel named Uriel, but she settled on a site that claimed to channel Uriel's music. The name attracted her, and the ethereal sound.

With the cushioned speakers of her headphones shutting out ambient sounds, she threw a cushion on the floor, sat cross-legged on it and closed her eyes, beginning the practice of breathing exercises Dr. Gold had taught her so long ago. He called it 'quieting the monkey mind'.

Five minutes in, the monkey was having more fun turning somersaults and jumping all over the place than being quieted. First, she saw Sage's blue, blue eyes gazing into hers the way they had at Osteria Monte Grappa. That did quite the opposite of relaxing her and made her feel all quivery. Next, she tried to focus on designing the fairy garden that she intended to create for Bella. No help there. Maybe she was being too logical and needed to let go of her left brain.

Dr. Gold used to suggest visualizing ocean waves. "Don't fight the thoughts that want to intrude," he had instructed. "Let them wash over you, then let them go."

Five minutes in, Jessica had the monkey wrestled into submission. Focusing in on her breathing, she felt it become deeper. Beginning the process of letting conscious thoughts go, the irony of the empty space in her head was irresistible. The murmuring voices that so often filled it had gone silent.

Behind her closed eyelids, the sense of floating in a vast and peaceful ocean.

Is there a guide for me? Is someone here with me?

She waited for an answer, continuing to focus on her breaths. In, out. In, out. Then, like a mild electric charge, a prickly sensation moved across her scalp, along her arms, and on the flesh below her right thumb and index finger.

If you are my guide, please step into my energy and merge with me.

She felt at once engulfed by a strong sense of transcendent love, like being wrapped in a wonderful cocoon. The closest she had come to such a feeling was when the angel spoke to her after she died in the car accident.

"We are always with you." The words telepathically impressed themselves on her mind.

Is there more than one of you?

"We are many. But we are one."

Are you the angel I saw when I had the accident?

"Yes, but there is not just a 'me'. I am part of the All, as are you."

Is that why I feel like I know you?

"We have known each other for as long as you have existed. For eternity."

Why can I talk to you now, when I couldn't before?

"You could have talked to us at any time. It is easier for you now because a part of your human brain became easier to access. You are more open to communication."

Was it because of my head injury?

"Yes. And other events in your life that have allowed you to let go of ego and listen."

Is that why I've been hearing all the voices?

"Yes. And no. Some in spirit who have chosen to remain in the earth sphere, who recognize that you can see and hear them, are impatient to get a message to their earth families."

Aren't they happy in heaven, or whatever you call it? Why are they so desperate to get through?

"Most people, after they shed the physical body, are content to move into the light. Some have unfinished business that they wish to address before they go on. Think of it this way. On the earth there are earthquakes. Sometimes many people die. If there was a quake and you could not connect with your sister by normal means, would you not do anything in your power to let her know that you had survived?"

Of course I would.

"As your friend Bella explained, you have to set the ground rules. Just because they are in spirit does not mean you have to allow them all to intrude upon your life."

You saw me talking with Bella?

"Of course." The angel's laughter vibrated through her. "Don't worry, we are not like those earthbound spirits, intruding all the time. We are with you as you need us to be."

He had answered her question even before it had fully formed.

Is this my imagination, or are you real?

The angel laughed again. "You must use your imagination to allow us to communicate with you. The power is in your own hands."

Can you help me find Ethan Starkey?

"Each one walks his own path. We cannot interfere in the

outcome."

What good is it for me to give people messages, if you won't help me when I need it?

"Help always comes when you need it. However, it is not always what you think it should be."

I need help now. *Why won't you help me?*

"You can talk to anyone. Their spirit can hear you when they sleep."

Can I reach Ethan?

"You can talk to anyone," the angel repeated. "We are here for your strength and support. We will never leave you."

That boy needs to be home with his mother.

"Do not confuse this boy with your own."

This is so frustrating. I thought you would help me.

A picture of a tranquil pond and a stand of trees came into her mind.

Oh, great. This is you helping me? Psychics always say 'I see the person near water.'

This is such b.s.

As the thought formed, the cocoon evaporated. Jessica ripped off the headphones and threw them down. She got up and went to the kitchen, snatched a bottle of Longboard from the fridge and chugged it.

What a load of crap. What's the point of being able to connect with the spirit world if they talk in riddles and don't answer your questions? Maybe I'm making up all this spirit stuff.

Shame and remorse jumped in to crowd the sulky defiance. The feeling of love that had suffused her was as real as anything she had ever seen or touched. She ought to be grateful. If she would get over herself, she might learn how to communicate with spirit better, as well as how to control her 'gift,' if that's what it was. She tossed the empty bottle into the recycle bin and located her phone.

"Hey, Zach," she said to his voicemail. "I need you to take me to where Ethan lives."

FOURTEEN

While she waited for Zach to return her call, Bella's words continued to ring in her ears: "I was so relieved they dropped the charges."

Googling 'Sage Boles,' Jessica accessed an *Ojai Valley Tribune* headline:

"*Ojai Muralist Arrested in Death of Artist Mother.*"

Her mouth went dry. Whatever she might have imagined, that was not it.

The article was dated eighteen months earlier.

"*Ojai resident, muralist Sage Boles, was arrested after his mother, sixty-five year-old Regina Boles, a renowned local artist, was found dead in the gallery where mother and son were preparing an installation. Ms. Boles' body was discovered by the gallery owner at the foot of a ladder, her neck broken. A neighbor told law enforcement that she had heard a loud argument just prior to Sage Boles, thirty-two, "storming from the gallery" and driving away at a high rate of speed. After being questioned by Ventura County Sheriff's detectives later in the day, Boles was taken into custody and charged with homicide. A source who wishes to remain anonymous reported that the younger Boles has a juvenile record, which was sealed."*

And a follow-up article, a week later.

"Local muralist Sage Boles, who was arraigned and booked into Ventura County Jail last Thursday, was released today when Judge Daniel Miles ruled that there was insufficient evidence to charge him in the death of his mother, Regina. In a statement to the media, Boles' attorney Ann Cunningham said, "My client's conversation with his mother had absolutely nothing to do with her death. She was still alive on the ladder when he left the gallery. He is devastated by these tragic events." To date, no funeral services have been planned for the artist."

Staring at the words, Jessica wished she had not read them; that Bella had never aroused her curiosity. She felt as though she had sneaked a peek into Sage's computer and found it stuffed with violent porn. Guilt ripped through her and tainted the hope that had just begun to flower—that real happiness was possible. Was this why he had told her not to be so quick to trust her instinct that he was a good person?

She had married Greg, she reminded herself. Her instincts sucked.

The phone rang and jangled her nerves afresh. Expecting to see Zach's number, she saw Sage's instead. The intuitive link that she already felt between them was undeniable and strong—not unlike her bond with Jenna. Had he somehow picked up on the turmoil fermenting in her gut?

It was impossible for her to talk to him in her present state, she knew that much. He would intuit that something was amiss. She needed time to consider what she had learned about him and figure out whether it made any difference.

Sage left a voicemail. Just a few hours had passed since they had parted in Ojai and he was asking her to have dinner with him tonight. She played it back a half-dozen times, mesmerized by his voice. The sexiness was there in spades, like warm honey oozing over her, but it was more than that. She wanted more than anything to see him again, and as soon as possible.

What can I say to him? I can't pretend not to know about his arrest.

What was the truth about his mother? The judge's ruling said there was not enough evidence to take the case to trial, which was not the same as saying Sage was innocent.

She texted back "Can't tonight." As soon as she sent it, she wanted to call it back; to say something less terse. As her fingers hovered over the keyboard, the phone rang again.

Zach.

"Hey chickadee, what the hell? Now you want me to take you to the Starkey's house?"

"Hey, Zach."

"What's wrong? You sound—"

Jessica pulled herself together and sent thoughts of Sage to the back burner. "How's Ethan's mom? I was watching it on TV. It looked like she passed out."

"Yeah. She's okay, just got caught up in all the emotion. Can't blame her. It's a tough situation."

"Take me over there. When can you make it happen?"

The line went silent. Sensing his reluctance, Jessica pushed him. "I thought you wanted me to work with you to find this boy."

"I do."

"Well, if I'm going to try and connect with him—and there's no guarantee that I can—I need to get in touch with who he was. *Is.* It might help to see his room, touch his things."

Again, the hesitation. "I know I asked you to help, but Abby's mom is pretty religious. She might be a problem."

"Does her mom have to know? Abby's desperate to know where Ethan is. Of course she'll go for it."

"If we do this, we can't tell Roland. Can you imagine the optics if the media got wind of what we're doing? It has to be strictly off the book."

"Yeah, I *know* that, Zach. We already had this conversation over Hailey Martin. Roland didn't complain when you found her body. Either you want me to work with you on this or you don't. The cost is the same either way. Zero."

"Of course I want you to, babe. I'll have to talk to Abby and pave the way. Let me call her and see what she says. I'll get back to you."

Jessica hated him calling her 'babe' and Zach knew it. She squelched the temptation to snap at him. If she reminded him that they were no longer a couple and he had no rights, he would know he had gotten a rise out of her. Instead, she asked how he planned to approach Abby Starkey.

"I'm sure not gonna tell her you're talking with dead people. That would freak her out. It would freak most people out. Guess I'll say you're a psychic and you've helped us on another case. She doesn't have to know the case was about Hailey Martin."

"I don't care, I want to help find Ethan. Let me know what she says. I'm gonna do some meditating, see if I can get a head start."

"If she goes for it, I'll set it up ASAP. Are you free anytime?"

"I'll make sure I'm free."

The Starkey home was located in Thousand Oaks, twenty-five miles northeast of where Jessica lived.

As she had predicted, Abby was unwilling to wait until the next day to meet.

"There won't be so much media at night," Zach said, as Jessica strapped herself into his Acura at eight o'clock that evening.

"And in the dark, anyone who *is* there won't be able to see me and figure out who I am."

"You got it." He gave her his goofy young Keanu Reeves grin. "You look like a cat burglar."

Jessica grinned back. She had twisted her bushy blonde hair into a knot and shoved it under a black watch cap. A long black sweater over leggings with boots completed the picture.

"Won't be the first time," she reminded him.

In the midst of her memory loss there had been an occasion when she wore the same getup while attempting to recover an important flash drive. On that night, she'd gotten caught, with painful consequences. Tonight, all she had to do was avoid a handful of journalists, not a security guard with murder on his mind.

Zach switched on the windshield wipers. "Hopefully, the newsies will stay in their vehicles. That should make it easier."

Once they hit the 101, due to the rain, traffic was lighter than usual for the time of night. With precipitation such a rare event in Southern California, when it came, it had a way of keeping the populace at home.

Forty minutes after leaving Jessica's house, they exited at Wendy Drive. Zach handed her his phone. When they were five minutes out, she texted Abby their ETA.

"There'll be a media van or two," said Zach. "If they come running over, ignore them. Act like they aren't there."

They turned onto Old Conejo Road. The rain clouds were wrung out and mist sparkled on the windshield. Zach slowed to locate Abby Starkey's street. A right turn, then a left. Their destination was easy to spot. Eyewitness News and KCAL 9 vans were parked along the street, concentrated around a two-story house.

The garage door rose as Zach turned into the empty driveway. Abby had been watching for them. Framed by the dim inside light, she stood in a doorway that led into the house.

"Go," Zach told Jessica. "Quick. I'll follow you."

She was out of the car and in the garage in a flash, too quick for the reporters to catch on. Car doors slammed, then the reporters were in the street, shouting questions as Zach followed Jessica. Abby hit the switch and the door rolled down.

Tonight, Ethan Starkey's mother was far from the well-put-together attorney of the press conference. Her shape was concealed under baggy clothing, her uncombed hair had lost its clip. Any makeup she wore for the cameras was long gone. Dark circles of sleeplessness outlined the pouches under her eyes. That, and the grayish cast of her face were the marks of stress.

Jessica introduced herself, hoping to feel a special fizz of energy when their hands met, a sensation might give her a clue to where Ethan and his father were. All she got was a keen sense of hopelessness.

The faint smell of alcohol trailed Abby as she beckoned them to follow her through the laundry room and kitchen. The interior lights in the front of the house were off but strong lamps shone through the closed café curtains over the kitchen window, which faced the front yard. The media, hoping for a glimpse.

Abby took them to a tidy den at the rear. No small boy toys

were in evidence. Hardwood flooring, a fireplace set in brickwork, wall-mounted TV; a turquoise sectional sofa, a recliner. French doors led to a patio lit by floodlights.

"I'm trying to make sure none of those news people sneak into the backyard," said Abby. "I've caught them peeking through the kitchen and living room windows, so I keep the lights off up front and stay back here. Or upstairs." She let go of a long sigh. "Thank you for coming tonight. Why don't you have a seat."

Zach took one end of the sofa, Jessica the other. She wondered whether Abby was a neat freak. Then she remembered that Zach had said she packed up everything belonging to her child. She had expected to put him in the car and escape whatever had driven her to make such a plan. The same as Jessica herself had done. She felt a renewed surge of empathy for Ethan Starkey's mother.

When they both declined her half-hearted offer of a drink, Abby looked relieved. She picked up a wine glass from the coffee table and drained the half-inch of red pooled in the bottom, her weary eyes roaming the room as though a waiter might show up with a refill.

Zach leaned in, drawing her attention to him. "So, Abby, like I told you on the phone, Jess thought she might be able to pick up something—"

"I'm not a professional psychic or anything like that," Jessica interrupted, not wanting him to speak for her. "Sometimes I see pictures of people in my mind. I'd like to hold some object that belongs to Ethan, maybe a piece of his clothing, or a toy. It might give me—I guess I'd call it a vibe. I'm *so* sorry for what you're going through. I understand how—"

Abby's eyes widened, sparking with sudden anger. "You *understand?* How the hell can you possibly—"

Jessica paid no attention to the silent warning Zach was throwing her way. She knew the roots of Abby's anger too well.

Well-meaning people said what Jessica had, but in most cases, they were talking out of their hat. Their ninety-year-old aunty passed away, or a friend died of an illness, or a pet. She had been angry too, when those people told her they knew how she felt after Justin's death. How could they possibly know? All grief is terrible but no experience compared to the upended order of things that is the loss of a child.

She tried again. "You're right, of course, Abby. What I meant was, I had a son a year younger than Ethan is now. And I was ready to take him one night and leave. We had an accident and I will never, ever stop blaming myself. So, it's true that it's not the same and I can't know how you feel. But I do know how it feels not to have my child with me. And I hope with all my heart that I can help bring Ethan back to you."

Abby's face fell, the anger melting. "What happened to your son?"

"He died in the accident."

Jessica heard herself say the words and marveled. Before Justin brought her the vision of himself and Mason at the beach, it was impossible for her to utter them. But now she knew he was alive in another form and another place. They had become mere words.

"Oh God, I'm so—I didn't mean—I didn't—"

"There's nothing to apologize for, Abby. I'm here to help if I can. I just wanted you to know that I do get it."

Tears spilled down Abby's cheeks. Sniffling, she wiped them away with the heel of her hand. "I'm kind of a mess right now, but I do appreciate you being here." She hesitated, hopeful but afraid to ask. "Are you picking up anything?"

"Not yet. I'm kind of new at this. Is there a photo of Ethan I could hold? I saw the one they showed on TV, but if you have one—"

"I gave my favorite to the FBI, but maybe this—" Abby got up and went to Zach's side of the sofa. She picked up a picture frame and handed to Jessica, face down. "I can't stand to look at him. I feel so damned guilty."

"You have nothing to feel guilty for, Abby," said Zach.

Turning the frame over, Jessica wondered which one she couldn't stand to look at—father or son.

The picture had been taken at a zoo enclosure. A blond man with a high forehead held a small boy with brown hair arranged in a bowl cut. His face gleamed with delight. His mouth was open in a wide "Ooooh" of excitement.

As she touched it, Jessica got an immediate, intense feeling that Trey Starkey's bland smile was phony, that it hid a darker side of his character. Was she imagining it, knowing that he had taken the child from his mother? The answer came quickly. No. The plain truth was, Trey Starkey gave her the creeps.

She set the picture back on the end table, glad to have it out of her hands. "Could I see Ethan's room now, please?"

"I'll take you," said Abby.

When Zach started to rise, Jessica put out a restraining hand. "I think you should wait for us here. It's better if we don't add more energy to the mix." It was one of those random thoughts that seemed to appear from out of nowhere and drop into her mind.

He shrugged. "If you say so."

Following Abby across the room, Jessica took a quick look back, glad to see that he was already doing something with his phone, checking email or texting. It was hard enough having to pretend a confidence she did not feel, without having to work with Zach and his on-again-off-again skepticism as an audience.

On the second-floor landing, where they would not be visible to the media people down on the sidewalk, Abby switched on a light. "We have four bedrooms," she said, pointing them out as they went. "This is our room. This one is Trey's home office. This is a guest room."

As they approached the door at the far end of the landing Abby's breathing became shallow. She stopped at the door, her hand grasping the lintel as if she needed the support. "This is Ethan's room. I got everything out of the car and unpacked his clothes and toys. I've put everything back where it belongs so he can see everything the same as always when he—" She broke off and stepped aside.

With a quick prayer that she would be able to open a channel to the little boy, or, if worse had come to worst, his spirit, Jessica took a deep breath and stepped into the room.

FIFTEEN

The brightly colored cartoon faces of Thomas the Tank Engine and his friends, each tucked into its own tunnel, grinned out from the wall behind a preschooler-sized bed. An applique of Thomas' big round face decorated the bedspread. The pile of plush animals in front of the pillow were a reminder that at four years old, Ethan was not far away from being a toddler.

Tall wooden letters tacked on the wall spelled out his name. There was a dresser painted blue. Hand-painted words and cartoon drawings named the contents of each drawer: pajamas, shirts, shorts and pants. Inexplicably, the bottom drawer bore a sketch of a helicopter.

"I had so much fun painting that dresser while I was pregnant," said Abby, following Jessica inside. "Trey was thrilled about the baby. It was all so good back then because I was always home."

Moving further into the room, Jessica tuned out the anxious blather. She closed her eyes and concentrated on the image of Ethan's face from the photo downstairs, speaking to him telepathically.

Ethan, can you hear me?

At first she felt nothing at all. Then a terrible ripple of fear ran through her body that left her shaken.

Ethan? I'm here to help you.

"*I want my Henry.*"

Everything is gonna be okay, Ethan. Who is Henry?

"Where is Henry?"

My name is—

"What's wrong?" The iron grip of nervous fingers around her wrist broke the spell and brought Jessica's awareness back into the room with a shock. Abby was staring at her, eyes dilated with fear. "Why are you crying?"

Jessica wanted to shrug her off, tell her to shut up and let her work. She moved away, so that Abby had to let go. "I need to tune in with him and that means I have to focus. I can't do that when you're asking me questions."

"But why were you crying? What's wrong? Is he hurt? He's not—"

Brushing away tears that were not her own, Jessica ignored her. The tears, she was certain, were an impression of Ethan's emotional state.

"Please," she said. "Let's just be quiet."

Relaxing her gaze, she allowed her vision to soften and blur, the way she did when she needed to access her right brain for her artwork. She turned in a slow circle, observing the room, letting the sense that she was on the brink of discovery tell her what to do next.

Dresser. Bed. Rocking chair. TV—

Isn't he a little young for his own TV? Focus, Jess. Concentrate.

Toys. Model of the Space Shuttle, gigantic box of Legos, Fisher Price jungle, tub of plastic jungle animals. Two-foot tall Tyrannosaurus Rex.

The T-Rex seemed to call her. She went and picked it up, hugging the hard plastic against her. "This is his favorite," she said with certainty.

Abby's smile came and went. "He loves that ugly thing to death. Takes it everywhere with him—school, the grocery. Wait a minute. How the heck do you know that?"

"Just a feeling I got."

"He fell in love with dinosaurs when Trey took him to the La Brea Tar Pits a while back." The more she spoke, the more animated Abby became. "He wants to grow up and be a paleontologist. Not that he can pronounce it—he says 'pelonist,'—but studying fossils turns him on."

"My sister and I took Justin to the Tar Pits," Jessica said, connecting with Abby over the shared memory. "He thought the mammoths were real. He wanted us to rescue them from the tar."

"They have that Fishbowl lab there, where you can watch them working on fossils." Abby sighed again. "Ethan would dig up the whole backyard if we'd let him."

Her words gave Jessica a small jolt. The FBI must have checked out the Starkey's backyard. If Trey Starkey had done the unthinkable, surely he would not have buried his son right outside their home. But then, who knew that he would steal his own child?

As if there was flesh and bone under the plastic, the T-Rex seemed to pulsate in her arms. Abby reached out and stroked it like a pet. "Ethan named him Henry. I have no clue as to why, or where he got that name. From TV, maybe."

"That's the name he gave me when we connected," Jessica said. "He misses Henry."

"You didn't tell me that." Abby's face crumpled. "He misses Henry, but he doesn't miss *me*? What else didn't you tell me?"

"When you grabbed my arm the connection got broken. It was too soon for me to get anything else. Abby, you've got to send him messages from your heart all the time; let him know you're thinking of him. Tell him you love him."

Once again, words were pouring from Jessica's mouth without her knowing where they originated. Maybe her spirit guides were helping after all. This whole mediumship-psychic thing was so confusing and upsetting. There seemed to be no rules as to when it worked and when it didn't.

She had to admit she was a rank novice and far out of her depth. What if—what if—what if—A child's life was in the balance and all they had to go on was her murky sense impressions. She could not stand to think it, but in the darkest reaches of her core, the accusation was there:

What if you're to blame for Ethan's death? Like you are for Justin's.

Jessica hugged Henry the T-Rex to her, wanting to reject the accusation. But it came from inside her and that left nowhere to go. She caught herself. If she did not quiet her thoughts, she would get nowhere. She began to inhale slow, deep breaths. One-two-three-four-five—

Ethan's bedroom disappeared.

Charcoal clouds painted a dusk sky. She was standing at the rim of a small body of water where the cattails were almost as tall as she was. More of a large pond than a lake—the place her guide had showed her earlier. Behind her was a split rail fence with a section of fencing broken out, large enough for a child to crawl through.

She looked down. As if they were her own, she saw short, denim-clad legs wearing Spiderman rain boots.

Hi, Ethan. My name is Jessica.

"Where's my Papa?"

Can you tell me where you are?

"I wanna go home."

I'll help you get home.

"I'm scared. I'm all alone. Where's Papa?"

Where are you, Ethan? Can you tell me—

Jessica broke off the question. Something was pulling at her from inside. There was no pain but the freaky sensation scared her. Nothing should be attached to the inside of her navel, trying to turn her inside out. She bent over, pulling back with all her might at the invisible cord. It stretched, then snap.

And just as when she died in the accident, then came back, Jessica was propelled back into her body with the speed of a lightning bolt.

She staggered backward, eyes still squeezed shut, reaching behind her, trying to remember how far she was from the wall. She backed up until her hands came in contact with the smooth surface and slid all the way down to the floor. Resting her forehead on bent knees, Jessica struggled to understand what had just happened.

"What's wrong? Jessica? What's wrong?"

Jessica ignored the shrill questions somewhere close to her ear. She was experiencing the now-familiar prickle tickling her hair; the sense of another energy blending with hers.

"It's okay, Mom, I'll help you."

Justin.

Her eyelids fluttered open. She was back in Ethan's room. Yet, not quite Ethan's room. This was a psychedelic trip, the colors too vivid, the surfaces rippling, twisting. The air felt liquidy, like soapy water.

"Jessica, what's wrong? Talk to me." Abby, who had been crouched at her side, jumped up and ran to the doorway, yelling down to Zach. "Something's wrong with Jessica. Hurry."

What had just happened? Was she stuck between two worlds? Her tongue felt thick and heavy, the way it had when she'd had the episode at Arial's Gallery.

The sound of heavy feet on the staircase.

Zach went straight to where she sat propped against the wall and crouched beside her. "What happened?"

"She started looking kind of weird, then she bent over and grabbed her stomach."

"Would you please get her some water?"

"Of course, I'll be right back."

Zach spoke quietly. "Jess? Are you having one of those episodes?"

Shaking her head yes brought on a wave of vertigo. Each connection she'd made with spirit so far had been unique. The pulling in her stomach was like nothing she had experienced.

Ethan's fear had come through loud and clear. She was confident he had connected with her. The question was, where was he connecting from? Was he alive? Or had he crossed into spirit? That, she was unable to tell.

She set down Henry the dinosaur, still clutched in her arms, and accepted the glass of water Abby offered.

"Let's give her some room," said Zach, moving himself and Abby out of her space.

Jessica gulped the entire glass, relieved as the colors relaxed into their original hues. The walls and furniture returned to their ordinary, inanimate state. The dizziness began to fade.

Zach and Abby stood in the doorway, looking at her expectantly.

"I was talking to Ethan and—"

An electronic roar shocked her into silence.

The T-Rex's jaws opened wide. The huge green eyes flashed red. It lumbered toward Abby, emitting one roar after another. With a shriek, Ethan's mother shrank behind Zach.

By the time he leapt to pick up the dinosaur it had reached the wall, its clawed feet still trying to move. Zach flipped the switch to 'off' and set it back on the floor, stepping away as if it might turn into a real dinosaur at any moment.

"You must have accidentally turned it on, Jess," he said accusingly.

"I was not touching it," she retorted, scrambling to her feet. "Nobody was near it."

"Omigod, he's dead," Abby moaned. "Ethan is dead and he's haunting Henry."

"I don't believe that for a minute," Jessica said. "He's trying to reach you through the toy."

How was she supposed to make a rational case for her impression that, somehow, using her energy to reach through time and space, Ethan's yearning for Henry and his mother was the force behind the dinosaur's startling animation?

Is he dead or alive? I can't let her give up hope until we know for sure.

"What did you see?" Abby demanded. "Tell me *everything*. Don't lie to spare me."

"I wouldn't lie to you. I felt Ethan. I didn't *see* him, but I felt that he was wearing jeans and a SpongeBob t-shirt with Spiderman boots and—"

"Yes," Abby uttered. "His Spiderman boots. He wears them everywhere. Where was he? Was he okay?"

"I'm not sure where he was. It was a rural-looking place. I saw a pond and very tall reeds and cattail plants all around it."

"Does that sound like any place you know?" Zach asked.

Abby's crestfallen face gave the answer. She shook her head. "No, it doesn't ring any bells at all. Are you *positive*? Wasn't there anything else?"

"I'm sorry. That's all there was."

If she tried to explain the weird tugging feeling in her solar plexus, it would make no sense to them. Neither of them would understand that it was like being connected to some unknown *thing* or *being* that was pulling her towards it. Maybe she should have asked her guides for protection before making the link. Her internet research and meeting with Bella Bingham had left her with more questions than answers. This was as difficult as dealing with amnesia.

Zach swung around at the slam of a door downstairs. Abby stopped him. "It's my mom. She doesn't like me being alone, so she's spending the night. We'd better go downstairs. Just don't tell her what we're doing. She'd have a hissy."

"Abby, are you upstairs?" the voice grew louder as Abby's mother plodded up the staircase. "Those darned reporters, they—oh." She reached the landing, preceded by a cloud of cigarette smoke. Seeing the three of them, she halted, her chubby face puffy and strained. "You didn't tell me you were expecting company, Ab."

This was the woman who had stood beside Abby during the press conference. She still wore the same sweatshirt and jeans, along with a trace of annoyance.

"Hi, Mom. Zach stopped by with his friend, Jessica. I was showing her Ethan's room."

"Did the reporters bother you on your way in, Mrs. Truman?" Zach asked.

Elaine Truman surveyed them all from the top step, her gaze resting on Zach. Her eyes narrowed, not buying her daughter's explanation for their presence.

"Every darn time I try to come here they keep yelling their dumb questions at me like they think it'll make me answer," she said.

"Keep ignoring them," Zach said. "They might not stop trying, but you'll have the satisfaction of not giving them anything."

"That's what I *am* doing. I brought a tuna casserole, Ab, but I don't think there's enough for—"

Abby and Zach spoke simultaneously.

"They're not staying."

"We were just leaving, Mrs. T. Don't let us disturb your supper."

Mrs. Truman's eyes landed on Jessica. "Have we met before?"

"Uh, no, I don't think so."

"You look very familiar. What's your name again?"

"Jessica." She held out her hand.

The woman held onto it a moment too long. "I have a very good memory for faces."

"It's true," Abby confirmed. "She's phenomenal. I always say she'd make a great witness in a criminal case."

"Maybe I just have one of those faces," Jessica said, wanting to look elsewhere. The scrutiny of Elaine Truman's mental microscope was making her uncomfortable.

"You said Jessica, right? Jessica what?"

"We really gotta be going, Mrs. T.," Zach interrupted, moving toward her in a blatant attempt to encourage her to move out of their path.

Refusing to take the hint, Elaine Truman stayed where she was, peering at Jessica with brows creased into a frown. She held up her hand. "Wait. Just wait a second; it's coming back to me. What's your surname, Jessica?" she asked again.

Jessica gave a sigh of resignation. "Mack."

The other woman's face lit up. "That's it! Not all that common. I remember now. There's a twin sister, isn't there? Another 'J' name?"

"Y-yes, Jenna. I'm sorry, but I don't remember meeting you."

"No, we haven't met. But I remember when you were in the news—oh, I'm not sure how long ago it was; quite a while back. It was a very big story—front page. About that senator and the drug company. The reason I remember it now is the connection. I recognized Zach the first moment I saw him, too. Of course, with this horrible nightmare of Ethan being gone, I didn't bother with it. But seeing you now, it's all coming back to me. Zach was part of the same news story with you and your sister." She turned to Zach as if he was to blame for her memory. "Weren't you, Zach?"

"Yes, ma'am."

"I remember. He got shot and you—"

"I'd prefer not to talk about it, Mrs. Truman," Jessica said, meaning it. Those terrifying days of not remembering who she was or that she had an identical twin sister; both victims in a plot carried out by a corrupt politician, and the experiment that nearly killed her and Jenna—she would rather leave all of it buried in the past.

"All right, hon, I understand. I wanted to be sure I got it right. You know how it is—you get an itch and it needs scratching. Well. So it *was* you. *And* Zach. Now I can put it to rest."

"Thank you," said Jessica, relieved.

With that, Elaine Truman turned around and they followed

her downstairs, where the aroma of the tuna casserole lingered.

"Is there anything new I should know about?" Elaine asked as Abby moved into the lead, taking the visitors to the door. "Is that why you're here? I should have asked before. Do you have some news?"

Zach rested a hand on her shoulder. "I'm sorry, Mrs. T., there's nothing to report right now. We just stopped by to see how your daughter was doing."

The sigh that gusted from Ethan's grandmother spoke volumes about how fed up she was with the situation. "I keep praying, I really do. I go to church every single day and ask God to bring our little Ethan back home safe. My priest tells me that God will watch over him wherever he is, but it's not good enough, Special Agent Smith." She turned her gaze skyward as if looking for reassurance from the Supreme Being. "I wonder whether he's even listening to me."

"Of course he is," assured Zach, although Jessica knew him as an avowed atheist. He gave Abby's mother a very un-FBI-like squeeze. "And I promise you, Mrs. T., we are doing everything we possibly can to bring Ethan home safe."

Jessica leaned up against the door in Zach Smith's car. "I don't think I can do this. It's too hard."

"Because of the episodes?"

"Not just that—though I have to say, this was a strange one. It's just—it's all the *emotion*. Abby, her mother. Ethan. It's hard to explain but, when I connected with him, it was like he was me and I was him. I felt what he felt."

Zach's head swung her way. "You mean, you were *possessed*?"

"*No*, dammit. You sound like Jenna. I was still me. But I was him, too."

"Okay, that's more than a little weird. So, what was he was thinking?"

"He was asking for his papa. And Henry the dinosaur— omigod, that was so freaky that it started walking on its own—and I did *not* touch it."

His skeptical glance told her he did not believe her. "*Something* set it off."

"It wasn't me. Anyway, I felt his emotions like they were my own. The poor little guy is scared shitless. I can't say where he is, but he doesn't want to be there."

"But all you saw was a pond and cattails? That's kinda vague, Jess. Where do you think could it be? A golf course?"

"I doubt it. The terrain wasn't manicured like a golf course. It was more—I dunno, wild. Marshy."

"Okay. I'll do some research, see if there's anything around here that fits the description."

"He's so scared, Zach. And it sounded like he was alone. I wanted to get him to tell me where he is, but then I started getting this weird sensation and popped back. I wonder where Trey is."

"He was alone? I hate to ask, but do you think he's dead?"

"How do I know?"

"Well, if he's not, how could you—connect—with him? Did you find a way to do it?"

"Look, Zach, all this psychic connecting stuff is pretty new to me and I don't know how to control it, or even whether it's possible to. I guess maybe I'm a medium or something because I sort of "plug in" to spirit, but—" Jessica paused to gather her thoughts. "From what I've read so far, all mediums are psychic, but it doesn't automatically work both ways. Not all psychics are mediums. So, I think I'm both. I just wish I knew whether he was here, or there, but I can't tell."

"Here alive, or—dead, you mean?"

"I'd rather think of it as being on the other side. Life after earth."

"That's still dead."

"Okay, alive or dead." Jessica glared at him. "It sounds worse to say it like that."

SIXTEEN

Sage called again the next morning. Again, Jessica let the call go to voicemail.

"Did I mess up?" his message began. "Am I being too pushy? Did I read you wrong?" He sounded so let down. The silence drew out as if he wanted to say more. "Okay, then, I'm not gonna bug you anymore. Call me if you want to talk…I hope you do."

What could she say if she called him? The episode at Abby Starkey's house had left her wiped out, emotionally flattened. A night of tossing and turning had done nothing to improve her energy or mood. The fact was, right now she had nothing left to give Sage Boles or anyone else.

Even work was not helping. After a few abortive attempts at sketching out the miniature she had in mind to make for Bella Bingham, it became clear that she was in no shape to produce anything decent. She crumpled up the paper and pitched it into the trash.

Sometimes you just had to step back and do something different.

The rain had ended in the night. Early morning fog drifted like a bank of smoke over the town, dampening the air and muting the traffic sounds. Driving out of her neighborhood, Jessica turned left at Harbor Boulevard and drove across the small bridge that led to Oxnard Harbor. Past the upscale homes that lined the Mandalay

Beach canals to her right. Past miles of sand dunes that stretched to Silver Strand Beach.

Ventura Beach was as deserted as it had been on her previous visit. A watery sun wrangled its way through hazy clouds but the waves were too small for surfers today. The iron-gray skies and low temperatures would discourage anyone seeking a tan.

It was eight-thirty a.m. when Jessica parked the Mini under the freeway bridge that crossed San Jon Road. She caught a green light and jogged back across Harbor to the bike path that ran alongside the sand, cold hands jammed in the pockets of her quilted jacket.

Keeping to the right, out of the way of the handful of stalwart cyclists and joggers, she strode into the invigorating wind with dogged determination and a strong dose of masochism. She was counting on the brisk air blowing in her face to clear her mind of Sage and Ethan, and that was that.

By the time she climbed the long wooden staircase up to the pier, the tension that had accumulated in her neck and shoulders was starting to let go.

The pier had suffered many insults in its hundred-year history and carried the scars of its adventures. Jessica liked to think of it as a grand old lady who had aged gracefully. She fast-walked the rough wooden boards that stretched a third of a mile from one end of the pier to the other and touched the wooden barrier for luck, hoping that she might age with as much grace.

There was something hypnotic in the agitated waves smashing against the pylons below.

Ethan. Can you hear me?

Nothing. No tingle, no images, no words.

She traced her way back along the pier and descended the steps back to the promenade, passing the empty playground on the sand. Still closed from the high surf brought on by the recent storms, it looked bleak without children playing on the swings. Justin would have loved the blue shell-shaped slide. Jessica summoned a picture in her mind of his little legs climbing the sandy stairs and—

"On your left," a deep voice called out from behind.

Turning her head, she was surprised to meet the gaze of the man with the Einstein hair, as she thought of him. He passed her and braked a few yards ahead, waiting for her to catch up.

"Hey there. Jessica, right?" he said.

"Yep. We meet again. Jay?"

"You got it. Two J's. You're looking healthier than the last time we met."

"Thank you. You were very nice to help a stranger."

He grinned. "Anytime, young lady, now that we're no longer strangers."

Jessica smiled. "I guess we're not. Well, nice to see you again. Don't let me keep you from your ride."

"That's okay. I'm a firm believer that everything happens for a reason." Jay stood there straddling his bike, regarding her with one eyebrow raised as if pondering an important question. Then, he said, "It's no coincidence we're meeting right now for the second time."

"Is that right? So, what's the reason for our meeting this time?"

"Good question. Give it time. It'll come to me. How far are you walking?"

"To the railroad bridge past Surfer's Point."

Jay nodded. "Good. That's the way I'm riding. We can meet up on the turnaround and find a bench, take a load off and see if we can figure it out."

As a rule, Jessica did not strike up conversations with strange men she met on the street, let alone one like Jay, with his wacky, wild man hair. But she liked him and they were out in public and she doubted he was a psychotic rapist. Of course, Ted Bundy the serial killer hadn't looked like one, either. She had read about him in her college psych class.

She heard herself agree. "See you then."

Twenty minutes later, Jessica reached the trestle train bridge that crossed the mouth of the Ventura River. She made the turnaround and had started back toward the pier when she heard her name called.

Jay rode up beside her and climbed off his bike. "I hope I don't smell all sweaty," he said, motioning her to a bench facing a small lagoon. "Riding my bike is one of my favorite things, but I'd hate to be socially offensive, especially to a pretty lady."

Jessica chuckled. She could feel waves of heat coming off him from exertion, but no bad smell. "You're fine."

"Am I glad to hear that!"

"What are your other favorite things?" Jessica asked, watching the sandpipers and gulls hopping around on sandbars, looking for food.

"I like traveling the world, been a few places. And driving a hard bargain at garage sales—I'm proud to admit it, I'm cheap. How about you? What do you like to you do?"

"I make miniatures, do some sculpting, painting."

He leaned away, his heavy-lidded eyes giving her a look of appraisal and, apparently, approval. "An artist, eh? Do you show your work?"

She told him about Ariel Anderson Arts and The Little Mermaid in Ojai. He was familiar with both galleries and spoke as though he knew quite a lot about art. It did not surprise her to learn that he had once owned an antiques shop.

The conversation began to wind down and Jessica was starting to get restless. She was ready to start again on the fairy garden for Bella Bingham. "Have you figured out why we were supposed to meet today?" she asked.

Jay shook his head. "Not yet. Keep talking."

His warm voice, his laugh, his unhurried way of speaking, put her at ease. Despite the unruly hair and a stubbly chin that had not met a sharp razor in a while, he was quite handsome in an older-guy, "rough diamond" way. Around her father's age, she thought.

Comparing this disheveled but palpably kinder newcomer to her life with her father—the distant banker in his finely tailored suit—was laughable. Even if they still had contact, which they did not, her father was the last person on earth Jessica would speak to about things of a personal nature.

Would it be dumb to confide in this stranger? She needed to talk to someone and there was no one else. Not even Claudia understood her the way Jenna did and Jenna was out of the picture. She made up her mind.

"Jay, since we're now such old friends, do you mind if I ask your opinion?"

"Fire away. I'm full of opinions." His eyes crinkled at the edges as he grinned. "They may be bullshit, but they're free."

"Okay, I'll take one." Jessica hesitated. "So…I just met this guy—"

Jay gave a knowing nod. "There's always a new guy for a gal as cute as you. I'm not coming on to you, I promise. But it's true."

She rolled her eyes. "*Anyway.* I'm super attracted to him and I can tell he feels the same. We don't know each other yet, but you know how you just know when there's 'something' there?"

"I sure do. I've felt that way more than a few times myself."

"The thing is, someone told me something about him that's bugging me. I can't decide what to do. I don't want him to know that I know, but it's a big deal—an elephant in the room kind of thing."

Jay nodded as she spoke, paying close attention. "Okay. "someone told you something." Just how did this someone come to tell you the something?"

"A friend he introduced me to mentioned that there was this, uh, problem. So, I Googled him, and a couple of newspaper articles came up."

"And? What did they say?"

Jessica cleared her throat, hesitating to say the words that would make it more real. She was considering withdrawing the request for Jay's input, then went for broke and blurted it out. "His mother died…and he was a suspect in her death."

The bushy salt and pepper eyebrows went up. "That's pretty big news all right. I can see why you'd be concerned."

"The article said he was arrested, but the judge said there wasn't enough evidence to go to trial. His friend was totally on his side when she mentioned it to me. The thing is, he had a juvenile record, so—"

Jay interrupted, "How did his mother die?"

"She fell off a ladder and broke her neck. But the problem was, someone had heard them arguing and—why are you looking at me like that?"

"Miss Jessica, I now know why we met and why we're sitting here on this bench right next to me."

"You do? Well, please let me in on the secret."

"Would I be correct in assuming that your new boyfriend is Sage Boles?"

Jessica had been staring at the sandpipers. She jerked around to look at Jay. "How do you know his name?" Then she relaxed. "Oh, you must have read about it when it happened."

"Yes, I do remember the case very well, but not for the reason you think. Sage and I go back a long way."

Now she was openly gaping. "Are you serious?"

"As serious as a heart attack. This was before I took early retirement. I was working at the California Youth Authority—juvie to most people."

His announcement left Jessica bowled over with shock. She couldn't stop staring. "I have to say, Jay, you don't look like a cop."

He grinned. "Not a cop, but I was a sworn officer of the law, got a shiny badge, the works. The part I hated was having to wear a uniform. You may have noticed I'm kinda on the casual side. I retired so I wouldn't have to shave. Anyway, I liked to think of myself as a babysitter."

"And you met Sage while he was in juvie?"

Jay nodded. "I worked graveyard, so the kids were asleep while I was on duty." He stopped himself. "Look, I'm sure you realize this is confidential information that I shouldn't be blabbing. But it was a long time ago and I have a good feeling about you, so I'm going to trust you. Anyhow, what are they gonna do, fire me?"

Jessica gave him a solemn look and raised three fingers. "I won't tell. Scout's honor."

"Were you a Girl Scout?"

"No, but I know how to promise not to repeat anything you tell me."

Jay looked straight into her eyes, taking her measure. He nodded again. "I know you won't. So, here we go. Sage had a hard time sleeping and I'd find him sneaking out of his dorm, walking around. Sometimes I'd let him come to the employee break room and we'd sit there and talk for a couple hours." He stopped for a self-deprecating chuckle. "Well, *he'd* sit there, anyway. *I* preferred to stretch out on the countertop. I'll tell you, Jessica, I love work. I could watch it all day." His eyes were twinkling. "Who'm I kidding? I'm basically a lazy sumbitch."

She wanted more information about Sage. "How old was he?" she pressed. "Why was he sent to juvie?"

Jay mused on her questions. "I've been retired for fifteen years, so, it was before that. Sage was around thirteen, fourteen; a super-bright, talented kid with some major problems. I think it was when he was around four years old, he went through some kind of terrible trauma. It fucked up—sorry, messed with his head."

Four years old. Like Ethan. Was this why he had used his aunt's money to establish the Center for Traumatized Children in his mother's name?

"What happened to him?"

"Dunno. I dealt with a shitload of kids going through CYA, but Sage was special. He stood out. We got pretty close, but he's never told me what happened to him. He might not even remember. Sometimes when there's something majorly traumatic, the kid can block it out. So, anyway, I heard that after he went to live with Mrs. Boles—"

"Wait, she wasn't his real mom?"

"No, he was adopted. It was long before we got him. I was never privy to the ins and outs of that, but I was told he didn't speak for the first year or so."

"Didn't speak?"

"As in totally silent. Whatever happened, they think he witnessed something so horrible, he couldn't verbalize it. He's a terrifically talented artist. That was how he expressed his emotions, through his drawings. Some of them were—I guess I'd have to say pretty bizarre."

"Bizarre how?"

"Gruesome. Violent. Trust me, young lady, you don't want the details."

Gruesome and violent. Jessica's hopes took a sudden nosedive. She had survived one violent relationship and vowed never to repeat that mistake. Even though she was already telling herself it was a lost cause, she had to ask, "What did he do to get put in juvie?"

"He cut a kid up pretty bad. According to Sage, several kids jumped him—a racial thing—obviously he's mixed race—his father was African American, his mother is Caucasian. Sage's excuse was that he was defending himself, and I don't doubt it was true. But this wasn't the first time or even the second that he'd been in trouble for fighting. He got into fights at CYA, too." Jay quirked a brow. "That boy had a lot of aggression built up. Kinda like a pressure cooker. It had to come out somewhere."

Jessica looked him in the eye so she might gauge his honesty when he answered her question. "Could he have killed his mother?"

Jay answered without hesitation. "He was totally devoted to her. Even as a young kid, he felt bad about getting himself locked up because he knew how much it hurt her. He's doing a lot of good things these days with the child abuse center and the other center back east."

"I know about the one in Ojai. There's another one?"

He nodded. "He spent a big chunk of his inheritance on them."

"You stay in touch with him?"

"We get together for a beer once in a while. Truth is, I love the kid."

"That's a pretty good recommendation. So, down to my original question. If I decide to see him again, should I tell him I Googled him?"

Jay sighed. "Honesty is not always the best policy, Missy. You asked for my advice. Here it is: give yourself a chance to get better acquainted before you make any big decisions about dumping him."

"Wow. You weren't kidding about no coincidences. I'm kind of overwhelmed right now."

"Anytime you need an opinion, remember, I got plenty of 'em and they're all free."

SEVENTEEN

Driving home, Jessica reached the conclusion that before returning Sage's calls, she needed more information and she knew where to get it. Claudia Rose.

"Are you free for lunch?" Jessica asked. "I need to see you. I'll treat."

"Is something wrong, Jess?"

"I'll figure that out after we talk."

"Okay, sure. Come on down. No need for us to go out, though. I made a big pot of vegetable barley mushroom soup last night, and Joel brought some fresh rolls from that bakery I love."

"I can be there by twelve-thirty."

"Okay, kiddo. See you then. Take care on the road."

Rather than battle the freeway, Jessica took the more scenic Pacific Coast Highway to Playa de la Reina. She was driving the same route that Annabelle took to the Regina Boles Center in Ojai, in reverse. If Annabelle's tire had blown on the two-lane winding roads, with nothing more than a low rail between the road and the water just a few feet below, she might have been badly injured or worse.

Jessica liked knowing that the girl's mother was watching over her. Her insistence on getting the message through might have saved Annabelle's life. Gratitude flowed through her, honored to be the one chosen to deliver it.

The voices had quieted down now that she had set up her working hours for the spirits. Following Bella's advice, she had set a neatly printing a card to set beside her bed, stating that she was not to be disturbed after midnight or before eight in the morning. Doing it had felt a bit silly until the spirits honored her request and no longer disturbed her sleep.

Besides, Ethan took up so much space in her thoughts that there was little room left for any others.

"I'm shamefully empty-handed," Jessica said, returning her friend's warm hug.

Claudia led her inside. "There's nothing I need. Except to see you, of course. Damn, Jess, it's been way too long."

"I know. I've been out of pocket for a couple of months."

They went straight through to the kitchen, where a big white stockpot bubbled on the stove. From the oven came an aroma that made Jessica's stomach rumble. Bowls and silverware were already laid out in the old-fashioned breakfast nook.

Claudia got a potholder and bent to slide a tray of hot rolls from the oven.

"It's about time you brought me up to date on what's been happening," she said. "And that includes how you knew Annabelle had a problem with her tire. First, get the butter out of the fridge please. Then, sit down, and start talking."

Half an hour later, they had finished their lunch and Claudia was up to speed. She had listened in silence, her eyebrows lifting a couple of times, but she said nothing until Jessica had finished telling her about the voices, including the dead women, Hailey Martin and Finley Hunter, and little Ethan Starkey.

"And you've been experiencing this all the time I've known you?" Claudia asked curiously, not judgy, like Jenna.

"Well, yeah. But that's not why I wanted to see you."

Up went Claudia's brows again. "Oh? You've just told me an amazing story. There's more?"

Jessica frowned at her, determined to be stern. "Don't give me that innocent look, Claudia Rose. I know what you're up to, and *that's* what we need to talk about."

"You're not going to tell me you aren't attracted to Sage?"

"No, I'm definitely not going to tell you that. But thanks for acknowledging your little matchmaking scheme."

Claudia grinned widely. "I was afraid I'd lost my skills. So, what's the problem?"

"You knew he was arrested in his mom's death, right?"

"Ah. The internet." She made a face. "Uncle Google knows all. Or thinks he does."

Jessica pinned her with a glare. "Well, duh. You think I would get with a guy, not knowing anything about him?"

"I was kinda hoping you would take my word for it. You know, good references."

"So you did know."

"Yes, I knew. Put it together, Jess. If I thought there would be a problem, I would never have tried to get you two to hook up. I know him pretty well and I don't have any doubts."

"Get into the twenty-first century, Claudia. 'Hooking up' means casual sex these days."

"And that's not what this is…"

"No way!"

"Sometimes you remind me of Annabelle. No. I don't see either of you as the type to be into casual sex. But I do see you together. *And* I've seen both of your handwritings, so I know you're compatible. Not that compatibility is enough on its own. There has to be a spark, too."

"Oh, there's definitely a spark. But why didn't you tell me about his mother?"

"What about her?"

"Starting with she's dead and he got arrested for it?"

"Oh. That."

"Is he violent?"

Claudia hesitated.

"What do you know?" Jessica pressed. "What aren't you telling me?"

"I have seen him get angry enough to be violent, but it wasn't against a woman."

"Oh, that's great; violence against a guy."

"Believe me when I say, the guy deserved it. Anyway, besides his handwriting—and you know I rely on what handwriting says about people to get to the truth—all I know is what he told me and I believe him. He and his mom had a big argument and he left. Next thing, the cops are coming to pick him up for questioning. I'm sure you know it didn't stick, that the judge—"

"Yeah, I read the stories," Jessica interrupted. "But there's a big difference between not enough evidence to go to trial, and being innocent."

"That's so. Remember, though, handwriting always tells the truth, and I didn't see any major red flags in his."

"What about minor ones?"

"No more than in yours." Claudia leveled a serious look at her. "You've both seen some serious shit; the kinds of things that are bound to leave baggage. And remember, the man Sage has grown into is based on what was done *to* him, not things he did to anyone else. Sure, he has some residual anger, but so do you. It comes from loss and the feeling of being helpless. That doesn't mean he's going to turn it against you or anyone else."

"Fair enough," Jessica conceded with relief. No one had ever accused her of being undamaged or lacking her own anger, not the least when it came to her ex-husband.

"When his Aunt Maddy appeared to me at Dr. Gold's, she did say she was proud of him."

"Well, duh, Jess. What does that tell you?"

"Okay, I get it. What happened to his birth mother?"

The abrupt way Claudia got up from the table and started clearing the dishes telegraphed that this was an uncomfortable topic for discussion. "If you have questions about his birth mother, you need to ask Sage," she said. "He might not want to go there. In fact, I'd be surprised if he did."

Jessica rose and tried to help, but Claudia raised a hand to stop her. "You relax, I'll get it."

"It feels like you're holding out on me, Claudia. What's the big secret?"

Like a mother admonishing a child behaving badly, Claudia threw a frown over her shoulder. "Read my lips. Talk. To. Sage."

Jessica drove down the hill from Claudia's house, listening to a traffic alert on the radio. An accident had clogged Pacific Coast Highway in the Pacific Palisades area. She would have to take the 405 north instead of PCH. The 405 was always a parking lot. A few choice swear words colored the air blue as she turned right onto Culver Boulevard.

A mile outside of Playa de la Reina, she was thinking over her conversation with Claudia and what had been left unspoken about Sage. Too late, she remembered the fork in the road coming up. The freeway entrance was accessed from the left fork. She was in the right lane with vehicles racing past on her left, leaving no way to change over.

Veering onto Jefferson, she parked at the curb. She had driven this road countless times. She knew better. That's what she got for driving distracted.

Then she heard a whisper.

Ballona Wetlands.

It was so obvious, she could have palm-slapped her forehead. She was sitting right next to the wilderness habitat. Ballona Wetlands sprawled across the landscape on both sides of the highway in the center of the city, while a mere hundred yards ahead of her on Lincoln Boulevard, cross-traffic flew past like the Autobahn. There were ponds and reeds and cattails just like those she had seen in that weird episode in Ethan's bedroom. She had been pulled here.

In its long and varied history, the Ballona Wetlands was once owned by Howard Hughes, whose heirs had intentions of developing the bulk of the original 1,187 acres. A protracted battle early in the twenty-first century had ended with the State acquiring and protecting more than 600 acres, including the tidal Ballona Creek and the marshy area surrounding it.

With Playa Vista, a planned community of multi-story luxury condos and manicured parks dominating the intersection of the two main roads to the east, and homes on stilts clinging to the hillside on the south, the wetlands stood as an outright contradiction to the urban neighborhood.

Had Trey Starkey brought his son here on the way back from Disneyland?

Back to *where*, though? Not home.

What has he done with Ethan?

The Wetlands was nowhere close to the places to Disneyland, where the missing pair were known to have visited. It made no sense, but an urge was growing in Jessica to get out and look for Ethan there. The urge swelled, pushing her the way an addict is driven to find a fix.

She sat in the car, checking out the area. Across the sidewalk was a split rail fence that surrounded the wetlands, protecting the wildlife from human invaders. There had been a split rail fence in her vision in Ethan's bedroom.

Jessica drove the few yards to where public access to the wetlands began and parked the car. At the entrance of the hiking trail, signposts stated that the area around the marshland was the only part open to foot traffic. She gazed across the distance, where the trail looped around the mile-long perimeter of the marsh. Too much walking for little feet.

Why would Trey have brought his child here? Or was she just inventing a story because if he had, it might provide a clue to his current whereabouts?

He might have been taunting Abby after learning somehow that she had intended to take Ethan and leave. Maybe he would show up tonight or tomorrow and pretend to carry on as usual, as if nothing had happened. He might just be showing her how easily he could take Ethan from her.

Jessica sighed. With Hailey Martin, she had felt quite sure of herself when describing to Zach what the dead woman showed her. It was different with Ethan. Everything around him was hazy and uncertain.

She called to mind the photo Abby had shown her: Trey, holding his boy in his arms like any good dad might, showing him the animals in the zoo cages. But she had seen a glint of evil in the expression he had turned to the camera. It was easy to imagine him making some smug remark. An "I know something you don't know, and it's going to hurt you" taunt.

Trey would not be bringing Ethan home. Jessica knew it as well as she knew anything.

Sauntering along the dirt trail, she opened herself to the energy of the wetlands. At mid-afternoon, midweek, the place was largely deserted. The trees and bushes on the street side muted traffic sounds. Far away on the other side, a jogger ran along the trail. The occasional bird whistle came to her on the soft breeze. It would be easy to lose herself in the wild beauty of the natural landscape.

Ethan, are you here?

A slight stirring? Maybe.

Ethan. Talk to me.

"*Sleepy.*"

Was the thought coming from the boy or was she making it up? Sometimes it was hard to tell the difference. Jessica inhaled three deep breaths through her nose and let them out through her mouth, focusing on the missing child.

Ethan, I'll take you home.

"*Momma?*"

I'll take you to your mom. Where are you?

"*Papa said I have to take a nap.*"

Wait, Ethan…

The brief connection had broken.

She continued on the footpath until she came to a chain link barricade on the inside of the split rail fence. It formed a three-sided border around a concrete culvert where clear water flowed, merging with a fuzzy green blanket of algae. She had never visited the place before but she knew it as if she had.

A *deja vu* experience.

Cattails, reeds.

In the section of fencing past the culvert, two of the crossbars were missing from the fence, leaving a four-foot wide gap. Enough space for an adult to climb through. More than enough for a child. The same as she had seen in her vision.

Following her gut, Jessica made a quick scan of the area to make sure no one was watching, then scrambled under the top railing. On the other side, a wide mat of flattened straw made a pathway down to the marsh.

On any other day she would have stopped to appreciate the winter wild flowers. On any other day, she would not have ignored the No Trespassing signs the way she was now, following the *deja vu* down the slight slope about twenty feet to the lip of the marsh.

Standing at the water's edge, Jessica sent out her energy to

Ethan the way the books she read instructed. The books Sage had bought her.

Don't think about him now.

Spirit guides, please help me find Ethan. How about a hint? I really, really need your help.

What if she could *choose* to have an episode like the one with the satanic cult victim, Finley Hunter? Just wake up and find clues in a miniature she had no memory of making. *Tada!* Wouldn't it be easier?

Nope. Bad idea. That whole experience of being hogtied had been demoralizing. And Finley Hunter was dead. She still had hope for Ethan.

For several minutes she stood there, listening and hoping for a sign of some kind. When nothing happened, she tucked away her disappointment and turned to leave. Cut short by a sudden strong impulse.

Connecting with the feeling, Jessica's gaze swept the vegetation around the marsh. She looked up into the branches of the trees above. Felt a nudge to look down at the muddy ground. Saw something she had not noticed before…

Less than a yard from her right foot, half-buried in the mud, was a plastic T-Rex.

"Where did you come from?" she said to the toy dinosaur, crouching on her heels.

The spade-shaped head and tiny arms, the bulbous body. It was the perfect size for a four-year-old fist to grasp. Jessica reached for it. The jolt of energy she got when her fingers touched the plastic so startled her that she almost fell over backwards.

With a soft, sucking slurp, T-Rex came free and the mud closed back over the hole.

EIGHTEEN

The plastic dinosaur was in a paper evidence bag in the trunk of Zach Smith's car and members of the Emergency Response Team were en route. Fish and Wildlife, who managed the wetlands, had given permission to conduct the search.

"You should have left it where it was," said Zach.

The rebuke set Jessica on the defensive. "Are you thinking about DNA? With all the rain we've had, would there be any?"

He shrugged. "Maybe not, but we like to see evidence *in situ*. I'll send it to the lab, see if they get anything off it. It could have belonged to *any* kid."

Jessica threw him a look of scorn. "Yeah. Except I was *pulled* here, and just *any* kid isn't likely to climb through the fence to the water. The same marshy water I saw in my head while I was in his bedroom. Oh, and in case you forgot, Ethan is a mini-paleontologist in training. *And* he has a special thing for T-Rex. *And* Abby ID'd the photo you sent her."

Zach rolled his eyes. "She said he had some dinosaurs like it, but they're in his toy box."

"*And* she said Trey would have gone and got him another one if he got upset that it got left behind. The one in the mud was like the one he had in his toy box. There's no shortage of toy stores, in case you didn't know."

"Well, I can't bring a full ERT out here just because your hand itched." Noticing her crestfallen face, Zach relented, letting her know he had been teasing. "Don't worry, chickie, I've got a smaller crew coming to walk the area. We'll do a thorough search." His phone rang then and he moved away to answer it.

She watched him listen to the other party, head bent, nodding, thinking how he had always reminded her of Keanu Reeves—appearing like kind of a goofball, but with more depth than it sometimes seemed. Zach was an important friend, but now that Sage had come into her life, she knew he would never be anything more.

He clipped his phone back onto his belt and ambled back to her. "Trey Starkey used his debit card at Dinah's."

"The diner on Jefferson? This proves they were near here." Jessica had lived in the area after her accident and had passed the historic restaurant countless times. Dinah's had been famous for their fried chicken and oven baked pancakes since the 1950s.

"Yeah, it proves it. I have to call Abby and find out if Ethan has a passport."

"You think Trey will take him out of the country?"

"At this point, I wouldn't—hold on; text…" Zach pulled his phone off his belt again and checked the screen. "The ERT is a couple minutes out. You'd better get going before someone sees you, Jess."

He looked past her shoulder, his expression changing to one of disgust. "Shit, fuck, dammit."

Jessica turned to see a TV news van pull up right behind her car. "How the hell did they know?"

"They monitor the police band, goddammit. They're here before we are. I've gotta set up a perimeter. Look, Jess, can you go and sit with Abby until her mom gets there? Make sure she doesn't try to come here to the wetlands."

"Does she know where you are?"

"I called her on my way here. It'll be all over the news."

"Okay, I'll text her that I'm coming."

"Thanks. You know the drill. Act like the newsies aren't there. Ignore them."

"Got it."

Jessica hurried out to the street. She was almost at the Mini when Keith Lewis, the TV reporter who had been at Abby's press conference, spotted her and jumped out of his media van. He reached the Mini first, blocking her driver door.

"Hi there. I'm Keith Lewis, Eyewitness News," he said, putting on a phony smile.

"I know who you are," said Jessica, not smiling back.

"Great. So, what's the story on little Ethan? Have they found something?"

"What do you mean? I was just walking the trail. Now, would you mind stepping out of my way?"

He stayed where he was. "Oh, come on, I saw you talking with Special Agent Smith. Did he tell you anything? What's your part in the story? Can you give me your name?"

Keith Lewis had a dozen inches on her but Jessica had learned early on that if she straightened her spine and put steel into her tone, it made her seem taller. She took a step toward the reporter. Surprised, he took a step back. Jessica raised her chin and narrowed her eyes.

"My name is get the fuck away from my car before I call the cops."

Driving away with a squeal of tires, she decided with a smug grin that the expression of stunned surprise on Keith Lewis' face was worth the irritation of being forced to deal with him.

"What if they find him in the marsh?"

Abby was the picture of hopelessness, slumped in her club chair in the den. Another dusk had fallen with Ethan away from home, out there in the world somewhere, away from his mother.

"What if he's all by himself in that muddy water? Oh, God, what am I going to do without him?"

Jessica cleared her throat, searching for the right thing to say. As much as she deserved to express them, Abby's emotions embarrassed her. Should she reach over and squeeze her hand or something? The gnawing despair Abby must be experiencing was all too familiar, but Jessica had never taken comfort in physical contact the way other people seemed to. After coming out of the coma and learning of Justin's death, she had wanted no one but Jenna within miles of her, let alone put their hands on her.

"You can't think that way, Abby," she said, settling for comforting words. "You've got to stay strong for Ethan."

"You're right. I just—my God, how did we get here? How did it all go so wrong?"

The questions required answers that Jessica did not have. She had glanced at the photo of Trey and Ethan on the end table as she sat down. It practically vibrated with negative energy and gave her the creeps just as much as it had the first time she laid eyes on it. She stretched for something intelligent to say that would not come across like some inane platitude; those meaningless "thoughts and prayers" that served to pick a wound raw.

"Sometimes, couples grow in different directions, Abby. Maybe that's what happened to you and Trey."

Abby leaned her head back against the chair, her long legs splayed in front of her. "I thought I was so grown up, dating the captain of the swim team. Trey was a junior in high school, I was in ninth grade. I was totally infatuated. He said I was his soulmate." The sigh she dredged up came from the depths. A faint smile ghosted her lips. "It's all so long ago."

"You've been together for a long time."

"He wanted me to wear his class ring on a chain around my neck, but as soon as I put it on, he got super-possessive. I made some innocent comment that my best friend's brother was cute. He went on this crazy rant, claiming I'd cheated on him. I was devastated."

Jessica nodded to show understanding, but inside she was cringing. She had made the same kind bargain with the devil as Abby had. Who was she to judge? Wasn't it too easy to examine someone else's life and think, 'Why would you stay with such a jerk?'

Abby was on a roll, letting out feelings that had been tamped down and hidden, maybe for years. "I kept calling and begging him to forgive me and take me back. How dumb was that? After *he* decided it was time to make up, I started working extra hard to keep the peace. I had to be super-careful with everything I said."

"Walking on eggshells," said Jessica, with the kind of understanding that comes from sharing a similar experience. "Making sure you never so much as looked at anyone else."

"I had to promise I would never go to my friend's house again."

"Ninth grade is so young. What did your parents say?"

Abby shrugged. "My father was having an affair with the company bookkeeper. He just walked out on us and was a deadbeat dad. That's why I became a lawyer, chasing men just like him. Of course, that was years later. Mom worked her butt off to support us girls. She cleaned houses for other families, which meant she was too tired to pay attention to us. She just wanted to go home and sleep. I know now she was depressed, too.

"I had to stay home after school and watch the girls. Trey always came over and I'd be trying to entertain him and get my homework done, too. He'd be sitting there watching TV, or else trying to get me into my bedroom."

Jessica let her talk, listening with half an ear, nodding where it seemed appropriate. The general pattern of abuse Abby described was well known to her. When she and Greg met, he had pursued her with expensive gifts and flattery, taking her to fancy restaurants. But once they were a couple, he sometimes stood her up or showed up late for dates, armed with pathetic excuses. She had been so ridiculously attracted to him that she made the mistake of overlooking those slights. When things were good between them, they were amazing. And there was the sex—she admitted it to herself now. He had always been able to talk her into bed.

Jessica recognized from the start that he drank too much. She fooled herself into believing his promises to quit after graduation— he needed the alcohol to help him deal with the stresses of school, he'd say. Then he graduated and he needed the alcohol to help him deal with the high-stress job as an architect. The drinking got worse. The more he drank, the more he bought her pretty things, jewelry, flowers to make up for his meanness while drunk. But the gifts never replaced what she wanted most—his love and affection.

No sooner had she decided to end the relationship than she discovered she was pregnant. Greg's excitement about the baby came as a shock. She was so sure he would want her to get rid of it. It was not until after he had talked her into getting married that she came to understand his need for control. That, more than his desire for a family, was what drove him.

He let her know in subtle ways that he saw her as weak and

under his thumb. But Gregory Mack failed to recognize Jessica's tough inner core, which eventually fought its way back to freedom.

Too bad she had not been clairvoyant then.

"We never should have gotten married," Abby was saying when Jessica came back to the present. "Poor Mom. She was thrilled when we got engaged, thinking I would be 'taken care of'—she's that old fashioned. It made her feel less guilty about neglecting us."

"She's here for you now," said Jessica, remembering how uncomfortable it had been to see her own mother at Justin's funeral. They'd had nothing to say to each other, no hugs. Lorraine had never made an effort to meet her grandson. She'd had to show up because it would have looked bad if she hadn't, and "image" was Lorraine's middle name.

Abby said, "Mom can't take a lot time off, or she'll lose her job. She's a nurse's aide. Anyway, since she pushed for the marriage, I don't like to rub it in her face that Trey turned out to be such a shit."

Privately, Jessica thought Abby's mother deserved to have her face rubbed in it, but it wasn't up to her. "Are you close to your sisters?" she asked.

"They call and we FaceTime. They all live out of state, have kids of their own." Abby pushed herself off the chair as if it took every ounce of strength she had. "How about some coffee? Glass of wine?"

"Coffee would be great, thanks."

They went into the kitchen. Large sheets of cardboard had been placed over the windows to block the reporters' view. Abby switched on the lights and started going through the mechanics of brewing coffee.

"Are you hungry? There's that casserole Mom brought over last night. I haven't touched it."

"I'm fine, thanks. You go ahead."

"I can't eat. I've lost five pounds." Abby pulled cups from the cabinet next to the sink and busied herself with small tasks. Either she had not finished with the conversation they had started in the den, or maybe she needed to keep talking to distract herself from what Zach and his crew were doing under floodlights at Ballona marsh. They both knew the possibility that they might come across Ethan's body there. Neither of them wanted to talk about it.

Abby set a cup in front of Jessica at the table. "Trey gets by on charm and good looks. He's super smart; could have done anything he wanted, but he's intellectually lazy. He never got that it's not that way for everyone."

"I'm surprised you were allowed to go to law school," said Jessica.

"When I told him that's what I wanted to do, he went ballistic."

"Because he knew he would lose control over you."

"He ranted that I didn't have to work, he would make enough to support me." Abby gave a mirthless laugh. "Then he said that if I had a job it would make me too independent."

"He wanted to isolate you."

"I stood up to him for once. Look, I care about my mom, but I couldn't allow myself to end up under-educated and poor like her. So, we compromised. I had to pick a school near home and wear an engagement ring. Trey took real estate courses. Then I started clerking at a law office and we got married. He wanted a baby right away, but I held him off for the first year."

"Was he excited when you got pregnant?"

"You'd think so, but it was like ninth grade all over again, only worse because now I was stuck. He started complaining that he was losing my attention. Then he made rules for what I was allowed to wear, how to fix my hair, everything. And you know how it is when you're pregnant—beyond exhausted."

"No energy, morning sickness."

"Exactly. Plus, working in a law office means you don't work regular hours if there's a trial going on. But dinner had better be ready and on the table the minute Trey walked in. He'd be furious if I was even five minutes late. No fast food, either."

"This sounds a lot like my marriage," said Jessica. "How did it go after Ethan came along?"

A dreamy look came into Abby's eyes. "That was an amazing time. Trey totally changed. He couldn't get enough of the baby. He bonded with him better than I did. I went back to work and they were together day and night." The smile disappeared and a tear welled up and slid down Abby's cheek. "Oh, Jess, I should have spent more time with him. I should have made him more important than work."

It seemed a cruel irony that Abby was now feeling guilty for the same reason her mother had—spending too much time at work instead of being with her child.

"Didn't you have a babysitter?"

"Trey wouldn't allow it. When Ethan was too young to walk, he took him in the stroller when he went to show houses." She allowed herself a wry smile. "A baby is a good selling tool. The clients think Trey is wonderful."

"He doesn't go to pre-school?"

"No. I can't imagine what's going to happen when he starts kinder—" Abby broke off and covered her face with her hands, sobbing. She took the sheet of paper towel Jessica tore off and shoved into her hand and blew her nose. She got up and went to the sink, splashed water on her face. When she turned back, her red, swollen eyes made her look like the "before" picture in a cosmetics ad.

"Trey was always a good father. But, a couple of months ago, I started noticing that whenever I tried to hold Ethan or wanted to play with him, he didn't want anything to do with me. He'd start fussing and squirming when I'd get near. He wouldn't even let me kiss him. He acted like he was scared of me."

"Do you think Trey—?"

"It was obvious to me that *something* was going on. I installed a secret nanny cam." Her face twisted with anger. "He was brainwashing Ethan. He would say, 'Mommy isn't home because she doesn't love us. She'd rather be with her friends at work.' Or, 'We're men, we don't like all that kissy stuff. You don't want to be a mama's boy, do you?'"

A photo of Trey posted on the refrigerator caught Jessica's eye. Again, he was playing with Ethan, looking the part of the loving father. She was not by nature a violent person, but someone messing with a little kid's head was enough to turn her into a monster. She would beat that arrogant face to a bloody pulp if she ever heard him say such a thing.

"Confronting him must have taken guts," she said.

"Even I have my limits. I wasn't about to let him do that to Ethan."

"How did that go?"

"At work, I never let on how things were at home, but I guess the strain started showing. My friend Donna kept asking what was wrong. When I finally told her about all the rules, she was totally scandalized. She said I was being abused." Abby huffed a short laugh. "I told her that was ridiculous and that if he ever hit me, I'd have left him right then."

"There are plenty of ways to abuse people without hitting them," Jessica said, having endured too many of them herself before waking up to the knowledge that her relationship with Greg was never going to improve. "Calling names, making threats. *Making rules...*"

"I know that now. But I was in so deep that I couldn't see it for what it was," said Abby. "Now that she knew what was going on, Donna wasn't surprised that Trey was talking crap about me to Ethan. I should have known better. I'm an attorney."

"Don't beat yourself up. It's easy to get in and way harder to get out."

"On top of everything else, I—well, I checked Trey's phone while he was in the shower. Maybe not my finest hour, but I'm glad I did. He was having an affair with at least one of his clients. I kept picturing him screwing around in our bed with Ethan in the next room. It tipped me right over the edge. I confronted him and said I intended to file for divorce and I was taking Ethan with me."

"The most dangerous time is when you're threatening to leave," Jessica said. She wished she knew what was happening at Ballona Wetlands marsh. And then, she didn't. She got up and poured herself a refill of coffee.

"No kidding. Trey got ice cold, which isn't like him. Most of the time he would freak out. He said if I ever left him, he would find me and kill us both. I grabbed Ethan and ran into the bedroom. Trey followed us. He had a gun." Abby started talking faster. "I never knew he owned one and he was pointing it at me. He said he would never let me leave him."

"Omigod, that's horrible. What did you do?"

"I was too scared to do anything, so I backed off. Ethan used to be the most loving child, but now—" She trailed off.

"Oh, Abby. I'm so sorry. You've lived under so much stress for too long."

"One night I snuck into the garage and called Donna. Trey burst in. I guess he thought he was going to catch me doing something wrong. He refused to believe I was just talking to a work friend. He kept insisting that I must be having an affair."

"That's like a thief accusing someone of stealing," said Jessica. Abby's story made her see her own life through a different lens and left her ashamed to have disregarded the warning signs for so long. Justin would be alive if she had left Greg sooner. Her culpability was a living thing that would gnaw at her soul for all the time she remained on earth.

"...then he wouldn't talk to me. That's his favorite form of punishment—shutting me out for days at a time."

She nodded sympathetically, but Abby's voice was stretching out like a slowed-down video, the words as meaningless as a foreign language. Jessica was back on that dark, hilly road, rain slashing against the windshield, Greg screaming at the car that overtook them. The red taillights of the semi in front of them—

She jerked herself back. She was here to support Abby, who might well be about to face her own terrible loss. She had to pull herself together.

"My sister and I made plans," she said, when Abby fell silent. "We were driving to San Francisco. The *plan* was, we'd get to the hotel and Greg would drink himself into a stupor like he did every night. I would call my sister, who would be ready and waiting outside the hotel. That was supposed to be the start of a new life."

"But you had an accident—"

"We had an accident," Jessica echoed. The silence lengthened, each of them lost in her own misery until Jessica once again reminded herself of her duty to Abby and pulled them back.

"How did Trey end up taking Ethan?"

"Same as you. I was ready to take Ethan and go. Trey found out somehow. He probably hacked my emails." Abby's voice pitched higher as she described the bombshell of finding her son missing, her plans nipped in the bud. "Donna came home from work with me so I'd have some backup, but they were already gone. I called the police—he wouldn't answer his phone. They said there was nothing they could do. I didn't have a restraining order, we're not divorced."

"That seems so wrong when he'd made threats against you."

"I was about to lose my mind, and then he texted me pictures of Ethan at Disneyland. I was relieved he was safe, of course, but I was beyond furious. I kept expecting them to come home. Like you, I planned to leave after Trey was asleep. He doesn't drink a lot like *your* husband, but he sleeps like the dead."

"But they didn't come back," said Jessica.

"I stayed up all night, waiting, but they never came home. I called the cops again. That time I told them about the gun and the threats. They treated me like I was making it up because I hadn't told them earlier."

"Why *didn't* you tell them?"

Abby's face reddened. "I guess I didn't want to cause him trouble."

"He threatened your life, Abby. Didn't you take it seriously? You know—gun?"

"I guess some part of me still wanted to protect him. Yeah, it scared me at the time, but I didn't believe he would go through with it. Now I hate him. I just want my baby back."

Yeah, I want my baby, too. I hope you don't have to pay the same price I did.

"Zach said they couldn't track his phone," Jessica said.

"Apparently, he removed the sim card. So, the FBI got involved."

"And here we are."

The heaviness of the atmosphere in the Starkey house was like attempting to breathe at the bottom of a pool.

A pool. A marsh…

Zach's ring tone interrupted. Without identifying her caller, Jessica rose from the table. If they had come upon the little boy's body, she did not want to take the news in front of his mother.

Excusing herself, she hurried to the den, her gut churning with anxiety, and answered the call.

"Don't say anything to Abby," said Zach's tense voice. "Just tell her we're continuing to search."

"Okay. What's up?"

"Right down by the water's edge, near the dinosaur, there was a Disneyland food wrapper."

NINETEEN

Elaine Truman was giving Jessica that watchful look again, as if she might steal the family silver. She had showed up bearing another covered dish while Jessica was on the phone with Zach.

"Beef stew," she said, stowing it beside the intact tuna casserole in the refrigerator, chiding Abby for not eating. "It's not that you couldn't stand to lose a few pounds. But this is the wrong way to do it. You've got to eat, Ab. You need your strength. Ethan needs—" She faltered to a stop.

Jessica came back to the kitchen. "Now that you're here, Mrs. Truman, I'm gonna head home. Abby, Zach said he'll call when he has some news."

"Thank you so much, Jess. It's not your job, you didn't have to come." Abby came over and hugged her hard. "I feel like I've gained another sister. I feel horrible for what you've gone through, too."

"Just be strong. Ethan needs you to be strong."

Hope lit Abby's face. "Have you felt him again? Is he—" She broke off with a gasp. Too late. Her mother's sharp voice cut through.

"What does that mean, Ab, 'felt him'? How could she *feel* him?"

"Nothing, Mom. It doesn't mean anything."

"You said it. It has to mean *some*thing." Elaine Truman's friendly gaze hardened into suspicion. She swung on Jessica, who was getting into her jacket. "What's she talking about, Jessica?

174

What did you *feel*? What are you *really* doing here?"

Jessica half-shrugged. "I have to go. Let's talk tomorrow, Abby."

Doubtless alerted by their colleagues at the Ballona Wetlands, reporters were out in full force again outside the Starkey home. Their presence underscored the dire situation. Waiting for a reaction from the bereaved mother if Ethan's body was in Ballona marsh.

They surrounded Jessica's car as she attempted to back out of the driveway, cameras flashing in her face through the windows. Shouting the same inane questions. "What's new with Ethan? Have the feds found Trey Starkey? How's Abby doing?"

Half-hoping they would not move out of the way and give her an excuse to run them down, Jessica gripped the steering wheel hard and backed up faster than she should. To her disappointment, they scattered.

She got on the freeway, wracking her brain, looking for a way to help Ethan. Yesterday's experience in his bedroom left her with little confidence that he was safe with his father. Why was he alone?

Please, spirit guides, please protect Ethan. Help me find him.

If anyone on the other side of life was listening to her plea, Jessica was not hearing an answer. But a clear picture of Sage's face materialized in her mind.

She could feel his disappointment at not having heard from her; his desire to see her. Was it a psychic sense or wishful thinking? A bleak wave of loneliness slammed into her.

She missed her sister, missed her son. She missed Sage. It made no sense; they didn't know each other that well. It was just, there was something so appealing about him. Besides the sexiness. Besides the good looks. Maybe it was infatuation. No. From the first moment they had set eyes on each other there had been a recognition, a sense of picking up where they had left off at some other time.

A karmic relationship? If it was true that soulmates met again and again through many lifetimes, maybe she and Sage... Jessica smiled a secret smile. *You really are going over the edge.*

His number was still in her phone.

"Jessica," was all he said, but he breathed so much into her name that it swept away the need for preliminaries or polite conversation. A flood of warmth left her body tingling from head to toe.

"I'm on my way home from Thousand Oaks," she said. "Can you meet me there? Or, if you're busy—"

"I'll be there. Have you eaten?"

"Not yet."

"I know you like Italian. I'll pick up some food."

"I have some nice wine."

"I'll help you drink it. See you soon."

As she ended the call, Jessica didn't need to ask herself what she was doing. Even if this—whatever *this* was—lasted just one night, it was what she wanted.

She woke in the wee hours wrapped in Sage's arms, knowing she belonged there. For the present, nothing else mattered.

Across the cottage, the kitchen window showed a sky the color of ink. As she lay there, content and a little spacy, the mental image of a jigsaw puzzle formed in the space above her: a black/white yin-yang symbol, male/female aspects in balance.

At the center, one puzzle piece was missing between the two dots, overlapping the white and black edges. As Jessica watched, the missing piece appeared and dropped into the space, completing the picture.

Yes. That's how this feels.

She had never believed in fate, but she had no doubt that she and Sage had been brought together by a power greater than their own. He stirred, murmured unintelligible words. Jessica ran her fingertips across his skin, felt him shiver. He reached out to her and they made love again. And later, again.

Spooning against Sage's long body, she let herself be engulfed by him. "I don't want anything to spoil this moment," she said.

His arms tightened around her, his face buried in her hair. "Nothing could spoil this moment."

His words sent a ripple of fear over her. *Tempting fate.* She forced them into the attic part of her mind, where she stored all the bits and pieces that were too painful to examine, and slipped back into sleep.

The evening before, she had arrived home from Abby's to

find Sage waiting with a big paper bag that held containers of mushroom ravioli, salad and garlic bread. The food had remained on the kitchenette counter top, uneaten.

There had been no conversation. Just immediate, hungry sex and then later, more leisurely, relaxed love making, rather than simply satisfying the wild animal desires that had driven them. A little sleep, then hours of lying together, holding hands, desultory talk.

An unspoken understanding kept the two of them rambling around the edges of Jessica's spiritual awakening, rather than revealing their personal secrets. There would be time for that.

Somewhere around daybreak, Sage said, "Being with you—making love with you—it's too familiar to be coincidence. You feel it, too, don't you? We've known each other before, in many lifetimes."

Jessica smiled, savoring the sheer joy she had felt from giving herself to him without reservation. "If someone else I'd just met said that to me I would run as fast as I could. I realize it sounds lame, but it's like being touched by magic. So many things that have happened in this life have become irrelevant."

Not Justin, of course. Never Justin.

She was going to have to tell Sage that she'd had a child and that due to her negligence, was liable for his death.

Not yet. Too soon.

"It's not lame," Sage said. "I feel the magic."

They rolled out of bed after nine and took turns in the shower, which was too small to accommodate them both at the same time.

"We'll have the pasta for lunch. It's always better on the second day, anyway." Jessica placed the container in the otherwise almost-bare refrigerator. "For breakfast, all I can offer you is oatmeal."

"Oatmeal is fine. Right now, I could eat the carton and not notice."

Sage came up behind her at the stove and pulled her close against him. He leaned down, his breath warm on her neck, his hands in her hair, caressing her shoulders with those long, elegant fingers, making her shiver in a way she was quite certain she had never done before.

He turned her around and kissed her slowly, as if there was

no hurry and no place in the world he would rather be. He kissed her, savoring her mouth as if her lips were fine chocolate, the only piece he would ever eat. He kissed her with childlike delight and she kissed him right back.

Sitting across from each other at her small table, eating oatmeal, they exchanged soulful glances like teenagers discovering love for the first time.

Once the food had been consumed and cleared away. They lay under the comforter together, arms and legs entangled.

"I guess you wondered why you hadn't heard from me," said Jessica,

"It doesn't matter now. I'm just happy you called."

"Me, too. I've been helping to look for that boy who's missing. Have you seen it on the news? It became all-consuming for a couple of days." She was not about to taint the moment by letting him know she had read the newspaper article about his mother's death. She imagined him being hurt that she had looked him up, going into a cold silence… *Stop mixing him up with Greg. Sage is warm and wonderful and…*

"Just so long as it wasn't because you were repulsed by me," he said, joking. Then his eyes opened wide in a look of mortification. "What a shitheel I am, making jokes when—do you think they found him?"

"Zach would have called. Anyway, if he's in the marsh, I don't want to know."

Would the little boy's spirit come to her if he had crossed over? She didn't know enough about how it all worked. In one of the books she had read, it stated that a loved one is always there to meet a newly crossed person, to take care of them, which was comforting. But in another it said there were lost souls, including children wandering around on their own, afraid. That had left her upset and worried for Justin, despite the evidence to the contrary.

She told Sage about the food wrapper Zach's ERT had come across at the marsh, and Trey Starkey's credit card being used at Dinah's.

"So, they were definitely there," he said. Today, his eyes were bluer than blue, the color of lapis lazuli. From the crook of his arm, Jessica tilted her head to look up at him. During the years of her marriage she had never felt safe the way Sage made her feel. If it were possible for them to stay just as they were and never have to think about missing children again, she would be the happiest person in the world.

As she was thinking that, a key turned in the lock. She bolted up. "What the—?"

There was no time to get to the door before Jenna swept in on a blast of cold air, Zach behind her.

"What the hell are you doing?" Jessica demanded.

Jenna stopped short, hands on her hips. "What the hell are *you* doing? Why aren't you answering your phone?" Then she noticed Sage. "Oh."

Sage did the standard shocked double-take, staring back and forth at the twins.

"My phone never rang," said Jessica, glaring at her sister. She turned to Sage. "Meet my sister. She forgot how to knock, and I forgot to mention we're twins."

While Sage introduced himself to the visitors, Jessica checked her phone. In all the commotion of yesterday with the marsh and Abby, then the much nicer distraction of the night, she had forgotten to put it on the charger. The battery was dead.

"*Sage*," said Jenna. Being the married mother of two little girls did not stop her from being impressed, if her frank appraisal of him was any indicator.

Zach introduced himself and the two men shook hands, eyeing each other like rival lions over a fresh kill. Neither said 'pleased to meet you.'

"What are you doing here?" Jessica demanded. It made no sense for Jenna to be here with Zach. She had nothing to do with Ethan. Unless Zach had brought her to cushion the blow of bad news. Jessica started trembling. "Have you found him?"

"No," Zach said. "We've called off the search. There's nothing at the marsh, other than what I already told you."

"I guess you've been too busy to watch the news," Jenna cut in. "You're trending, Jess."

"*Trending*? What are you talking about?"

Rummaging in a purse the size of a small suitcase, Jenna pulled out her phone and tapped keys. The screen she pointed at Jessica sucked the breath out of her:

Psychic helping FBI find Ethan.

"How did they find out? Who would tell—oh, hell. *Elaine.*"

"Who's that?" Jenna asked.

"Abby Starkey's mom," said Zach angrily. "Why the hell would you tell her?"

The unfair accusation bruised Jessica more than it should have. She flared back at him. "I *didn't* tell her. Elaine came over last night while I was at Abby's house—because *you* asked me to be there—*remember?* Abby let it slip. Dammit, I *knew* Elaine was going to drag it out of her the minute I left. But why would she blab it to the media?"

"Probably thinks her daughter is going to hell because of what you're doing. And she'd probably be right."

Zach shot Jenna a dirty look. "Knock it off, Jen."

For a half-second, Jenna's face collapsed with fatigue and the strain of uncertainty. The breezy mask fell back in place, but not before Jessica saw what her twin was hiding: genuine worry.

"You came all the way over here so you could tell me I'm trending?"

"We came because we couldn't get hold of you and I have a key to your house *in case of emergency.* And now, I'm leaving. I don't see any emergency here."

Jenna pointed an accusing finger at Zach. "Next time you can't reach her, don't call me." She sashayed to the door, turning back with a beauty pageant wave. "B'bye, *Sage.*"

They watched her go in silence.

"Have you found anything new since the food wrapper?" Jessica asked, as the door closed behind her with a sharp snap.

Zach's face was pasty grey with exhaustion. Dark circles smudged the skin beneath his eyes, the thick, black hair greasy and uncombed. The signs of working all night at Ballona marsh with his team. He glowered down at her. "I'm no longer allowed to discuss the case with you. If you want to know anything, ask your brother-in-law. Or turn on the news."

"You're acting like it's my fault that you asked me to connect with Ethan." She heard the peevishness in her tone and wished Sage did not have to witness the childish exchange.

Zach heaved an injured sigh. "No, Jess, it's not your fault I asked for your help. But you and I get to bear the consequences of my mistake. I'm not allowed to ask for your help again, and can't share any information. Roland is doing damage control right now, seeing if he can save my fucking job. He's telling the media—with her permission—that it was Abby who called you in. But they've got your name *and* who you and Jenna are. They know you were the one with amnesia and she was the kidnap victim who got the brain implant. I advise you to keep a low profile. You can expect it to get insane once the newsies figure out where you live. Your services are no longer needed. Don't call me and I won't call you."

With a curt nod to Sage, Zach walked out, shutting the door behind him harder than he needed to.

"I'm sorry," said Jessica.

Sage pulled her into his arms. "There's nothing for you to be sorry for. Maybe I shouldn't say it, but is your sister always such a bitch?"

That made her laugh. "Not always, but lately, way too often."

"It's incredible how alike you two look."

"I intended to tell you about the twin thing, but it's been kinda busy." Jessica sighed, feeling as bruised as if her twin had used her as a punching bag.

Sage released her. "I know about your amnesia, of course, but—Jenna had a *brain implant*?"

"Not right now, okay?"

"No need to say a word until you're ready."

"Thank you. I can't tell you how much I appreciate that."

"Sure. But what's with this Zach guy? He has a thing for you." He released her and took a step back.

In a flash, her shields went up, her shoulders stiffening out of habit, ready to defend herself from a verbal assault.

He's not Greg.

Thank God.

Drop the shoulders. Release the breath. "He *had* a thing for me. We were together for a while several years ago. We're just friends now."

Sage gave her a small smile. "The way he looked at you, it's not over by a long shot. Not for him."

"I don't want to think about Zach. Or Ethan. If I'm not allowed to help on the case, I need to get him out of my mind."

Jessica reached up, stretching on tiptoes, and took Sage's face in her hands. She pulled him down and kissed him, sweetly at first, then with growing intensity. She should not be wanting him again already, but an urge to make up for lost time melded with the urge to strip off their clothes and start all over again. The way his body responded told her that he felt the same.

Much later, she wiped away beads of sweat gathered on her skin, congratulating herself on finding such an effective way to rid her mind of the painful scene with Zach and Jenna. Sage was flat on his back underneath her, panting.

"You're gonna wear me out," he said. "Not that I'm complaining." He caught one of her long curls and wound it around his index finger, drawing her down to him until their noses were close. "I love your hair," he murmured, "It's so wild."

"Untamable," she agreed.

A slow smile spread across his face. "Mmm, kinda like you, I bet."

She nodded. "Like me."

He didn't know yet that being untamable was a source of pride for Jessica, and had been as far back as her memory would take her. The first time she had defied their mother's order to put on the same dress as her twin, they were three years old—the same as Emma and Sophie now.

Lorraine had planned to show off her identical little dolls to the garden club ladies. Jessica's obstinate refusal to wear the pink ruffled dress with its big flouncy bow had set off one of her "spells." It turned out that locking herself in her room with a fifth of vodka and lime slices in a bowl of ice was not the punishment Lorraine intended. The twins had taken it as an invitation to watch as much TV as they wanted.

"Hey, where'd you go?"

She rolled off him and lay beside him, feeling his skin, still damp. "A quick trip down memory lane."

"What did you find there?"

"An alcoholic mother who parented at her convenience. The

good news is, she wasn't our birth mother."

Sage turned on his side, resting on his elbow. "You're adopted, too?"

"From six months old. We don't know anything about our birth mother or why she gave us up. Have you ever looked for yours?"

A shutter came down over his face, giving him a harsh look that startled her. Remembering what Jay the bicycle man had told her about his youth, she tried to take back the question with a kiss. Not a kiss of passion, but the kind she would have given Justin for a scraped knee.

"I'm sorry if that's off-limits."

Sage shook his head, letting her off the hook. "We both have our baggage and we'll talk about it all sometime. Regina was my *real* mother. That other woman was just an incubator, a means for me to get here. And, I didn't have to look for her. Regina told me about her as soon as I was old enough to understand. I've met her."

"You have? How was it?"

Growing up, Jessica and Jenna had countless discussions about their birth mother and who she might be. On their eleventh birthday they'd made a pact never to question their parents, never to search for their birth mother, fearing what they might find. That way, the loving fantasy woman of their own construction—the tragic mother, forced to give up her babies through some terrible circumstance, would always be theirs.

Sage lay back and stared up at the ceiling. "I didn't have any feelings for her. It wasn't like, oh, Mommy, I love you, or anything close. I went to see her for one reason: I wanted her to tell me what happened to my siblings. She refused to see me at first, but I hounded her until she told me how to find them."

The conversation had brought the woman he did not love into the cottage with them, draining some of the warmth from his voice. "My sister died young. Drugs. My brother was the middle kid. He's doing great. We were separated too young for him to remember me very well. I got in touch with him through his Facebook page. He was totally psyched to hear from me. He got married last year and became a dad."

Jessica grinned. "Which makes you Uncle Sage."

"Yeah, it does. One of these days soon, I'll take you to see the baby. They live in Silicon Valley." He leaned over and touched a fingertip to Jessica's lips. "Now, let's get some shuteye and when we wake up and I see your beautiful face, everything will be perfect again."

She kissed the fingertip. "It's perfect now."

Her curiosity about his childhood itched like a healing scab that she wanted to pick at, to understand what Sage had been through to make him the beautiful man he was today. His friend, Jay, had said he was adopted at four and didn't speak for a year. What had that child witnessed that was so terrible he couldn't speak about it, drawing violent pictures years later? Four years old.

Ethan's age.

The wintery mid-afternoon light dribbled in through the kitchen windows, the intermittent rain a mild drumbeat on the roof. In a matter of seconds Sage's breathing had slowed to a light snore. Curled next to him, Jessica rested a hand on his chest, preoccupied with the remarkable strangeness of knowing that she was already precious to him.

The dream started soon after his soft respirations lulled her to sleep, too.

Consciousness faded and she was Ethan, running on skinny little legs in the cold black night, choking on a suffocating terror the likes of which she had never known. Then, just as abruptly, she was no longer Ethan.

She was nothing. Alone in an abyss so complete, it had no end. She was nothing. Had never existed. The world she remembered was nothing more than a dream.

Reaching out through the roiling black brume, her hands touched nothing, her eyes saw nothing. Her body was tormented by unendurable pain, and fear that terrible punishment must come as a result of diabolical deeds, although she did not know what they were.

For eons, she floated in cold darkness, deprived of sensory stimuli, until at last, the maw of hell opened below her, releasing the silhouettes of other humans. She and they were faceless zombies, their humanity wiped away, walking the streets of a ghost town.

Whether or not the others saw her, too, so consumed were they by their own misery that they had nothing left for the suffering of anyone else. She reached out to touch one but her hand passed straight through its body. No communication, no connection.

What am I doing here? What have I done to deserve this?

"You know." The voice echoed through her, reverberating with the beat of a kettle drum, penetrating every cell. Other voices called out. "Come with us, we've been waiting for you."

A group of shadowy figures gathered around a door that had materialized in the distance.

"Come on in," they called, beckoning her to enter through a blinding light that seemed to surround the door. "Come with us."

Anything must be better than the ghost town. Floating over, she passed through the doorway and emerged into a long, dark tunnel. The light that had attracted her was extinguished as she entered, leaving a charcoal fog.

Unable to see, she tried to pull back, crying out in revolt. *I don't belong here.*

The figures encircled her, ignoring her protests, pushing and shoving, dragging thorny nails as rough and sharp as broken glass against her skin.

"You are nothing," they taunted. "You have *nothing* to look forward to."

A miasma of pure evil enveloped her. "You are *nothing*," whispered a rasping breath, unleashing a smell so foul there were no words to describe it. "You must come with us."

Somehow, she knew that the only hope was to cling tight to the last vestiges of her soul. Her mouth opened wide, sending commands to vocal cords that paid no attention. In her mind she screamed, *"Let me go! I want to go back."*

With harsh cries, snarling and gnashing their razor-sharp teeth, the creatures released her and slithered back into the void.

Out of the darkness, a hand reached out and took hers.

"Come, Jessica," a voice sang out with the sweetness of healing water poured onto parched land. "You do not belong there. Come."

Without waiting for a second invitation, desperate to put as much distance as possible between herself and the stark horror of that place, she flew back the way she had come, toward the light.

Jessica awoke naked and confused near her worktable. Her arms burned like fire. She grabbed the back of her work stool as the room tilted, and waited for the floor to settle under her feet.

How did I get to hell, then back here?

The same way you went from the worktable to the patio. Call it what it is, dumbshit—a fugue.

That damned snarky voice, always barking an answer she would rather not hear. The voice had no name, but she had accepted it long ago as a particularly obnoxious part of herself that always insisted on being right.

A fugue. She might never have known what a fugue state was if it weren't for the retrograde amnesia that temporarily robbed her of memories of life before the accident.

"Fugue," Google had instructed her, was *a rare psychiatric disorder characterized by reversible dissociative states that may last from hours to months.*

As usual, Snarky was right. The recent episodes were more and more like fugue states—longer and deeper than earlier ones. But never had she gone as far as Hell.

An abrupt surge of longing for her twin made her hurt all over. They used to share everything. Even when they disagreed on a subject, the argument was good-natured bickering. Jenna had always been the conservative one, but becoming Roland's wife and mother to her twin girls had turned her into someone Jessica felt she no longer knew.

She glanced at Sage asleep on the futon, with a pang of envy. His chest rose and fell evenly beneath the covers, one foot carelessly sticking out from the comforter. She would give a lot to be able to sleep that soundly. It was hard to remember a time when she had not gone to bed afraid that she might awaken in some strange place, having done things she was unaware of, but which might alter her future.

The dream had felt so real, her stomach churned. The empty wine bottle that stood by the bed was nowhere near enough alcohol to account for the sick ache in her gut, nor the way her head was hammering, as if roofing nails were being pounded into it.

Jessica stumbled to the bathroom for the bottle of ibuprofen in the medicine cabinet. She turned on the light and held her arms in front of her, nearly puking at what she saw. Deep scratches ran from elbow to wrist, leaking pinpricks of blood. Across each palm was a thick black X. Gulping back bile, she turned on the cold faucet and washed her arms clean.

Had she gouged those lacerations into her own flesh? Or had she really experienced a run-in with demons from hell? *Why me? Why now? Why? Why? Why?*

She pumped eucalyptus-scented soap onto her palms and scrubbed at the Xs until her hands were raw. The medicine cabinet held a tube of aloe vera gel. She squirted it onto her palms and arms, breathing a sigh of relief as the sting began to subside. What would Jenna say about those Xs?

"*You have the mark of the Devil.*"

And she would be right, wouldn't she? What else could it be?

Jessica took four Advil with water from the faucet, spilling more down her chin than she swallowed. How was she going to tell Sage she had gone to all the way to hell and back? In their short acquaintance he had been nothing but kind and compassionate, far more than she could have expected or asked for. But even he must have his limits. What better way to kill a budding relationship than to tell him what she had experienced? Yet, there was no way to keep it from him. Her teeth were chattering, her skin, clammy with fear, alternating hot and cold.

She did her best not to disturb him as she slipped under the comforter, but Sage rolled over and slipped an arm underneath her. "Whoa, you're an icicle. What's wrong?"

The terror would not let go. "I—I—"

Sage gathered her close, rocking her like a child. "Shhhh, baby, baby, it's okay, you're safe. You're not alone, Jess, I'm here with you."

She had become so accustomed to being alone since Jenna got married that it took more than a moment for the words to sink in. He went on murmuring, reassuring her in a voice so low and calm, that soon, she relaxed into him. Sage rested his chin lightly on her head. He rubbed her exposed shoulder and arm, continuing along the length of her body until the gooseflesh smoothed, her pulse slowed to normal again. With a shuddering breath, the shivering stilled and the words started pouring out.

"I went to hell. It wasn't a dream, it was real. I went to sleep here, with you, but I woke up over there, at my worktable. Look—" She showed him her damaged arms, the Xs on her hands, told him everything.

His hands closed around hers, tenderly hiding the reminders of the dream. "Do you have any idea what it means?"

"Remember I told you how I *became* Hailey Martin who was murdered, and Finley Hunter, the cult victim? It was like that, only quadrupled. But what's weird—among all the other weirdness—at first, I was Ethan, I was seeing through *his* eyes. Then it…well, it…was different."

"Different how?"

"I wasn't him anymore. I was—" Jessica sat up so fast it made her head spin. The dawning truth made her drop her voice to a near-whisper. "In hell, I was Trey Starkey."

TWENTY

"Are you sure?" Sage asked.

Jessica huffed a humorless laugh. "*Sure*? I'm not sure of *anything* anymore. Maybe it was all a horrible nightmare."

"But you don't think so."

"No, I don't think so. It was absolutely real." She touched the scratches on her arms. "If that's hell, I will vow right this minute never to sin again."

"We make our own heaven or hell when we die," said Sage with confidence. "That's what I believe, and what Bella's spirit guides have told her. If Trey Starkey *is* in hell, then obviously, he's dead. And if he believes he deserves the kind of hell you described, he's created it with his mind. You don't have to make it *your* reality."

"If he created what was in my dream, he's in a *very* bad place." The further she was able to separate herself from the infernal force that had taken hold of her, the more the fog started to clear from her mind.

"It's no better than he deserves, considering what he's done," said Sage. "Jess, if he *is* dead, what about Ethan?"

Jessica was asking herself the same question. The sensation of *being* Ethan, terrified and running away—she shuddered. Earlier, he had said he was alone. What was he running from? If Trey was dead and she had literally inhabited Trey's spirit in his version of hell…

"I've got to call Zach," she said, already swinging her legs over the side of the futon and reaching for her phone.

Sage got up, too, and handed her the clothes she had discarded the night before. The mood had been far different then, so charged with passion and anticipation before she had gone off into another world again. Now, with Ethan Starkey still missing and the possibility that she had the means to help locate him, Jessica told herself, she had no right to pursue those feelings.

"Answer the phone, Zach," she muttered as it went to voicemail. She left an urgent message for him to call and started dressing.

Sage, already in his Levis and cashmere sweater, shot her a troubled glance. "Do you think maybe he's blocked you?"

Jessica stopped zipping up her jeans and frowned, not comprehending his meaning. "Blocked me?"

"He told you not to call him."

"Zach wouldn't do that to me." Sounding more confident than she felt, she grabbed the phone back and keyed in a text, deflating at the words "not delivered" that appeared on the screen.

"We have to *do* something."

"You don't believe Ethan is at the marsh now?"

"I have a strong feeling that he's not—he was, but—I can't tell where he is now."

"Zach said they've already stopped looking there. What can we do if we don't have any clues?"

Before he had finished speaking, Jessica was already shaking her head no. It didn't matter if there were no clues, she would find some. She had to focus on locating the missing child, not spend her time reliving how Sage's hands felt, exploring her body. She loved how those hands...

Stop it. Keep your head in the right place.

She was zipping up her second boot when her phone rang. She snatched it up without looking. "Zach—"

An unfamiliar female voice cut her off. "Is this Jessica Mack?"

"Who's this?"

"Hi, Jessica, this is Mercedes Thompson from Eyewitness News L.A. I wondered if I might get a statement from—"

"No, you might not," Jessica snapped, wishing she could slam the phone down like an old-fashioned landline. As soon as she set it down, it chirped again. Then again, six more times. One reporter after the other asking the new question: "Are you Jessica, the psychic?" She powered down the phone and stuffed it in her pocket. "Let's hit the road before they start showing up here."

Sage put up a restraining hand. "Okay, fine. But Jess, before we go anywhere, I have a question. You said when you woke up you were at your worktable. Why? What was there?"

Her gaze flicked in that direction and back to him. "Honestly? After the whole Finley Hunter crime scene monstrosity, I was afraid to look."

"Shall I check?"

She scrunched up her face. "Wouldn't *that* make me a total chicken?"

The ghost of a smile flitted across Sage's lips. "How about we look together?"

The suggestion stippled her skin with a rush of heat but she heard herself say "Okay," in a voice not quite her own.

He held out a hand and she took it. Bigger, stronger, it swallowed hers up. Was it pathetic to be this needy? The fact that he was so willing to accept all the crazy she had dumped on him made him a star in her book.

"You're just curious to see what kind of mess I've made this time," she said, trying for lighthearted and not quite making it.

"Yeah, you caught me." He squeezed her hand. "Gotta admit, you're nothing like other women I've met."

"I bet," she said darkly, then stopped short, pulling Sage back. "What's that doing there?"

She pointed to a cardboard shipping box and die-cut foam liners littering the area next to her worktable.

"You didn't leave it there?" said Sage.

"No."

The mess on the floor must have been there when she awoke, but Jessica had not noticed it. Hardly surprising, given the trauma she had gone through in the hellish dream. Her heart was hammering as they approached it, knowing there was no way to escape whatever was on her worktable.

She had left her sketchbook out, and some pieces of charcoal. Not her sculpting tools and the lump of drying clay, which were now on the tabletop, too.

For sure, she had not placed a log cabin there. Her stomach sank.

Around five by seven inches, it rested in a nest of delicate green cloth, which had been artfully arranged so that it appeared surrounded by shrubbery. An oval mirror lay on the desktop near the cabin, creating the illusion of a body of water.

"A log cabin," said Sage, stating the obvious. He let go of her hand and leaned down to inspect the primitive building. It was constructed of three long logs on each side, broken by closed shutters. The ends were made of shorter logs with a single door at one end.

Jessica stared at it. "It's a kit I bought a while back in case I needed it for some future project. It's been on the top shelf for months. I'd forgotten about it."

"That's quite a coincidence." Sage gazed at her with an expression that was hard to interpret.

Malignant vibes seemed to radiate from the little cabin. It was not her fault that she had unwittingly created what Jessica instinctively knew was another crime scene, but it might as well have been. If it was possible, she would back away from the worktable right now. She would run all the way out to the street and keep running.

"Is this connected to the dream?" Sage had echoed her thoughts as eerily as if he read her mind.

"I guess we'd better find out." Afraid she would lose her nerve if she delayed, Jessica took a step toward it and lifted the slanted roof.

"Fuck me," murmured Sage. His mouth kept moving, but ten thousand bees droned in Jessica's head, drowning out his voice.

Inside the log cabin were two rudimentary cots. A clay figure clad lay on one of them. Clad in a plaid shirt and denim pants, its head was a black lump, oozing a sticky red substance onto the pillow. An impossibly tiny handgun, also fashioned from clay, lay on the cabin floor.

Making a supreme effort, Jessica silenced the bees and asked Sage to repeat what he had said.

"There's no Ethan."

"What do you mean?"

"In the scene. There's one figure, not two, and it doesn't look like a child."

Jessica's mouth was as dry as if she'd eaten a spoonful of talc. "He's got to be here. If Trey killed him, he would be in the cabin, wouldn't he? He's gotta be here somewhere. Where is he? Oh, Ethan, where—"

The one-room cabin had no place to hide. Jessica switched on the desk lamp and began frantically picking through everything on the worktop. She picked up the cabin and set it aside, shook out the green cloth, swept aside tools and paints. There was no second, smaller figure hidden anywhere on the desk.

If what the Trey figure depicted was true, what if she sculpted the little boy and placed him far away from the cabin and the terrors it held? Would that make it true?

She picked up the lump of clay and studied it. Twisting off a small piece, she rolled it between her palms, forming it into a ball the size of a grape. Next, she took up a wire end modeling tool and began to meticulously shave the clay. Within seconds it had taken the shape of a head with rough features. She squinted at it briefly before selecting a detailing tool.

"Where the hell is he?" she murmured absently, going to work on the face, using minute, delicate strokes to sculpt eyes, nose, and sweet bow lips from what she remembered of the photos of Ethan. The features began to take shape.

She felt the light touch of Sage's hand to her back.

"Do you think this is for real, the cabin?" he said. "That he really shot himself?"

Jessica closed her hand around the clay head and squashed it back into a formless lump. She dropped it onto the table and smashed it flat with her fist. "How the fuck do I know?"

The look of stunned surprise on Sage's face brought her back to reality and she heaved a big sigh. "I'm sorry. I didn't mean to yell at you. I'm not always a crazy person. I'm just scared out of my wits for that boy."

He squeezed her shoulder. "You don't have to be sorry. Let's just figure out what to do next."

"If we're going to find him, we have to talk to Abby. You drive. I'll call her and arrange a place to meet."

His keys were in his hand before she finished her sentence. "Let's go."

They narrowly escaped the media vans, which were cruising the street, looking for places to park. With no sidewalks in the neighborhood they were out of luck. Homeowners parked in their own driveways, the streets to narrow to allow much visitor parking.

"I bet they'll offer the neighbors a bundle to park in their driveways," said Sage, as two of them parked illegally in front of homes. His own car was around the corner, where some street parking was permitted.

The gathering darkness made it easy to slip unnoticed past the TV crews setting up their equipment in front of the Victorian. Jessica had wound a scarf high around the lower half of her face as they walked away. "Imelda's gonna have a fit if they start ringing her bell," she said, fastening her seatbelt.

"Who's Imelda?"

"One temperamental landlady."

"We can worry about her later." Sage turned north onto Victoria and headed in the direction of the 101. "First things first."

Jessica switched on her phone. Of the dozen voicemails, none were from Zach. She tapped in Abby's number, worried that he might have told her to block Jessica, too.

She need not have been concerned. Ethan's mother answered right away.

"Oh, Jessica, I'm *so* sorry about my mom. I never thought she would—"

"Hi, Abby. Can you talk?"

"Not privately." She was half-whispering. "Listen, I saw her talking to those creeps and tried to stop her, but she was loaded for bear. I still can't believe she did that."

"Forget it; we have more important things to think about. Can you leave the house? I don't want the media to see us there. They're already camping out around my place."

"Okay, sure. Where should we meet?"

"Thousand Oaks Mall? That's close to you. We can sit in the parking lot and figure things out."

"Let's meet at the Hillcrest Drive entrance of Macy's by the road. I'll watch for your car."

"I'm not in my car. I'm with my—friend." She darted a look at Sage. One night of fantastic sex might not make him her boyfriend, but he was more than a friend-friend. She turned away from his amused glance as she described his car to Abby.

"We can be there in thirty minutes if traffic is okay."

"See you then."

They made it in forty. Ethan's mother, wearing a pink knit hat and puffy down parka, was waiting under a lamppost next to her car. Sage parked in the space beside her.

Jessica rolled down the window and waved.

Sage went around to open the back door and introduce himself. Even under the stressful circumstances Jessica caught Abby looking at him with a bemused stare. Something she was going to have to get used to. The good thing was, Sage wasn't a jerk, flaunting his good looks the way Greg had. He didn't seem to notice.

"It's so great to be outside and nobody knows who I am," said Abby, climbing into the backseat. "Nobody chasing me for a comment."

"You're sure you weren't followed?" Jessica asked, as if Abby were a spy who had successfully dodged the bad guys and made it to the secret rendezvous.

"There's nobody hounding me for comments, so I'm assuming—"

"You didn't tell Zach you were meeting me, did you?"

"You're joking, right? He's already mad that I let the cat out of the bag with Mom. Have you ever been read the riot act in complete silence? He couldn't say too much, but I knew he was *fuming*."

"It was his idea for us to meet; he can fume as much as he likes."

"True, but I don't want him to be in trouble at work."

If Zach had not blocked her calls, Jessica might have cared more about his work problems. She changed the subject. "What's the situation with your mom now?"

"When I left, I told her to go home and not come back until I say so. Which you can be sure isn't gonna be anytime soon. Believe me, I'm not going to tell her about this meeting."

"Okay, good. Now, let's talk about Ethan and Trey."

Abby grabbed onto Jessica's seat back. "Have you seen Ethan again?"

"Yes, for a quick second." Abby did not need to hear about her trip to hell or the bloody-headed corpse she had sculpted in her fugue state. Or the fact that her child was nowhere in that scene.

"I'm going to try again to locate him, but I have to find a way to connect with his energy. I was thinking maybe if we talked about the places where Trey might have gone—"

"But I've already given all that information to the FBI. If they couldn't find him, what makes you think you can?"

"I don't know whether I can or not, but I'm going at it from a totally different angle. If I visited some of those locations, I might get a sense of whether they were there."

Abby looked dubious. "I guess. But—"

"Someone's already gone to his parents' house, right?"

"Yes, they live in Phoenix. He wouldn't go there anyway. They haven't talked in years, ever since he conned them out of some money before we got married. They never forgave him. They've never even met Ethan."

"Any siblings or cousins?"

"No, and he doesn't have any close friends, either. Zach already checked out the women he's been involved with—the ones I know about, anyway—none were serious enough relationships for them to risk hiding him and Ethan from the feds."

As Abby spoke, Jessica attempted to tune in to her energy using a method she had read about. Nothing pinged back. "Trey is in real estate, isn't he?" she asked. "What about his clients?"

"Zach has talked to them, of course. I can't imagine any one of them would hide Trey. They're just clients, not close friends."

"What about vacant properties?"

Abby paused to think about it. "The only one I can think of is a house in Benedict Canyon. Zach already went there."

Benedict Canyon. The name rang a bell. "He mentioned it the other day. He was going out there on Sunday."

"The owners are out of the country and not coming back until summer. Zach tracked them down and got permission to go inside and look around. I gave him the key code for the lockbox and the alarm. Trey keeps his files at home, so it was easy enough to find."

"Did they find anything?"

"Not so much as an eyelash."

"Does Trey often sell homes that far away?"

"No, Benedict Canyon is definitely out of his usual territory. The listing was a referral from a client whose house he sold. The guy was so thrilled with the deal he got them that when a friend wanted to put his house on the market, he sent them to Trey. He's a shitty husband but a super realtor."

Abby talked on about the house and the clients and Trey but Jessica had stopped listening, her attention turned to a familiar tingle on her scalp. The other woman's voice collapsed, receded. The car's rich leather interior disappeared, along with its occupants.

Her energy began to expand until it reached to the edges of the universe, lifting higher and higher. For a second, the hazy outline of a large house appeared to her. Then it was gone; Ethan's face appeared and was gone. She was back in the car, not fully tethered to reality.

She soundlessly deflected the questions Abby and Sage were hurling at her with their eyes, waiting for the spaciness to dissipate. When it had, she said, "I need to go to that house. Benedict Canyon. The empty one. Do you have the address?"

"Yes, of course, I'll take you there."

"That's not a good idea."

"Why not? I might be able to help."

"I don't mean to sound harsh, Abby, but have you looked in the mirror? You have dark circles under your eyes, you're exhausted. It won't help if we end up having to take care of you. You'd be much better off waiting at home in case anything changes and Zach needs to get hold of you."

She was talking too much, overselling it. The truth was, she didn't want Abby along in case they came across her husband's dead body. And she was quite convinced that Trey was dead.

Oh God, I don't want to see that either.

But Ethan. It always came back to that innocent little lamb, caught up in the mess of his parents' ugly problem.

"Jessica's right," Sage added. "Besides, it gives you plausible deniability. The less you're aware of what we're doing, the better off we'll all be. You'll have nothing to tell Zach if it goes south. Nothing for the media to grab onto. You'll be totally out of it."

"I'm already high on his shit list," Jessica added. "No reason for you to be, too."

"I guess." Abby looked like she might argue with their logic but either she saw the wisdom in what they said or was too exhausted to press the issue. "You have to promise to tell me if you find—even if—"

"We will. Promise." Jessica reached over the seat to seal the promise with a press of Abby's hand. "We'll keep you posted, whatever we find."

"Thank you, Jess. I know this isn't your job. You're not getting paid to do it."

"I don't care. Ethan needs to be back with you. The sooner you can get us that address, the sooner we can go look for him."

"It's still in my phone from when I sent it to Zach." Not bothering to wipe away the tears running down her face, Abby texted the address to Jessica, along with the lockbox and alarm codes.

Within fifteen minutes of their arrival, she was back in her own car and Sage and Jessica were on the road.

TWENTY-ONE

"And if it does 'go south,'" said Jessica, "are you sure *you* want to be caught up in it? There's still time if you want to back out."

Sage turned the long-lashed, blue-blue eyes her way and gave her heart a flutter. "Are you kidding? I wouldn't miss it for a billion bucks."

"A billion?"

"Well, maybe for a billion. But not one cent less."

Jessica smiled. "Thank you, Sage. I'm glad you're coming with me."

"Excuse me, lady, this is *my* car. *You* are coming with me." Then his expression grew somber. "It drives me nuts to see a kid being abused."

She reached over and squeezed his hand. One day soon, she intended to find out what had prompted him to build a center for traumatized children. For now, though, she would allow him his secrets, just as she protected her own.

According to Google Maps, the Benedict Canyon address lay thirty-five miles east of the Thousand Oaks Mall. Their route would take them back on Highway 101, continuing south to Beverly Glen, where at some point they would turn onto Mulholland Drive, twisting and turning until they reached Benedict Canyon Drive in Beverly Hills.

"Benedict Canyon is where Charles Manson's gang killed a

bunch of people," said Jessica, reading what Wikipedia had to say about the area and its history. "There was a pregnant actress named Sharon Tate. It says she was married to a director—Roman Polanski, who got exiled because of underage sex." She read further. "That's way before we were born. 1969. Oh, look, here's a name I know. Adam Levine from Maroon 5 lives there."

"Oooh, *now* I'm impressed." Sage sent her a grin. "Why don't you look it up on Zillow? We can get an idea of what we're going into. By the way, what *are* we going into? Do your woo-woo feelings have a plan for when we get there?"

"Nope. I just know I have to go. It's like someone *pushing* me. Like I don't have a choice."

"Gotcha."

They hit evening rush hour traffic, sat in a sea of red lights, reaching their exit over an hour later. The road into the canyon was only a little wider than the street where she lived and not well lit. The gleam of Google Maps in the darkened car showed a densely populated, sprawling neighborhood, thinning to the occasional home before curving into gulp-inducing hairpin turns.

"Nothing under a million," said Jessica, perusing the listings in the area. "Here's one for *thirty million*. Who pays thirty million bucks for a house?"

"Someone with money to burn. What about the one we're going to? What's it listed for?"

She checked. "A measly million-six. They must be the poor folk in the neighborhood."

"Must be."

They drove for a time without talking on the curving road. The Tesla's headlights picked out towering hillsides and old growth trees and shrubs jutting from both sides, punctuated by fences or walls behind which homes hunkered down. The further into the canyon they drove, the more the homes were built up or against the hillsides, with backs of houses and garages facing the winding road, no space taken up by sidewalks.

"You looked pretty intense back there with Abby," said Sage, pulling onto a straightaway. "For a minute I was wondering where you'd gone."

"The moment she mentioned Benedict Canyon I got a super-weird vibe. So—look, I've just started learning how this stuff works, feeling my way. I wish Justin would come—" she stopped herself. Sage did not know about her son.

"Justin—?" he prompted.

"Not now. I can't talk about it now. I just can't. I need to concentrate on Ethan."

"Okay, no pressure. We can talk whenever you're ready. Or never."

"Thank you," she said, grateful for his understanding. She consulted the GPS. "Get ready to turn in three hundred feet."

Sage tapped the brake and made a sharp right onto an even narrower road that wound upward. He slowed as Jessica read the mailbox numbers and kept checking the onscreen map.

"Another six hundred feet. Three hundred. Okay, stop; it's right here."

They turned onto the steep driveway in front of an ivy-trimmed garage. Sage killed the engine.

"Give me a sec."

Jessica turned inward and waited for the touch of spirit, a message that would tell her what their next action should be. What felt like ages went by with nothing happening. She shrugged. "I guess we go look."

A six-foot unfinished wood fence surrounded the property. As they entered the gate a bright security light came on, spotlighting a storybook house with ivy-covered walls, dormer windows on the second story. Small by Beverly Hills standards—a mere 1,600 square feet, according to the MLS listing.

They climbed the slight incline to a brick veranda. Three steps up brought them to the shiny black front door. Using the light from her phone, Jessica tapped the code into the lockbox keypad and got the key. She unlocked the door and Sage entered the burglar alarm code Abby had provided.

They stepped into a narrow entry hall with dark hardwood floors, a staircase to the right. Sage located the light switch. A wide arched entry led to a great room on the left. Jessica took a quick look inside, absorbing the atmosphere. Emptiness bounced back at her.

"Anything yet?" Sage asked.

She shook her head. "I'm not getting *anything*. Maybe I've brought you on a wild goose chase."

"Don't give up. What you felt when Abby was talking about Trey's client—"

"What I felt then was overpowering. Now that we're here, there's nothing but a big, fat blank."

"We're here, let's check out the house." He grinned down at her. "Maybe we'll want to buy it."

"Why, do you have a spare million-six lying around?"

He gave her a one shoulder shrug and another smile. "You never know."

What am I getting myself into?

They began their self-guided tour, moving through the downstairs. The owners might be away, but someone was keeping the place ready for prospective buyers to see. Designer touches throughout left it ready for an *Architectural Digest* photo shoot.

The great room faced the backyard and led to a sunroom. A small kitchen done all in white opened onto the dining room. The chunky wood dining table held a vase of red silk roses.

Coming back to the staircase, Jessica noticed a light prickle of static dancing across the crown of her head. She was learning to recognize the sensation of someone ruffling her scalp as a sign, a prelude to spirit contact. She waited for some kind of guidance.

An invisible hand pushed her toward the staircase with the force of a strong magnet. She glanced at Sage. "We need to go upstairs."

He gave her a nod and followed close behind her.

The master bedroom and a guest room on the second floor were sparsely furnished. A few black walnut pieces, no personal items on display, which seemed appropriate for a house on the market and the owners away.

A third bedroom had been turned into a den. The cream-colored fabric of the eight-foot sofa looked brand new, no saggy cushions from years of family members vegging in front of the big screen TV in the built-in entertainment center. No glass ring marks on the polished coffee table. Who had white upholstery, anyway? If any kids lived in this house, their parents must be OCD.

Jessica took it all in from the door, all at once reluctant to enter the room. She half-turned to Sage, who was right behind her, reminding her by his presence that she was not alone in this. But in fact, she *was* alone. He could not feel the invisible hand that was pressing her to go in, or the other hand pulling her back.

Enter or back out? The decision was hers alone to make.

What if she turned away from this responsibility now? If she did, regardless of how it turned out, it would be impossible to forgive herself.

Jessica grabbed Sage's hand and squeezed it tight. Letting it go, she stepped across the threshold, passing through an invisible veil so cold it made her gasp. An unwholesome effluvium saturated her soul, sucking her dry of the desire to make any connection with the spirit world or look for Ethan Starkey.

This was a waste of time. Why bother to look for someone else's child when she was permanently separated from her own?

"You are nothing. You don't exist."

Where had she heard those words recently? She sank onto the sofa, her head lolling back against the puffy white cushions as she struggled to remember.

She should not be here. It was all a waste. Nothing mattered.

"You are nothing. You don't exist."

"What's happening, Jess?"

As Sage's words touched her and bounced off, it came back to her: the visit to hell. Was she back there, inhabiting Trey's energy again?

"Jessica? Can you hear me? Jess!"

Did Sage intuit the vile presence that sapped her will to answer? She could not summon the energy to ask him. Coming to this place was an exercise in futility. They should end this worthless search. If she just closed her eyes and drifted away…

Strong arms slid behind her back, under her thighs. Her limp body was being lifted and carried, bouncing against the rough texture of Sage's jacket. Down the stairs. Out into the cold evening air. Her eyes opened to a starry sky, a full moon.

Sage had brought her to the privacy of the backyard, where the security lights reflected off the pool water, winking and sparkling. She looked up into his face and tried to smile. The muscles around his mouth, bunched with anxiety, relaxed.

"Are you back? Are you okay?"

"I think so." The sludge in her brain started to clear, the power returned to her limbs. "Seems like these days, people are having to ask me that question too many times."

He set her down. "What were you feeling back there?"

"It was so eerie. I was back in the hell dream, but not exactly. It was the feeling of the dream without being there. Like death. It's too hard to explain." She made a supreme effort to sweep away the remnants of the unnerving experience and gather her thoughts. "One thing I'm sure of is, they were here. Trey and Ethan were here."

"So, you were picking up what he was feeling while he was here?"

She glanced back at the house with a convulsive shudder. "I'm sure of it. I didn't make a specific contact, but it was Trey's energy I felt, I'm positive. It doesn't make sense that it's anything else."

"What did you feel? I know it wasn't anything good."

"He had nothing to live for. Nothing. Sage, I think we're too late."

Sage looked around the small, stone-paved backyard. "There's no cabin here."

"No."

A swimming pool took up most of the available space. On one side, a low rock wall butted up against the pool's edge. Rising above it on the hillside was a cactus garden, a few trees. At the far side of the pool was a table and two chairs. No place they would find Trey with his head shot off. No little boy.

"I should try again to reach Ethan," said Jessica. "Not inside, though. I'll never go back in that house."

She sat at the poolside table and put her hands in her lap, palms up. Taking three deep, long breaths, she pushed away all other thoughts and brought a picture of Ethan into her mind as she had last seen him in the vision. Still wearing his SpongeBob shirt and Spiderman boots. His toddler face tear-streaked, eyes round with fear.

Help me spirit guides. Please help me find this child.

She waited, got nothing.

Please listen to me. I'm asking for your help.

She tried until her hands were freezing and she had to put them in her pockets. She hunched into her jacket, turtle-like. "I keep hearing a tinkly bell and am thinking of Bella."

"My Bella? The psychic medium?"

"She's the only Bella I know of."

Sage nodded. "Maybe your guides want you to get her to help."

"I'll try anything. Do you think she would mind if we called her?"

He said she would not, and called up her number in his phone. The Reverend Bella Bingham answered right away. Sage told her he was putting her on speaker so they could all hear each other and explained the situation.

"I saw you on TV," said Bella, her accent sounding stronger over the phone. "I remember you said you wanted to locate a little boy, but I was surprised to hear the reporter say you were involved in looking for the one that's been missing."

"His grandmother outed me to the media. She's very religious and doesn't like psychics."

Bella tsked, then said, "I had a funny feeling I'd be hearing from you."

"A psychic feeling?"

"I suppose you might say that. My guides gave me a message for you."

Jessica glanced at Sage, who wore a knowing smile. "Why didn't they just tell me to call you? Why play charades with a bell ringing that reminded me of you?"

"Ah, that's a question for another time, luv. For the present, we need to hurry. The message I've got for you is this: there's a séance tonight at 9:00 in West Hollywood and you need to be there. That's not far from where you are now, is it? See how that worked out?"

"A séance? You mean, sitting around in the dark, contacting the dead? That kind of séance?"

"The only kind, ducky. I've been told you should go. Remember I mentioned Russell Levine to you? Shall I give you the address, then? I c'n give him a ring and ask him to put you on the list. You won't get in unless you're recommended and on the list."

Jessica hesitated, not at all sure she wanted to attend a séance. For one thing, it felt like an irrevocable step toward the development of her mediumship. But there was her promise again, nagging at her conscience. She had vowed to do anything within her power to get Ethan back.

"Thanks, Bella, please go ahead and call him."

"All right then, dear. Give us a minute, I'll ring you back." Bella chuckled. "Now don't you two go snogging while you're waiting."

"Snogging?" Jessica said when they ended the call. "What's that?"

Sage grinned. "British slang for making out."

"Oh, jeez."

He shifted the second chair closer to her, getting into her space. "We might have time for just a *little* snogging."

"Maybe it's not a good idea to get started."

Jessica's feeble protest died away as he put an arm around her and pulled her close, his eyes holding hers. "I think it's a *really* good idea," he murmured, leaning in until the tip of his nose was touching hers. He stayed there, teasing, waiting until her need to kiss him was so strong, she couldn't *not* lift her lips to his.

Bella's callback interrupted before they'd had enough.

"All right luv, yeah? I've got it all worked out for you. Well, it was *spirit* who got it worked out, I'm quite sure. Now, are you ready?" The address she recited was five miles from their location as the crow flew, which was at least a half-hour on the L.A. freeways.

"Now, listen to me carefully, this is important. You've got to be there before 9:00 or you won't be allowed in. Once the door is closed, it's closed and locked until the séance is over. Nobody gets in or out while it's going on."

"But what if we get stuck in traffic or lost?" Jessica protested. "Can't we call ahead and ask him to wait for us?"

"No, dear. There's no excuse that will open that door after it's been closed. I had to call in a favor to get you in, spirit or no spirit. Russell will be expecting you. You'd best make sure you're there on time."

"Thank you so much, Bella, we'll be there."

"Well, the way spirit's been tweaking my ear tonight, there's certainly a reason for you to be there. I swear, if you two hadn't a' called me when you did, I would have called you a minute later.

Now, don't be frightened. You'll be in pitch darkness, but you mustn't let that worry you. Just do as you're asked and all will be well."

"When someone says 'pitch darkness' and 'don't be frightened' in the same sentence, it frightens me," said Jessica when they were back in the Tesla and on their way to West Hollywood. "What did she mean? Have you ever gone to a séance?"

"No, but I've always wanted to. I'd love to see ectoplasm up close."

"You mean that slime stuff in *Ghostbusters*?"

"Uh, not quite. I've seen some YouTube videos and read some websites that say it's a substance that comes from the medium's body—the pancreas, I think."

Jessica stared at him, aghast. "Comes from *where*, exactly?"

"It can come from any orifice. In most mediums it comes from the mouth or nose."

"Eww, that sounds *gross*."

"It can take on different shapes and spirit can use it to materialize a body and talk to the people at the séance. In one of the videos I watched, a sitter said he was at a séance where ectoplasm took the shape of a hand and he shook it."

Jessica tried to imagine shaking a spirit hand. It was one thing to see an apparition, quite another to reach out and touch spirit "flesh" made from ectoplasm. The idea both attracted and repelled her.

"What if the sitter was gullible?" she said.

"He was a very well-respected lawyer named Victor Zammit, and seven other people saw it, too. It wasn't like a ghost, where you can't touch it. There was a red light on and they could see the hand. It was well-formed and solid, every detail, even the fingernails and the hair on the back of the hand."

"That sounds scary to me. You believe Bella knows what she's talking about, sending us there? It's kinda strange, isn't it?"

"Says the lady who sees dead people. And yes, I'm sure Bella knows what she's doing. Do we have any other options?"

Jessica wasn't ready to stop playing devil's advocate. "Isn't it an amazing coincidence that he's having a séance *tonight*, at the exact time we need it?

"A coincidence that Bella's guides must have been aware of. Do you want to blow it off?"

"No. Yes. No." Jessica sighed. "Let's get there and see how it goes."

"Remember what Bella said. After the door closes, nobody in or out. So, you'd best decide right now whether you want to do this. Are you sure you'll be okay in a dark, confined space? You're not claustrophobic, are you?"

"I'm not sure of anything, except that I *have* to go." An inadvertent giggle escaped her. "I'm like a psychic bloodhound following a scent."

Sage rolled his eyes. "I guess that's one way to look at it."

They located Russell Levine's address at eight forty-five.

The house, an early twentieth-century wood Craftsman bungalow painted yellow, stood on a corner flanked by apartment complexes. The price range in this area was far below Benedict Canyon, but the bright floodlight shining on the driveway over the one-car garage was similar to the house they had visited. A dusty red Honda of uncertain vintage faced in and left no space for another vehicle. Lined with cars on both sides, the street was as closely packed as sardines in a can.

"We're going to miss it," said Jessica.

"No, we're not. We're supposed to be there, remember?"

"Well, in case you haven't noticed, there's no place to park and it's almost nine."

"Concentrate. Ask the parking gods to help us."

"You're kidding, right?"

They turned the corner and drove slowly along the street. "Try it," said Sage.

"Okay, fine, but I don't see…"

Three car-lengths from the corner of the short block, red backup lights came on at the curb. A Prius pulled out and Sage squeezed into the Tesla-sized space.

Jessica stared at him. "How did you do that?"

He shut off the engine with a triumphant smirk. "What'd I tell you?"

"I can't believe that happened. I want to see you do it again."

"Oh, ye of little faith."

They hurried back to Russell Levine's house around the corner. According to Jessica's phone, it was 8:56 when they rang the doorbell, which sounded remarkably similar to the tinkling bell she had heard earlier.

The door was opened right away by a man who must have been six-five and twice as wide as Sage. Late 40s, early 50s. Piercing dark eyes. Hawk nose. Long, silver-grey hair that had a "just-washed" shine. He was dressed in faded jeans and an olive drab t-shirt that bore a cartoon drawing of a man in sixteenth-century clothing. The word "Nostradamus" was printed underneath, with a thought bubble above the man's head that read: "You're all screwed."

What had she expected, a wizard's gown and cap like something out of Harry Potter? She could practically feel Sage's elbow jabbing her with the same thought.

"Glad you made it," said Russell Levine warmly, ushering them inside. "I was afraid I was gonna have to lock you out. C'mon through."

The tiny living room was no more like Jessica had imagined it would be than Russell himself was. No Victorian furniture, heavy curtains or crystal balls in evidence, no tarot cards. An IKEA-type couch, a pair of matching recliners in front of a 55-inch TV. Nicer than his slightly tatty appearance suggested, and nothing to indicate that a séance was about to be conducted on the premises. Weren't other people supposed to be present?

"The séance room is out back," said Russell, answering her unspoken question. "Everyone else is already there." He guided them through the living room and into the kitchen, where he handed them each a gallon-size clear plastic baggie from a box on the worktop.

"You'll have to leave your phones, purse, any jewelry in here," he said, showing them a wooden box that already contained several similar bags filled with phones, watches, wallets, rings. "It's like the airport; nothing in your pockets, please," he continued. "We check everyone that comes in. It protects the integrity of the process and makes sure no one is trying to pull a fast one."

"Is that a big problem?" asked Jessica.

"Debunkers, you know? They sometimes come in acting like

they're genuine seekers and think they can trick us. You're more than welcome to inspect the séance room in whatever ways you want to. We're completely transparent."

"No need," said Sage. "You're a friend of Bella's. That's the best recommendation you could get."

Russell nodded. "I can say the same of you. Now, your coats stay here. You'll need to remove your boots in the séance room."

They hung up their coats on a rack with several others and then Russell showed them a scanner wand.

"You weren't kidding about it being like the airport," said Sage, removing his belt and ring and placing them in the baggie. "Is that a metal detector?"

"Yep. Stand still and hold your arms out." Russell ran the wand over each of them and, after asking permission, gave them a brief all-business pat down.

This is getting serious, Jessica thought, still considering backing out.

"It's like getting into Fort Knox," Sage said.

"We have to be careful for our protection and yours. So, I'll need to see your ID."

"Are you kidding?" Jessica said.

"Nope. Anyone new is required to show ID."

"Wow. Okay. Here's my driver's license."

Sage showed his, too. Russell gave each card a cursory look and handed them back.

"Thanks, guys. Now, let's go on through. Follow me."

He took them out the back door and through a yard so small it might fit in one of Jessica's miniature scenes. "The séance room is an addition to the house. We've had a ton of offers from builders who want to put condos on this corner, but the lot is perfect for what we need, so we keep putting them off."

A Do Not Disturb sign was posted on the add-on room door, with "No entry for any reason" written underneath. When Russell opened it, Jessica was surprised to be faced with a second door behind the first.

"Extra security," he said with a smile when he saw her expression. The trio entered and he locked both doors behind them.

It's a good thing I don't *have claustrophobia,* thought Jessica, noticing that the two windows had blackout curtains closed over them. The room was larger than it appeared from outside. Two dozen people were seated on metal folding chairs arranged in a circle. Two of the chairs were empty, but not together.

They looked like an ordinary collection of folks, various ages, dressed down like the medium himself. At one side of one of the empty chairs was a woman in her twenties in a backwards Dodgers cap over waist-length blonde hair was already giving Sage the once-over, her eyes resting too long on his crotch, Jessica noted with amusement. She was getting used to women checking him out and he always seemed oblivious to the attention.

On the other side, a middle-aged, heavyset woman sat next to a thick-lipped bald man around the same age. Next to the other empty chair was a woman who might be anywhere from thirty to fifty, wearing too much makeup, short-clipped hair too black to be natural. Jessica tried not to stare at her long, black and gold striped fingernails. How she drove with those talons was a mystery.

The other attendees all blended together.

"This is Sage and Jessica, everyone," said Russell. The group chorused "Welcome." Some waved or nodded.

Hovering by a table set next to a small alcove at the back of the room was a slightly-built, olive-skinned man in head-to-toe black. Long, black drapes hung from the ceiling on each side of the alcove, a Mission-style wooden chair between them.

Russell said, "This is Miguel. He'll be in charge. I'll be the one in the cabinet."

Jessica was tempted to ask why he would be in a cabinet, but Russell had gone on to remind them to remove their boots and leave them by the door with the various footwear already there.

"I don't know how much Bella has told you," he said, as they complied. "But our development circle has been meeting every week for the past seven years. We're all very serious about our mediumship and we expect guests to be, too."

"Oh, we're totally serious," said Sage. "No problem there."

"Great; have a seat. Now, so you know, Bella didn't tell me anything about you two or why it was so important for you to come tonight, just that it was." As Jessica started to reply, Russell stopped her. "We don't *want* to know anything, so please don't give any information that might interfere with the integrity or the transparency of the process. Okay?"

"Okay. Sorry."

She went to the empty chair between the two women. They introduced themselves as Marlene, and Fawn, the one with the baseball cap. Sage took the last seat between a man named Bob, and Tanya, the woman with the talons.

Russell ambled over to the alcove. "This is the cabinet where I'll be sitting," he said. "Have either of you attended a séance before?"

"No, never," said Jessica, fascinated despite her misgivings.

"Séance virgins," said Fawn, pointing a benevolent smile at Sage.

"The best kind," said Russell. "Don't worry, there's nothing to be afraid of."

Why is everyone talking about being afraid?

A cardboard box sat in the center of the circle. It contained an assortment of children's toys and on top, an object that resembled a skinny dunce cap.

"Once in a while, children in spirit come to visit," said Bob, following her glance. "They come out and play with the toys. Last week, we had the father of a girl who passed in a car wreck come to visit us. She was in the front seat when they got T-boned. The other driver was the one who got cited, but the father couldn't stop feeling guilty. His daughter walked out of the cabinet and sat in his lap and kissed him. She told him she was happy in the world of spirit and that she loved him."

"The best thing was, she told him she didn't want him to feel bad, that it wasn't his fault," Fawn added.

"That father was in tears," said Marlene. "In fact, there wasn't a dry eye here. His daughter's visit gave him so much comfort."

"It must have been—I don't even have words for it," said Sage. He appeared to be enthralled, but Jessica was too choked with emotion speak. The story had resurrected the memory of her own accident, of her death and return to life.

She had noticed that most of the time the spirits' motives in coming back with messages for their loved ones was simply to let them know that they were okay, or that there was no need for guilt.

There was nothing big and profound in what they had to say. They just wanted their people on Earth to know that they loved them. Even the father of Mean Grocery Store Guy.

"Sometimes, several of them show up," Tanya said. "Children, I mean. 'Specially at Christmas. We put up a tree and all the decorations. When the lights are out you can hear them playing, squealing and laughing, throwing the balls around, ripping open the Christmas presents we bring them. It's incredible."

Jessica smiled and nodded, but it was thoughts of whether Trey had killed his son that filled her mind. If Ethan was dead, would he come through tonight and sit on her lap? He didn't know her, so it was doubtful. Would Justin? She thought she would not be able to bear it if he did.

"Okay, folks, let's get started." Russell, who reminded Jessica of a grizzly bear, looked too large for the cabinet, sat on the chair and placed his hands on the arms, talking as Miguel fussed around him. "Let me tell you a little about how it works. Miguel is gonna tie me down so I can't get up and also so I won't get hurt if the spirit team decides to move the chair." He must have noticed Jessica's alarmed expression. "Once in a while when I'm in trance they'll pick up the chair and spin it around or even send it across the room. I never remember any of it, of course."

Spinning chairs? Don't be frightened? Oh, sure.

"I'm gonna ask our newcomers, Jessica and Sage, to please test the ties? After you've done that and made sure there's no hanky panky, everyone will sing some songs to build up the energy and raise the vibration. Miguel handles the music. He'll be sitting near me so he can make sure everything is okay and I'm not having any problems."

Jessica's anxiety climbed a little higher. *What kinds of problems?*

"I have to say one important thing," Miguel added in a slight accent; South American, she thought. "Not all of the time, but sometimes there is ectoplasm coming. I have to warn, if you see, you *must not* touch it."

"Okay," said Sage, "but why?"

"Ectoplasm, he is part of the medium's body. Any contact can make severe injuries to Russell. If is touched or bright light comes, the ectoplasm, he go fast, back into the body. It make dangerous.

No photograph, no touching."

"I got burned once before," Russell said. "One of those secret debunkers grabbed at it, which is another reason why we're so careful about who comes in here. I'm not ready for that to happen again, believe you me."

"Literally burned?" Jessica asked.

"*Very* literally. Second degree. I ended up at urgent care. Same warning if a spirit comes out and touches you—they always ask permission first—or if you see a trumpet floating around, don't touch. Is that okay with you? If not, now's the time to say so."

"I didn't know there would be trumpets," said Jessica. She was beginning to detect a kind of energy in the atmosphere that was making her skin hum and the fine hairs on her arms stand up. Did that mean there were already spirits present? She glanced around, not seeing anyone who looked other than corporeal.

Miguel went to the cardboard box and took out the object that looked like a dunce's hat and showed it to her. "This is trumpet. Not the one you play a tune. Is okay to touch now. You check, make sure no tricks."

Jessica took the trumpet from him and turned it all around, inspected it inside and out, one end and then the other. It was comprised of three collapsing sections, was open at each end and made of lightweight aluminum painted a luminous blue.

"The trumpet, he make the sound louder," said Miguel, mixing up his pronouns. "What is the word?"

"Amplify," said Bob. "It amplifies the sound. Spirits have no physical human voice box after they cross over, so the trumpet helps them communicate with us."

"Ectoplasm can form into a voice box, too," said Tanya, making a shape in the air with her long nails. "They can speak through it, but it's not easy for them to do. They have to remember what their human voice sounded like."

"They forget what they sounded like?"

"If you didn't speak for a long time, then got your voice back, you might have to practice sounding like you used to. It's called direct voice mediumship."

Someone else piped up. "When the spirit body is coated with ectoplasm, they say it's like trying to talk with your head under water."

"There's a lot of competition in the spirit world. They line up, wanting to get through," said Russell. "But it means they have to get in touch with feelings from when they were last on the earth plane, and sometimes that's not so easy. So, if they're going to get up the energy to come through, they have to really want to do it."

"I never knew any of this," Jessica said, getting more than a little excited about what she was learning. She glanced over to see whether Sage was listening but he was distracted, examining the trumpet.

Miguel came over then with four heavy-duty plastic cable ties and showed them around the circle, then returned to Sage. "These the police use for handcuffs. You try to stretch."

Sage complied, showing everyone that despite his best efforts, the tensile strength of the cable ties made them virtually impossible to stretch or break.

Miguel took the ties and bound Russell to the chair at his wrists and ankles. Russell did a convincing job of straining to move his arms and legs. Again, the ties stayed intact.

"Okay, some final info for you new folks," Russell said. "It's important for everyone to be upbeat, in a good mood, and be open to the spirit energy. Otherwise, this won't happen. We work in complete darkness, except for a red light that might go on after the room lights are off. That's only going to happen if there's a materialization. Think of it like a photographer's darkroom. White light impedes the process of spirits developing, the same as photos."

There was that word again, *process.* He had used it several times now. Jessica had expected to sit around a table with a Ouija board, everyone touching their fingers to the planchette and making it move, the way they did in scary movies. Half of her was champing at the bit to get started. The other half still wanted to jump up and run, locked doors or not. She flicked a glanced across the circle at Sage. His spellbound gaze was fixed on the medium in the cabinet.

"My control is a spirit named Graham," said Russell. "When I go into trance, that's who you'll hear first."

"Graham is our circle guide," Fawn explained. "He's lived

on Earth before. Freddy also comes in. He's ten years old. He died of the Spanish Flu after World War I. If someone wants to materialize, Freddy's the one that will help them. He's in charge of the ectoplasm."

Marlene reached out her right hand to take Jessica's left. "We all hold hands. It completes the circle and makes sure everyone is where they're supposed to be. No monkey business." She gave a big grin. "Not that anyone in this room would cheat, of course, but we still do it that way, every single time." Fawn stretched her left hand, which was cool and firm, quite the opposite of Marlene's soft, warm one, and took Jessica's right.

Russell closed his eyes and began to breathe deeply.

"Everyone is quite happy?" asked Miguel, taking his seat beside the cabinet. He started fiddling with an iPod on a small table next to him, then turned off the lamp, plunging the room into a darkness so deep that nothing was visible. This must be how it felt to be blind.

"He's unscrewing the white light bulb," Marlene whispered to Jessica.

"Why would he do that?"

"So it can't be turned on accidentally."

Then the music started, *Girls Just Wanna Have Fun* blaring loud and raucous from the speakers. Everyone else laughed, but the unexpected noise made Jessica jump, despite the hands firmly holding hers on either side. Apologizing, Miguel adjusted the volume down.

It felt wrong to be lighthearted at the same time she was seeking a missing child, but the Cyndi Lauper song got the group laughing and singing, and Jessica let the music loosen her up. The last thing she wanted was to be the person to drag down the energy and ruin the séance.

Marlene was off-key but enthusiastic, pumping her hand up and down in time to the music. A clear tenor that Jessica recognized rang through the darkness, rising above the other voices. Sage could do better than carry a tune. The man had a multitude of talents, not the least of which he had shown her all through last night.

Not the time or place, Jessica.

They sang *All You Need is Love, Good Vibrations, Don't Stop Believing*, and *Happy*, for what seemed ages but was more like twelve or fourteen minutes. Jessica shifted her rear on the hard metal chair, trying to get comfortable. How many songs did it take to get the energy level right for the spirit visitations to start?

You've Got a Friend in Me drew to a close and the room filled with silence and the sounds of their breathing.

A minute or so passed. Somebody stifled a cough. Then, seeming to come from above them, a deep baritone voice spoke ponderously in a cultured accent that sounded like a 1940s British film actor. Graham had arrived.

"Good evening, friends and visitors. I bring greetings of peace from the World Unseen. In these days of great fear and trouble, you may wonder whether you are alone on this earth, or whether there is a God who cares for you. You may wonder what will happen when you leave the earth plane, and whether life continues in another place or another plane. We wish you to know and believe that there is merely a thin veil between this world and the next. That you have nothing to fear. If you wish to know us and be close to us on this other side of life, you have only to call on us and ask for our help. A spiritual connection is not as difficult as some of you would make it. There is no need to wait for a grand display of angelic power for you to connect with us. You are so close, you have only to lift your minds and hearts and we will be here to meet you as we are now. Call upon us. We are only a whisper away. We are glad you ask us to come and work with you."

A dim red lightbulb came on in the room, providing just enough illumination to show that Russell was still bound in his chair. And as she watched, awestruck, a gauzy white film issued out of his mouth and spilled like a long scarf to the floor. *Ectoplasm.*

Graham directly addressed several people in the room, answering questions, making jokes, and with permission, placing a hand on the shoulders of two of the sitters. They thanked him reverently, marveling at how large his materialized hand was, formed by the ectoplasm.

The friendly way the sitters interacted with the spirit came as a great surprise to Jessica, who had expected a somber, sedate event.

"Would you like me to put my hand on your shoulder,

Jessica?" The unexpected question startled her. Graham must have known that her mind had been wandering through the esoteric dissertation he had been giving about the density of the physical world compared to the vibrational field of the spirit world, and decided to surprise her.

"Y-yes, please," she stammered. The feeling of a heavy hand molded itself around her shoulder and felt as real as any earthly hand. "Er, thank you, Graham. I can feel it. It's very, uh, large."

"Do not worry, my dear. You are in the right place," said Graham's voice. "Be patient."

"I will, thank you." The pressure of the hand left her shoulder and for ten seconds there was silence. Then a high cockney voice that sounded like a ventriloquist's dummy called out, "'ello everyone."

The sitters all answered in unison, "Hi, Freddy."

"'ow's everyone tonight, then?"

For a while there was a lot of giggling and bantering with Freddy, who was something of a comedian. Jessica, who was still stunned by being singled out for Graham's touch, was finding it hard to focus on Freddy's chatter about his childhood and how things had changed over the years since his death. He joked and laughed and had the sitters sing another song. Then, when it seemed they must be getting near the end of the séance, he called for the trumpet.

"Marlene, luv," Freddy said. "There's a young lady sitting to your right—well, not all that young." There was laughter at that. "But she's not old, either. Someone over here on our side wants to talk to her. Is your name Jessica, luv?"

"Yes."

"All right then, give us a minute. Graham's helping me sort things out. We've got to get things connected."

There was a slight metallic rattle and from the toy box, the séance trumpet rose and flew high above their heads, its luminescent outline glowing in the dark. As Jessica twisted to watch, the trumpet made a full circuit of the room, stopping near her face.

It hovered there, energy emanating from it like an energetic field, reaching out to touch her. From the cabinet came a loud sucking sound, which she supposed was the ectoplasm doing who knew what? Her grip tightened on the hands she was holding. Fawn and Marlene squeezed back reassuringly.

A whispery voice spoke from the trumpet quite near her ear. "You will not find the person you're looking for on the earth plane."

If Jessica's nerves were strung any tighter, they would have snapped. What was she supposed to do? This was what they had come here for and she had no clue what the protocol was.

Fawn said in a low voice, "It's okay to ask questions."

"Is—is Ethan still alive?"

The trumpet remained quiet, floating near her. She tried again, her voice just above a whisper. "Can you tell me where to find him?"

The breathy sigh came again, then the whisper. "You'll have to go to the mountain."

"What mountain? Where?"

"To the east. There is house close to a lake. Another house. You will need to go there." The hoarse words, barely more than a whisper, were hard to make out.

"Another house? Do you mean a house owned by the people where we just came from?"

"Yes, those people. Go to the lake. Now, there is someone here with us who has recently come to our side. He wants to say he's sorry."

Jessica knew she was gripping the hands holding hers too tight, but if she let go, she would not be able to stop herself from reaching out and trying to grab hold of the entity speaking to her.

"Trey," she said. "Where is he? Where's Ethan? How can we find him?"

The trumpet dropped at her feet with a loud bang.

"Wait, Trey!" Her voice echoed too loud in the quiet room. Whoever had materialized the voice in the trumpet was gone.

"You mustn't be upset, luv," said Freddy's childlike voice. "Just do what he said and you'll get what you need. All right, then?"

"But how do we know what mountain, what lake?"

"You'll know. All right?"

"Yes. Thank you." What else could she say? What good would it do to argue with the spirit that she needed to know more than just "lake and mountain"?

Freddy went on to bring through someone for another sitter, but Jessica's mind was churning over what the whispery voice had said. Would Abby know what it meant?

There was a final prayer and the séance was over. The overhead lights came on. Jessica dropped the hands that had held hers for the last ninety minutes. As she rose from her chair, she heard a small object fall from her lap and hit the floor. She stooped to pick it up.

Fawn had heard it, too. She stared at the little object with a look of awe. "Look, you guys. Jessica got an apport."

"I got a what?" said Jessica.

"An apport," Bob answered, coming to look. "It's a gift from spirit."

"But how did it get on my lap?"

"You were searched and wanded before we came into the room, weren't you?"

"Well, yes, but—"

"We all were, too. So, it didn't come in with you or any of us, did it? Spirit produced it."

Tanya edged closer, the talon on her forefinger pointing. "Can we see what you got?"

Bewildered, Jessica held out her hand for their inspection. Resting in her palm, right in the center of the faded X, was a gold cufflink she had never seen before.

"Whose initials are those?" someone asked, as they all crowded around to get a look. Fawn and Tanya were practically jumping up and down with excitement.

Jessica turned the cufflink to display the flat square surface. She read the three letters engraved there:

"*TBS.*"

TWENTY-TWO

"You know this person?" Miguel asked. "This 'TBS'?"

"Yes, I think so. I'll verify it with his wife, but it makes sense."

"We are very happy you came tonight," Miguel said. "To have this happen, it is a great honor." He told her the item belonged to her. "This is a rare thing. Spirit move an object from one place to another, it means a big gift. Someone is trying to give some help."

He photographed the cufflink from every angle and texted the pictures to her phone.

Russell, who stayed in the chair, was looking the worse for wear. Miguel explained that the sessions zapped his energy. He would show him the photos later.

In a daze, Jessica thanked them. She had come to the séance to make contact with Trey Starkey. She had achieved that goal.

They sat in the Tesla, rehashing what they had experienced.

"Well, that wasn't at all what I expected," she said. "Trumpets and raspy voices. All that singing and joking around. If it wasn't for this—" She unclenched the hand where the cufflink had left an imprint in her palm. She kept expecting it to disappear, to dissolve back into thin air or wherever it had come from. "I can't get over the way it just *appeared*. Was that for real?"

"What else could it have come from?"

"I didn't feel it fall on my lap, yet it was just *there*. and now there's a monogrammed cufflink here in my hand. How can it be?"

"What's your guess about how it happened to be on your lap?"

"I don't have any guesses. Russell said Bella didn't tell him anything. But what if she did?"

Sage snorted derisively. "You think Bella called him a half-hour before we got here and told him to go get an engraved cufflink complete with a middle initial, which, by the way, *we* don't even know is Trey's? Maybe Russell keeps a boxful of blanks, in case they're needed? Maybe she arranged the séance, too? Even if there was any way that might be true—and it's not—Bella doesn't operate that way. She's the real deal. She wouldn't have sent us here if she hadn't been guided."

He was right, of course. There was no disputing the reality of the cufflink; she was holding it in her hand. Everyone in the circle had been holding hands. None of them had an opportunity to place it there. The red light had been on at that time. She would have known if Miguel, or anyone else, had been walking around the room. Miguel had never once left the chair at Russell's side.

"Okay, okay, I believe you. It all *seemed* above-board and transparent. And everyone was so nice. It's just—"

"Easier to believe when it's *you* channeling the spirits?"

"Exactly," said Jessica, shamefaced. "Now I know how Jenna felt when I told her about my so-called 'gift.'"

"There's one easy way to settle it. Text the picture to Abby and see if she recognizes it."

A car drove past, looking for a place to park. Sage started the engine and pulled away from the curb, leaving an opening for the driver. "I was thinking about what the spirit said. You know—about the lake and mountains? Next to that log cabin you made, remember the mirror? It looked like water."

Sage was right. She had been so intent on looking for a second little figure that everything else had faded into insignificance. "I was so freaked out by the body in the cabin, I forgot about the mirror." She nodded, warming to the idea. "It could definitely represent a lake. In fact, it makes perfect sense with what the spirit said."

"Abby should be able to find any other properties this family owns," said Sage. "She said she's got Trey's files."

"Good idea." Jessica texted a photograph of the cufflink to Abby with the message: *Does this look familiar?*

To Sage, she said, "If Trey killed himself—and if that *was* Trey coming through at the séance, he is dead—then *where* is that poor kid?"

"Jess, let's face it, Trey may have killed him, too."

"Oh, please don't say that. There was only one figure in the cabin miniature."

"Yes, but that spirit was apologizing. Maybe they weren't in the cabin when he did it. Maybe he did something to Ethan somewhere else. Maybe he went back to the cabin afterwards and shot himself."

"Let's not think that—" Jessica's phone chirped. She broke off and answered, putting Abby on the speaker.

Abby's voice was high and tense. "Where did you get that cufflink? Have you found my baby?"

"No, Abby, I'm sorry. We haven't found Ethan yet. But the cufflink, it *is* Trey's?"

"Of *course* it's Trey's. He got it for being salesman of the year in his office. I've waited for *hours* to hear from you. You promised—"

"We had to make an unexpected detour. It was important."

"Was the cufflink at Benedict Canyon?" Abby asked, giving up on her complaints. "Zach didn't find anything there, so that means they were there after he checked."

"There wasn't any sign of Trey and Ethan at the house, but—"

"He forgot his cufflink? I don't understand. Why would he even take them with him when they were going to Disneyland?"

"Would you please check and see whether the other one is there?"

"Why would it be here? If he took them—"

"Please, Abby, humor me."

"Okay. I'm heading upstairs to our bedroom. It would be in his valet box. Did you pick up any vibes, or whatever you call it, at the house?"

"Enough that I'm positive that they were there."

"But that's obvious if he dropped a cufflink there," said Abby, frustration building in her voice.

Was there any benefit in sharing the details of how Trey's dark energy had affected Jessica in the house, or about the séance? Why get Abby more worried and upset than she already was?

They listened to the sounds of her rooting around in Trey's valet box. She came back on the line. "One of the pair is missing. The mate must have dropped into his suitcase without him realizing it. How the hell?"

It was unimaginable that Trey's spirit had somehow removed the cufflink from the valet box in his bedroom, apported it through time and space, and dropped it on Jessica's lap in Russell Levine's house. Yet, if the experience was not real, the only other reasonable explanation was that the entire séance had been a fraud. With all evidence pointing in the opposite direction, Jessica knew she had to accept the easiest explanation.

The séance room had too many safeguards. Besides, if Sage trusted Bella Bingham, so did she. The piece of gold jewelry winked up at her in the light of her phone's screen.

"I have a more important question for you," said Jessica, interrupting Abby before she got more wound up. "Is there a way for you to find out whether the Benedict Canyon client owns any other properties?"

"Why are you asking that?"

"Just trust me, please? Would Trey's file include that kind of information? Can you look?"

"I'll look, but it wouldn't be in the file unless they were wanting to list it for sale. Are you thinking Trey's taken Ethan to some other place these people own? What makes you think that?"

"It's just a feeling I got; something it might be worth looking into. Maybe the client talked to Trey about a vacation home. A lake house; a cabin in the mountains."

Abby hesitated. "Should I tell Zach about Benedict Canyon?"

No, don't say anything to Zach. He'll shut us down. She did not say it out loud, but she was shaking her head even though Abby could not see her. Aloud, she said calmly, "You can if you want, but there's nothing for him to see there."

"Except the cufflink proves they were there."

The quaver in Abby's voice gave Jessica a pang, but not enough to make her back off. If Zach started interfering now, they would never find Ethan. He would not be as accepting as she and Sage were of apported jewelry, and she could imagine his reaction if she told him she had received it, not at the Benedict Canyon house, but at a séance.

"Trey and Ethan aren't there now," said Jessica. "And he'll be pissed if he hears I'm involved after he told me to stay out of it."

There was a long, exhausted sigh. "I guess you're right. I just thought—"

"I promise, you'll be the first to hear if we find anything for Zach to investigate—physical evidence. Then you can tell him. Meanwhile, *please* check the file?"

"Okay, sure. I'll go look. Anything that might help find Ethan. If there's nothing in the file, I'll check online. They might own a place and not have it up for sale."

"Great. We're in Hollywood right now. We'll hang out here until you call. No point in us heading back right now. We'd just have to turn around if you find anything useful."

When Abby went silent, Jessica regretted that she'd revealed their location. The lawyer's brain was already creating a mental map, figuring out where they might be, she could feel it. Abby's next words confirmed her feeling.

"If you had to turn around, you'd be going east. You mentioned a mountain cabin or a lake house. What are you thinking, Big Bear?"

"I don't know, Abby. It could be Big Bear or Arrowhead. They're both in the San Bernardino Mountains, which isn't too far. They both have lakes. And tons of people keep homes or cabins up there for skiing and boating. Or, it could be some other place altogether. I'm hoping for some kind of vibe."

"I'll go look and call you back."

"Bye."

"If the family did have a place and Trey knew about it, they're too far away to know he used it," said Jessica, ending the call.

"If he killed himself on their property, obviously, they're going to find out."

Sage turned left onto La Brea and drove into a McDonald's parking lot. It was past eleven and they were open for business. Jessica realized she was hungry, which meant Sage must be famished.

"I could use a Big Mac," he said. "Are you hungry?"

She slid the phone into her pocket. "Yeah. Too bad there's nothing more nutritious open this late." That sounded ungracious. She tried again. "You're so patient. Most men would have been griping by now."

He locked the Tesla and took her hand as they walked to the restaurant. "Oh, just you wait, Miss Jessica. I promise, I can gripe with the best of them."

For Hollywood, eleven o'clock wasn't all that late and McDonald's was doing a brisk trade. They got in line, placed their order, waited for their food, carried the tray over to a booth in the corner. Abby had not yet called back.

The aroma of hot, salty fries wafted up Jessica's nose and stimulated her appetite. She stuffed a few in her mouth. "If Ethan's not with Trey, where can he be?" Asking the same question and getting no satisfactory answers was getting old.

Sage shrugged. "Who knows what that kind of parent is capable of? But if he loved his kid, I can't see him blowing his brains out and leaving the kid to deal with it."

"Is it any better to kill the kid first and then himself?"

A woman in the next booth twisted around and gave Jessica a shocked look. She gave the woman a weak smile and lowered her voice. "—if my crime scene was accurate."

Sage leaned toward her so his voice wouldn't carry. "Why wouldn't it be accurate? The other one you told me about—the cult murder—was."

Involuntarily, she opened her hands. The Xs on her palms glowered back, blaming her for creating the horrible death scene in the log cabin. She wanted so desperately to find Ethan, to gather him up in her arms and return him to his mother, as she wished Justin could be returned to her. Maybe there would be some form of redemption for her if she succeeded.

She dug the apported cufflink from her pocket—half-surprised it was still there—and took another peek. Miguel said it meant that she was getting help from what the first spirit, Graham, had called the World Unseen. She hoped he was right.

"What's taking Abby so long?" She squeezed a puddle of ketchup onto her fries, then pushed it away again, repulsed because it had the consistency of congealed blood.

"Maybe she had to do an internet search," Sage said.

Jessica fidgeted on the molded plastic bench. Now that they were no longer running around, her mind full of how to contact Ethan, and with the séance behind them, Justin had tucked himself firmly in the forefront. She sighed and licked salt off her fingers. If she waited much longer to tell Sage about him, it might well be too long. She was afraid to open up to him now and damage the fragile bond that was already forming. But when would it ever be the right time?

She pushed her bag of fries to the side and wiped her hands, worrying that she would say the wrong thing, knowing she had to try. "Sage, I need to tell you something. Finding Ethan means more to me than you know."

He glanced up from his Big Mac. "I can see how much you care."

"It's not just that. I—I had a son a year younger than Ethan. He died."

Sage set his half-eaten burger in its box and wiped his hands on a napkin, turning the full bore of his attention on her. "Jess, I'm so sorry."

"It was my fault." She watched closely for signs of judgment, but nothing in his expression changed. Another little piece of the ice in her heart melted.

"What happened?" he asked.

"I was married to a high-functioning drunk and I waited too long to end it. On the night I planned to leave him, he wrecked the car. My son, Justin, was killed because I was in a hurry to get going and I was desperate enough and foolish enough to trust Greg to properly clamp the safety seat. When we went over the cliff, the car rolled and Justin was thrown out, still in his car seat."

"This is the accident that caused your amnesia?"

She nodded. She heard her voice drone on in a monotone, emotion leached from it by the enormity of what she was revealing. "They told me he died instantly, but who knows whether that's true? I died, too, but I came back. While I was over there, I watched him go into the Light. It *seemed* like it was instant, but how can I know for sure? The only way I can stand it is to believe that."

Sage started to reach across to her, but she shook her head, refusing comfort that she did not deserve. "In the last few days, Justin has started coming through to me." She paused to give him a wry smile. "The upside of being a medium. He's shown me how he's growing up on the other side." Jessica could see the concern in his face and knew it was genuine.

"Wow, that's fantastic. I mean, it's kind of ironic, but—how old was he when he crossed?"

"He was almost three. He's eight now. He's forgiven me, but I'll never forgive myself." Jessica hesitated. "Look, I understand if knowing that changes the way you see me—"

Sage reached out again, and before she could protest, took her hand in his. "No, Jessica, it doesn't change anything for me. We all have things in our past that we regret." He hesitated the same way she had. "The last time I saw my mother, we had a huge argument and I stormed out. Right after I left, she fell off a ladder and broke her neck. I torment myself over it constantly. If I hadn't left when I did, maybe she would be alive now."

"How horrible for you," Jessica said. Then decided that she might as well lay it all bare. "I read that you were arrested."

"I figured you would get there sooner or later. I would have told you about it."

"I know you would."

"Except for her dying, that was the worst time of my life. Locked up for days, interrogated like a criminal. Knowing that in some way it *was* my fault that she was dead, even though I didn't kill her. Same as you believe about your son. Does that change the way you see me?"

"Of course not."

"Well, there you go." He produced a thin smile. "Maybe *this* will: my birth mother has been in prison for most of my life."

Jessica gave a small start of surprise. She ran all the clichés through her mind, but *this too shall pass* or *keep your chin up* just didn't cut it. "She must have been an adult. Whatever she did, you aren't responsible for it."

"Of course not. But as they say, the apple doesn't fall far from the tree. Maybe evil genes can be inherited."

"Evil? That's pretty extreme. Can I ask what she did?"

"First, she—"

Jessica's phone rang. Sage broke off.

Abby, sounding excited.

"You were right, Jess. There *was* paperwork in the file for a brand-new listing. The family is moving to Europe and selling everything they own. Trey hadn't gotten around to filing it with the MLS, but all the information is here. It's just what you said, Jess, they own a place in Big Bear."

TWENTY-THREE

Abby's phone call left Jessica with a buzz of energy and a certainty that they were headed in the right direction. Big Bear Lake was a little more than a hundred miles east of their current location. Two hours in decent traffic. The freeway would be clear at this time of night, but if they ran into bad weather, delays were possible.

"Weather.com says there's snow on the mountain," Jessica said, after checking her phone. "Do we need to get chains?"

"The good news is, I went skiing a couple of weeks ago and took some with me. They're still in the trunk."

"I don't suppose you have snow clothes in that trunk, too?"

"None small enough to fit you."

"Hey, small but mighty."

Sage threw her a grin. "I have definitely learned that already."

Google found them a nearby Ross Dress for Less that was open until one a.m.—only in Hollywood. They raced through the store, gathering up what they needed for the cold mountain weather—gloves, heavier socks, sweaters, knit hats, including toddler-sizes in the shopping cart, too. There was no telling how well-prepared for the mountains Trey had been. Abby said he had been a good dad. Surely, he would dress Ethan warmly. Assuming they did go to Big Bear.

Please help us find him. Let him be alive.

Back in the Tesla, their purchases stowed in the trunk, Jessica started thinking out loud. "Maybe this is the point we should tell Zach what's up."

Sage messed with the GPS screen and brought up the route to the Big Bear address Abby had texted. He turned in his seat to give her a long look. "If we find Trey dead, you'll have to tell him anyway."

"So, you think I should?"

"I'm just saying it's probably the right thing to do, *and* I can imagine his reaction. 'Another waste of time.'"

Jessica bristled. "The marsh was hardly a waste of time. The dinosaur, the food wrapper, remember?"

"*I* know that. I'm on your side."

"Okay, fine, I'll text him and cover myself."

"He'll know we got the address from Abby."

"Who cares? If we find them—"

"Use my phone. The number isn't blocked."

She tapped out a message: *It's Jess. Going to Big Bear. I think he's there.*

She included the address of their destination and hit send as they entered the I-10 East.

Ten miles later, a reply pinged back from Zach:
Stay the hell out of my case.

"Well, that's a pretty clear message," Sage said. "So, we've done our duty and informed him. Now, let's go find this asshole. If Trey Starkey is as dead as we think he is, the local authorities can inform Zach."

"I don't think he can get any deader." Jessica did not mention Ethan again; didn't need to. The missing four-year-old's essence was riding with them in the backseat of the Tesla.

They drove on in silence, each wrapped in their own thoughts. She wanted to ask why his mother was in prison for so long. A long sentence meant it was serious. She must have killed someone. The conversation with Jay of the mad scientist hair came back to her. As a small child, Sage had witnessed something so terrible that he hadn't spoken for a year. What had he seen? Was it the event that had put his birth mother behind bars?

Their conversation about Justin wasn't finished either. That would wait for another time.

The long, difficult day was catching up with her, starting with the stress of Jenna and Zach bursting in, their argument. The meeting with Abby, Benedict Canyon, the séance.... The headlights of oncoming vehicles and the freeway signs flashed past. Hypnotic. Jessica leaned back against the headrest and closed her eyes. Everything drifted away.

"You okay, Jess?"

Sage's words pulled her back from wherever she had been going—drifting off to sleep? A fugue state? Sometimes it was hard to tell.

"Yeah, I'm fine. I think I'll try again to connect with Ethan."

Following the instructions from the book, *Opening to Channel,* which she had downloaded, Jessica concentrated on her breathing and opened her mind to the little boy. She made a careful blank space for him to come in, asked her spirit guides to contact his guides and connect them. Waited.

Nothing happened.

Either she was doing it wrong or worse, there was no connection to be made. She tried to swallow the lump of emotion that came into her throat and push away the fear as the powerful Tesla chewed up the miles. They roared past El Monte, West Covina, Pomona, Ontario, Riverside, hooking onto State Route 38 without any flashing blue lights coming up behind them. Then they were curving around the mountain, a sheer wall rising on Sage's side.

He took the hairpin turns with confidence but Jessica clung to the armrest, white-knuckling it through the darkness that pressed around the vehicle. She could not see the steep drop beyond the low guardrail but she knew it was there. And knowing it made her sweat.

The same type of guardrail had not prevented Greg Mack from driving straight through it.

The actual memory of sailing off the cliff, of her head slamming into the windshield, was lost to her, but not the dread—the realization that it was about to happen. Nor had she forgotten dying and communicating telepathically with an angel. And the one memory that would always stay with her. Justin rising into the Light.

Sage's voice broke in, once again jerking her back to reality.

"You okay, Jess? Want me to slow down?"

"Huh? No, it's fine. Go as fast as you can. How much further?"

"An hour. You can already feel the temperature change. I'm gonna turn on the heater."

He was right. The distinct nip in the air had not been present at lower elevations. The higher the elevation, the colder the temperature. Big Bear City was close to 7,000 feet up the mountain.

"I learned to drive in snow last year," Sage said, and Jessica figured he was trying to distract her from the drop. "It was in Maine, where I met Claudia. We got stuck in a really nasty blizzard."

"Is there any other kind?"

"Not as far as I'm concerned."

"I'm glad you know what you're doing."

He grinned. "Hey, I didn't say I knew what I was doing."

"You're a barrel of laughs," Jessica said. "I'm going to try to reach out to Ethan again."

"Again?"

"It doesn't make any sense to keep trying, but it can't hurt."

"Go for it," said Sage. "I'll be sending good vibes, too."

"I think you should keep your mind on the road."

"Yes, ma'am."

This time, she said a prayer first and asked God to help her make a connection with Ethan Starkey, or even Trey. She and God had never had a strong relationship, and Justin's death had not improved it. But that did not prevent her from hoping He— or, She—would understand Jessica's wishy-washy attitude and overlook it.

Apparently, God did. Once she slowed her breathing and began the routine of opening her chakras, a clear image of Ethan landed in her mind, curled into a fetal position, sucking his thumb. Jessica was well aware that traumatized children tended to regress to an earlier stage of development. She could think of no greater trauma than what this child may have suffered. The image broke her heart.

As if she were locking him onto a tractor beam, she aimed all of her concentration on the boy and began transmitting messages to him:

Ethan, are you there?

For several seconds she felt and heard nothing but her own breathing. Then, *"I'm scared."*

I know, sweetie. We're coming to get you.

"But I'm f-f-fwighten."

You're a very brave boy, Ethan. Can you tell me what it looks like where you are?

"Want Mama."

You'll see her soon. Ethan, are you inside the house?

"Don't feel good. Head hurts. Sleepy."

Ethan, can you hear me?

He began to cry, the soft sobs of a scared little boy who had given up hope.

Jessica couldn't help thinking of the fairy, Tinkerbell, drinking a cup of poison to save Peter Pan, her light fading, extinguished as she dies. In the story, all that was needed to bring Tink back to life was to clap your hands if you believed in fairies. A stray tear trickled down Jessica's cheek. All the clapping in the world would not help Ethan if it was too late. An arrow of fear shot through her. What were they going to find at the cabin?

"Could you tell anything about where he is?" Sage asked, when she told him what she had seen.

"No." She hated the utter helplessness of being stuck in a car, still too many miles from their destination. "The darkness was too intense. I can't tell whether he's dead or alive, but it's down to freezing. We have to get there fast."

"I can't take these turns any faster, Jess."

"I know."

After that, although she tried and tried again, nothing evoked any response from the boy. Had he actually responded to her at all? Maybe rather than "hearing" her in his head, he had felt her presence and not understood what it meant. Of course he couldn't understand. How could he? Poor little lad.

The night stretched ahead of them as black as the inside of a coalbin. If it were not for the occasional light post in the distance reflected off the headlights in the falling snow, they might have been driving through a wall of fog.

The Tesla's tires gripped the slick road even without chains. Still, Sage slowed down more on the curves.

"Shit."

Snow crystals had begun to splatter the windshield like white rain. The road soon looked like cotton. What they had been able to see of the horizon disappeared. Snow piled on the windshield, swept smoothly away, but the wipers had no effect on the frozen chunks that stuck to the hood like crushed ice from a Coke machine.

"What if the cabin affects you the way the Benedict Canyon house did?" Sage asked, once again reading her mind.

"I can't let it affect me," said Jessica. "I have to stay alert."

"Okay, but it couldn't hurt to say a prayer of protection before we go in. "

"Fine by me. Do you know any?"

"The specific wording isn't important. We can work on it later."

It seemed a lifetime before the GPS directed them onto Big Bear Boulevard. They passed the airport, the Convention Center. On the road that ran alongside the dark lake, the top of Jessica's head started tingling with the ruffling of her hair, a sign that spirit was touching her aura. It was hard to believe she had accumulated so much knowledge about the world of spirit in a few short days. And yet, for all she had learned, she knew next to nothing.

For an instant, the full moon appeared through the clouds, huge, and low in the sky, spilling a shaft of silver light across the water like an omen. Jessica shivered. What might such an omen portend?

On each side of Big Bear Boulevard, plows had pushed the snow off to the sides of the wide road. Unlike the jam-packed cities at the foot of the mountain, there were open spaces between buildings here, occupied by towering pines. They cruised past darkened churches, a post office, fire station, Denny's.

"Everything is so dark," Jessica said. "Shouldn't there be some lights on, at least in the Denny's? They're always open."

Sage agreed. "Just the traffic lights are on. The power must be out."

"How can traffic lights be on if the power is out?"

"Backup batteries. Can you read the street signs?"

The snow was coming down harder now, soft flakes turned to ice pellets bombarding the body of the car.

"They're too dark to see. Does this road ever end? I don't remember Big Bear being this big."

"Population 30-k, give or take."

They kept rolling through miles of endless business district, coming at last to residential streets where homes were built on wooded lots that allowed for plenty of privacy. The snow plows had not made it this far out and a white mantle camouflaged everything in sight—roofs, vehicles, hedges, trees.

Abby had already texted twice to ask their progress. She had sent a photo of the A-frame they were aiming for. It might have been more helpful if the sun had been up. In the wee hours and in snowfall, all bets were off.

Banked snow on the road made it impossible to see street corners. The prim GPS voice counted down the number of feet before the turn but they bypassed the street anyway.

"I'll have to put the chains on before we head back," Sage said, clenching his teeth when the tires began to slip and they were forced to make a U-turn.

The muscles in Jessica's already tense shoulders tightened some more. "I hope we can get the hell away from here, fast."

"That's the plan."

At last through the trees, the headlights picked out what appeared to be the right place. By the time they turned in by a glow-in-the-dark snow pole marking the driveway, it was past 2 a.m. The good news was, they were no longer being pelted by ice.

The A-frame stood fifty yards back and away from any other dwellings. It was painted a dark color, either green or black, which had made it hard to see. The steep pitched roof on the front section came close to the ground. At the front, a small wooden deck perched on five-foot-tall stilts. Sliding glass doors allowed entry from the interior.

Another section behind the first one had the higher roof of a second story. Icicles hung from the eaves. Packed snow on the roof looked like frosting.

"A gingerbread house," Jessica murmured, overcome with sudden dread for what awaited them inside.

She had not thought to ask Abby the make and model of Trey's car but it would have made no difference if she had. The vehicle parked in the driveway was mostly buried under a mound of snow.

Contemplating the A-frame from the warmth of the car, Sage peered through the falling snowflakes. "The entry must be around back. Ready?"

Jessica had no answer. An unpleasant impression of heat and darkness seemed to issue from inside the top of her skull. Slowing neurons, dendrites, axons to a crawl, busy drilling into the deep structures of her brain. Thinking was too hard.

"Jessica?"

She heard his voice but engrossed with the ooze, she did not reply. Thick and sludgy, like overused oil, it brought the heaviness of bleak despair, even worse than she had experienced in Benedict Canyon.

By the time she caught on to what was happening to her, her facial muscles were beginning to numb. The sensation moved inexorably downward. She struggled to alert Sage, her lips as stiff as if they had been injected with botox.

"Now would be a good time for that prayer of protection."

Without asking questions, Sage reached over and grabbed hold of her hand, speaking in a strong voice. "Father-Mother God, we come here in the name of love, light, peace and truth. We ask that the power of the Holy Spirit uplift and protect us as we enter this property and attempt to find Ethan Starkey. Surround us with light and cast out any negative entities that would stand in our way."

And just like that, the brewing darkness arrested. The energy that had been sapped out of her returned. Jessica gazed at Sage in awe. "That was freaking amazing. Did you make it up?"

He shrugged. "It's partly from a prayer Bella uses sometimes. She got it from another British medium named Brian Hurst. I ad-libbed the rest."

"I love it," she said, meaning it. "I *feel* protected."

"Good. Now, we need to figure out what we're going to do. Knock on the door in the middle of the night?"

"We can't wait 'til morning. I think we should take a walk around the place. Maybe we can see inside."

"And hope not to get shot." Sage tapped the steering wheel. "Okay, Miss Jessica, if that's what you want. Let's go do it."

She reached for the Ross sack in the backseat and got out the

SHEILA LOWE

items they had purchased, including a flashlight. She had installed the batteries and torn the price tags off the knit hats and gloves during the drive. Sage pulled his hat down over his ears and Jessica did the same.

Falling snowflakes landed on their faces and melted into ice water. The frigid air burned her throat. Jessica leaned back into the car and snatched up a woolen scarf. She wrapped it around her neck and over her lower face, grateful for the warmth.

Together, they moved toward the building. Low-lying cloud cover hid the stars in the silent night and made her think of the vision she had seen of Ethan surrounded by darkness. She knew they were close.

It must have snowed for hours before their arrival at the upper elevations. The drifts piled two feet high. They crunched their way through hundred-foot-high conifers, following a path around to the back of the A-frame. Two windows were set high on the side of the house. Too high to see into without a ladder. An enclosed porch at the rear of the house stopped them.

The porch door stood open.

TWENTY-FOUR

Protect us. What was it Sage had said in his prayer? *Surround us with light. Protect us. Surround us with light. Protect us.* Maybe if she kept repeating it...

Leading the way, Sage mounted the wooden steps and disappeared through the porch door. Jessica gave him a few seconds to return. When he did not reappear right away, she followed. The inner door leading into the house was open, too.

The interior was as cold as outside and quiet as a soundproof booth. Still holding on to the faint hope that she was wrong about Trey, she considered the possibility that he and Ethan might be asleep upstairs.

Then she remembered. In the log cabin scene, he'd had a gun. What if he woke up and thought they were intruders?

Surround us with light. Protect us.

The doors to the A-frame had been left open to the freezing air. It seemed unlikely they were asleep. But what if they—

Surround us with light. Protect us.

Keeping the flashlight pointed low, Sage swung it around the entry, showing a staircase that led to the second floor. Beyond it was a small kitchen and a short hallway to the living room. The flashlight beam revealed a cozy, updated decor. Leather couch with big throw pillows, and a multi-colored knitted afghan in a heap, the way someone might leave it after getting up from a nap.

On the opposite side of the room, a wide screen TV stood atop an Asian-style media cabinet. Matching side chairs and an upright log table between them faced the sliding doors they had seen from the car. A free-standing, wood burning fireplace made a pleasant hearth in the corner nearest the deck. Sage opened the glass door in front, showing freshly laid kindling waiting to be lit. He pulled out the ash drawer. Clean.

Why were the doors open?

Jessica felt along the wall until she found a switch and flipped it. Nothing happened. Their suspicion that the bad weather had caused a power outage, seemed to be on target.

Sage motioned her to wait for him where she was, and tiptoed up the staircase.

The A-frame was small enough that searching the two bedrooms and bath went fast. He came back down and reported seeing no sign of Ethan or Trey.

"Are you *sure* they came here?" he asked.

"Yes, I feel it as strongly as I've ever felt anything."

"Then where the hell are they?"

"I think we can safely assume it's his car under that pile of snow. They can't be far." If Ethan was outside in this weather—panic flooded her. There was no way he could survive alone in the snow, regardless of how well he was dressed—assuming Trey had dressed him properly for the weather.

She had to stop the crazy. She had to turn inward and ask for a message.

For the first time, she found tuning in to her psychic sense similar to finding a radio station. The voices were the static. Once she got past them and listened carefully, she heard, "*Go outside.*"

With the words came a *knowing*. Beckoning Sage to come with her, she walked out to the porch, following a magnetic pull. It was a similar feeling to what she had experienced in Ethan's bedroom, except this time, instead of pulling at her from inside her abdomen, it was an external pulling, as if a cord was tied around her waist, leading her away from the A-frame and into the trees.

They walked as fast as the ankle-deep snow allowed. Thirty feet behind the house, partially hidden behind the trees was a rustic structure the size of a one-car garage. With the exception of the door being on the side of the cabin between two windows, rather than at one end, it bore a strong resemblance to the log cabin Jessica had assembled in her trance state.

They exchanged a look—a question and an answer.

"He's in there," she said quietly. "Trey is inside. I feel him."

A roof overhang kept the snow from the porch, but the three stone steps Sage mounted were blanketed with the white stuff. He knocked hard on the door and called out, "Trey? Trey Starkey?" His voice reverberated in the silence. They were too far away from other dwellings for the neighbors to hear. He knocked again.

While he was shining his flashlight in the window to the left of the door, Jessica climbed the steps and tried the doorknob.

"The door's open," she whispered.

Sage swung around, his flashlight arcing across her face, blinding her for a moment. "Don't go inside," he said hoarsely. "You don't need to see it."

Jessica stared at him. "What did you see?"

"You were right. Your scene was right."

Her heart lurched. "Ethan."

"Wait, Jess, don't go—"

If Ethan was inside and Trey... She had no intention of waiting for anything. She pushed open the door, started to step over the threshold. Sage wrapped his arms around her and jerked her back.

"It's a crime scene. You can't go in there."

"But Ethan..."

"Remember, Ethan wasn't in the scene you made. He's not here." Holding her behind him in the doorway, Sage swung the flashlight around the cabin.

"You don't have to protect me," Jessica insisted, straining against him. "Let me see."

"If you're sure—"

She stepped into the doorway, her gaze raking over the plain furnishings. Two cots, an oil stove, a cheap-looking two-drawer chest. And Trey Starkey, face up on the cot closest to the door—though not much was left of his face. Jessica's stomach lurched. She turned away, afraid she would hurl.

She put a shaky hand on Sage's arm, taking several deep breaths through her scarf to steady herself. "The log cabin scene—"

"Yeah."

Blood spray and tissue had splattered on the wall behind the body. There was no ambiguity about what had happened: Trey, stretched out on his back, had placed the handgun under his chin and pulled the trigger. The gun had landed on the floor in the very spot where the clay one had been placed in the scene she'd constructed.

Sage moved the flashlight beam to show the second cot. A slight indent in the pillow showed where a small head had lain. A powder blue blanket drooped over the side of the cot, sponging up blood that had pooled on the floor. The light of the flashlight gave it a grisly tie-dye effect.

"How does a father do this to a son he supposedly loved?" said Jessica.

"People do all kinds of evil things to the people they supposedly love. Revenge on Abby was more important to him than his child. Selfish motherfucker."

"Where can Ethan be? There's no place to hide in here."

Sage pointed the flashlight at the chest of drawers. "Look."

An amber colored pharmacy container stood on the chest, its white childproof cap next to it.

Jessica wanted to rage at the corpse on the cot, to grab him by his bloody shirt and shake him until he told her where his son was. But Trey was past any human response. At least a few hours must have passed since his transition to the world of spirit. Linear time did not exist over there. He had come through with a message for her at the séance. Was it possible Trey had already been there long enough to rid himself of the selfish need to hurt Abby through their child? Could she reach him?

Where is he, Trey? Where is Ethan?

"I'm sorry. Tell Ab…"

The line of communication was shaky. That she received an answer at all astonished her. She fought to hold onto the connection, knowing that at any moment she might lose him.

I will tell her, Trey, I promise. But please, let me help Ethan.

A shimmery image of the A-frame appeared to her, almost immediately replaced by one of Ethan. As she had seen him earlier, the little boy, thumb in his mouth, was curled in a tight ball, surrounded by darkness.

Is he in the house somewhere? Is that what you're telling me?

"My son...sorry...sorry."

The connection broke like a bad cell phone signal, leaving behind the heaviness of guilt and sorrow. Jessica knew in her gut that Trey would not reconnect. She turned to Sage and spoke urgently. "We have to get back to the main house. Ethan is there."

"But we already looked in the house."

"I don't care. He's there."

"Okay, let's go."

She gave him a quick glance, loving the way he trusted her without question. Sage closed the door on the hideous tableau and hurried back through the woods.

Jessica took the flashlight, while Sage used the flashlight app on his phone. Inside the A-frame, they split up and explored every room again, calling Ethan's name, listening to the silence.

She opened bedroom closets and even drawers that were too small to be a hiding place. The linen closet in the bathroom. Cabinets under the sink. A storage chest that contained summer bed linens. They met back where they had started, in the living room.

"We've looked everywhere, Jess. He's not here."

"He's got to be. We must have missed something. I'm not leaving until we find him."

"We need to call the police. They can help look for Ethan. If he's in the woods—"

Jessica interrupted, "He's *not* in the woods. Trey showed me this house and Ethan. I wish we had better light."

No sooner had the words left her mouth than the living room lights came on. Startled, they blinked at each other, their eyes adjusting to the sudden change.

"I must have left the switch on," she said. "And the power came back on."

"That makes things easier. I'm going to look around some more."

Sage left the room and Jessica went upstairs again, going back over ground she had already covered. Once more, she looked under beds, in closets, in every drawer.

She was opening the linen closet again when Sage called up from the hallway.

"Jess, come down here. Hurry."

She rushed back to him at breakneck speed. He was crouched next to the triangular space under the staircase. Bending down, she followed his pointing finger. A door no more than three feet high was set flush with the wall.

She held her breath as Sage reached out and gently opened it.

TWENTY-FIVE

Jessica fell to her knees. The cupboard under the stairs extended several feet back. It was full of darkness, too dense to see inside.

"Shine the light to the side, Sage, not directly inside," she said softly.

The beam bounced off the wood flooring, bringing sufficient illumination to light up the space. Crouching on all fours, she peered in. She was just about able to make out his face, so pale it was almost luminous. His eyes were closed, long lashes dark on chalky white cheeks. They had found him and he looked dead.

He can't be dead. He can't be dead. He can't be dead. If she said it enough, would it be true?

"Ethan." Jessica spoke just loud enough to be audible. "Ethan, everything's going to be okay."

"Let me get him out of there," said Sage.

She backed out of the space, refusing to believe they were too late. "I'll go get the blanket off the couch."

"Good idea."

He took her place, kneeling on the wood flooring. As Jessica hurried away, Sage was stretching his long arms into the cupboard.

She seized the afghan and sped back to the hallway. Sage was holding the four-year-old in his arms, his ear bent close to Ethan's mouth. He seemed to be listening for the child's respirations.

"Please tell me he's alive," she said, noting that the boy's lips had a bluish tinge.

"He's breathing, but slowly," said Sage.

Jessica nearly fainted with relief. How long ago had Ethan woken in the cabin and seen the horror that must have sent him running for the A-frame? How long had he been holed up in the cupboard under the stairs with inadequate protection against the freezing weather? The legs of his footed fleece Spiderman pajamas were damp and speckled with brown spots.

Between them they bundled the afghan around the boy, pulling it up around his head so that only his face was visible. Her hand brushed against the icy cheek.

"He's lost too much heat," said Sage. "We've got to bring his body temperature up."

"The afghan should help. And I can go get the clothes we brought him."

"That will help, but this is hypothermia. He needs to be warmed on the inside, too. We need to get some warm fluids inside him." When Jessica looked at him in surprise, he added, "I had to take pediatric first-aid training before we opened the Center."

Grateful that he had, Jessica took one small, cold hand in hers and rubbed it, then the other. Ethan squirmed and moaned. "Thank God," she murmured.

Sage ran out to the car and brought back the bag with the warm clothes they had purchased.

"We need to get him back down the mountain," Jessica said, as between them they got Ethan changed into fleece pajamas with feet and a puffy down jacket and knit hat. They wrapped the afghan around him again.

Sage said, "There's an emergency room at Bear Valley Community. They're open all night."

"Can't we take him home?"

Ethan moaned again and his eyes fluttered open, unfocused, then closed again. "I had a bad dream, Mama," he murmured and went back to sleep.

Jessica stroked his forehead. "I know, baby. You're okay now. Everything's gonna be okay."

Keeping her voice to a whisper, she said, "Let's get him back to Abby. Taking him to a hospital is going to add to the trauma.

At this hour traffic won't be bad and we can be there in a couple of hours. He already feels warmer."

"Your call, Jess."

"I'll check in the kitchen and see if there's anything I can heat up for him."

"Okay, but let's hurry."

There were a few canned goods in the kitchen cabinets, but the prize was a clean thermos bottle and a box of individual packets of cocoa. Thankful that the power had come back on, Jessica zapped water in the microwave and poured it into the thermos. Her hands were shaking and she spilled some grains of cocoa powder onto the counter. The truth was, she was close to losing it. All that was holding her together was gratitude for the role she had been given to play in this drama. There would be plenty of time later to break down and sob the way she needed to.

With no child safety seat, Jessica climbed in the Tesla's backseat and Sage belted Ethan across her lap. It was not ideal, but she held him against her, rocking him a little, the way she used to rock Justin. And as she rocked him, she called his mother and gave her the news.

Then she called Zach Smith.

TWENTY-SIX

Three weeks later

"You wouldn't have found him without help," said Jenna.

"Help from the spirit world, you mean? It's going to take a while for the poor little guy to work through everything that happened—what he saw." Jessica sipped coffee, her eyes on her two little nieces who were playing with their Barbies on the other side of the den.

"I'm so glad Sage was able to take Ethan into the program. Abby rented an apartment for them to stay near the Center. She's been taking him over every day for school and therapy."

"Does she get to stay at school with him?"

"It's out of the norm, but Zebediah evaluated him and gave Abby special dispensation. She sits in the back of the classroom so he can see that she's there. For the first week, he wouldn't let her out of his sight. He would wait outside the bathroom door for her to come out. He's still having nightmares, but he's starting to loosen up in class and looking for her less and less. Annabelle is working with him one-on-one, too. He's starting to make friends."

"I can't imagine a parent doing what Trey did," said Jenna, revulsion written across her face.

"I know. I like to think he was trying to redeem himself by telling me at the last minute where to find Ethan. He'd given him several Ambien—the bottle was on the dresser in the cabin. He must have expected that Ethan would die in his sleep and never know about him shooting himself. It's amazing that he *didn't* die. I think he must have a very good guardian angel watching over him."

"He *would* have died if you and Sage hadn't ridden to the rescue the way you did. Why do you think Trey didn't just do it in the house, instead of going to some ratty old cabin out in the woods?"

"We'll never know for sure. All I can think of is, he had some misguided sense of duty to his clients, and didn't want to mess up their house by killing himself and Ethan in the A-frame. They would have had a hard time selling it after that."

"Misguided is a nice way to put it. Can you imagine that little boy finding his way back to the house, drugged and freezing?" said Jenna.

"He was so cold when we found him. God knows how long he was hiding with no heat and just his damp jammies. We hauled ass back down that mountain, as much as you can haul ass with chains on. We were so lucky the snow had stopped. The chains came off as soon as it was practical. Then we *really* hauled ass. We got back to Thousand Oaks around five in the morning. I thought Abby was going to come unglued. I sure would have."

"Yeah, me, too."

They talked about Jessica's hellish dream and the X's on her hands. She got a big surprise when Jenna said, "That's not the mark of the Devil, you doofus."

"It's not?"

"No. The X is the mark of Christ. It's a symbol of the crucifixion wounds where the nails went into his hands." She reached over and grabbed Jessica's hand. "He was protecting you."

Jessica tried to speak but emotion clogged the words in her throat. She remembered the hand that had reached out and taken her away from the demons that tried to hold her. If only she had trusted her sister and asked her sooner.

A commotion across the room drew their attention and, with a final squeeze, Jenna let go of her hand.

"Emma, don't put your doll in the flowerpot. She's getting dirty and you're making a mess, getting soil on the floor."

The cheeky little face with the pert nose turned to her mother. "But she's digging her garden, Mama. She has to plant some pretty flowers."

Jessica grinned. "That's my niece."

"I'm having a really hard time right now not saying 'why can't you be clean, like your sister?'" Jenna said in a stage whisper.

"Please restrain yourself. I had to hear that the whole time we were growing up."

"I know you did, and I'm sorry." Jenna took a deep breath. "And I'm sorry for everything I did to mess things up between us. You're my other half, Jess. I have to have you in my life."

"I'm sorry, too. Look, I get that it's hard for you to deal with me hearing spirit voices. It's not something I can turn off at will. I wish I could make you understand that they're not *evil* spirits. They're just people who are trying to get a message across to someone they love."

Jenna did the thing with her lips where Jessica knew she was battling her emotions, too. "I'll work on it," Jenna said. "I promise I will."

Jessica put down her coffee, leaned over and hugged her twin. "That's the very best I can ask for."

She drove home from Jenna's house, grateful to have her sister back and at least a move towards spending some time with her nieces.

That night, Sage brought dinner to the cottage. He said he wanted to spend the evening with the two most important people in his life, and invited Jay. Afterwards, when the conversation was finished, the food and wine was cleared away and Jay had driven off in his Prius—he didn't just ride a bicycle—Sage and Jessica resumed the conversation they had begun on the night they rescued Ethan Starkey.

"I want you to know why I built the Center," he said as they snuggled together under the comforter. "I've never told anyone before."

"I want to know. And I'm glad you want to tell me."

Jessica pressed against him, steeling herself for something

that she knew instinctively was going to be hard to hear. His arms tightened around her. "Some of this is pretty hazy, but other parts are like it just happened. I was four. My birth mother—Roxanne, and this guy—I don't know whether he was my father, I just think of him as 'asshole.' They were having a huge fight—pretty much a daily occurrence as I remember it. He was always beating her up. There was a difference this time, though. He started beating on my little brother, too. I tried to pull him off. So, he turned on me.

"Roxanne was screaming. She pulled me away from him and told me to take Jade and the baby to our room and stay there. All the screaming scared the shit out of me. But then, it was him screaming, not her." Sage faltered, then continued. "I wanted to protect her. I shut the little ones in the bedroom and snuck back to the kitchen. He was on the floor and she was straddling him. I remember her arm pumping up and down. Over and over and over. Blood everywhere. On her face, her clothes. The walls, the cabinets, a puddle on the floor. There was this gigantic knife in her hand. Well, it looked gigantic to my eyes."

No wonder he had been unable to speak for a year, Jessica thought, remembering what Jay told her. Wanting more than anything to erase the memory from his soul, she put her hand over his heart and sent him every bit of healing energy within her.

"I couldn't move," he said. "I was petrified. Then asshole stopped screaming, stopped moving. I must have made a sound. Roxanne turned around." A single tear leaked out of Sage's eye. It ran down and landed on Jessica's cheek, as if they were the same person.

"I'll never forget her eyes when she saw me. I thought she was about to pull that knife out of his chest and come after me next."

"What happened after that?" Jessica murmured when he fell silent again.

"All I can remember is, we were driving around and around for what seemed like hours. She must have cleaned the blood off herself. We stopped in some neighborhood I didn't recognize and she got out of the car. She took the baby with her. I couldn't see where she went. But when she came back, no baby. Then, she kept Jade with her and left me with Regina. They were friends—they'd met as teenage runaways. Regina told me all about it. They stayed in touch, but went in very different directions." He sighed. "I never knew what happened to Jade until last year when I confronted Roxanne in prison and made her tell me. She dumped him off at a mall and told him to find a cop. She'd left the baby at some random house where there were toys in the yard and hoped they would take care of her."

"I can't begin to imagine what you went through," said Jessica, suffering over the three little ones abandoned by their mother and for what Sage had been forced to witness.

He reached up to stroke her hair. "I was the lucky one, having Regina raise me. There are too many kids who go through much worse than what we did. I know I can't fix them all, but I intend to spend the rest of my life doing everything in my power to help as many of them as I can. I hope you'll want to be a part of it."

Jessica raised herself onto her elbow and laid her hand on his chest, drew his eyes to her. "I want to be a part of everything you do."

Sage rolled on his side to face her. His hand rested on her hip, drawing her to him. When she lifted her face to his, his lips tasted of the faintest hint of wine.

"You're all the proof I need," he murmured. His hands were in her hair, then tracing the contours of her face with his artist's touch, making her breaths come trembly and shallow.

She drew back just far enough to gaze into his incandescent blue eyes, which were shining in a way she had not seen before. "Proof of what?"

"That in spite of all the ugliness in the world, in spite of the evil, goodness exists. Kindness, sweetness, beauty exists. They're all in you."

Just then, a voice sounded in her head, speaking over the others.

"I like him, Mama, he's nice."

Me, too, baby. Me, too.

Love had found Jessica Mack and she was no longer afraid.

AFTERWORD

Dear Reader,

Thank you for reading *Proof of Life*. I hope you enjoyed it.
If you haven't yet read the "prequel," *What She Saw*, click here to share Jessica's journey from when she first wakes on a train, not knowing who she is or where she's going, to discovering why her memory has been wiped clean.

To stay updated with news about my books:
Join my mailing list: https://bit.ly/2CrifYw
Like me on Facebook: https://bit.ly/2RuR4pY
Follow me on Twitter: http://www.twitter.com/sheila_lowe
Goodreads: https://www.goodreads.com/SheilaLowe
My Amazon Author Page: https://www.amazon.com/author/sheilalowe

And if you have a moment, please consider leaving a short review of *Proof of Life* on its Amazon page. Tell other readers why you liked the book. This helps me because when Amazon sees readers enjoying a book, they boost it. Authors like that a lot. At least, this author does!
Finally, visit www.claudiaroseseries.com often, where you can read my blog and keep up with my various goings-on.
Thank you again for being one of my readers. I hope we'll be together again soon.
Happy reading!

HOW I BECAME INTERESTED IN THE AFTERLIFE

When I was seven, my mother started studying the Bible with a fundamentalist religion. They teach that *any* contact with the spirit world was demonic. This doesn't make a whole lot of sense to me now, as the Bible is filled with tales of spirit contact—people talk to angels all the time. Growing up, we were instructed that meditation was bad because if you emptied your mind, it would leave room for the demons to come in and take over. Having learned from such an early age to blindly obey what the organization said, I simply accepted what I was told and was afraid.

Fast-forwarding through a really difficult marriage to an elder in the church and, despite the religion, a divorce, I was raising three kids on my own, struggling to "keep the faith." My oldest child, Jennifer, had more than just the usual teenage "issues" and we had a love/hate relationship for many years as she struggled through numerous abusive relationships. She was in high school when she brought home a Ouija board. I freaked out, terrified that the demons were now in our house. Of course, nothing bad happened, but I insisted she get rid of it.

I count myself fortunate to have been kicked out of that religion on my 35th birthday, told by the elders that I was "clearly a danger to the congregation." They practice shunning, cutting off all contact, including family (now 90, my mother still does not allow any communication), so I had to find a new support system. Soon, one of my wonderful new friends took me for my first psychic reading. When I did not find myself demon-possessed afterwards, I was emboldened to learn how to read the tarot for myself. I was exploring a whole new world and I liked what I was learning.

Perhaps that "opening up" was to prepare me for the nightmare to come. On February 19, 2000, Jennifer, then 27, became the victim of a murder-suicide by her boyfriend, Tom Schnaible. That's when my exploration of the Afterlife began. I am positive that's what saved me.

Now that my mind was open, I was ready and grateful to receive the many signs Jen sent, letting me know that she was still very much alive. Her perfume would suddenly scent the air, lights would flicker. My phones rang, both landline and mobile, and when I answered, there was only static and a distant voice whose words I could not make out. I knew she was trying to get through to let me know she was okay.

There were many other manifestations, too—the car radio volume increased when no one touched it. The overhead light in the car going on by itself, etc., etc. On one occasion, I *saw* her walk past my kitchen door. On another, I heard her call me outside my ear. As a skeptic who is not quick to believe this sort of thing, I assure you, these events were not my imagination. I was not asleep. They were quite real. My sons experienced similar contacts from their sister, too.

At that time, I began meditating daily and reading every book I could find on life after death. My first favorite was *One Last Time* by John Edward, who picked me out of a crowd of a thousand people with very specific and astounding messages from Jen. Those who say he does research or reads your mind have no explanation for the things he told me that even I did not know until a week later. James Van Praagh's books were also helpful. A year after her death, Jen arranged for him to come to my house and tape a segment for his show.

Six weeks after Jennifer crossed over, as scheduled, I hosted a handwriting analysis conference—it was too late to cancel—and then started a year-long book tour to publicize my first book. At the end of the tour, when I stopped running and finally faced my daughter's death, I became very sick with mononucleosis and was pretty much toast for the next month. After my recovery I found myself unable to meditate, which was frustrating, as I'd felt I was making good progress in my spiritual journey. Somewhere along the way, I gave up on all of it. Not consciously, the spiritual stuff just drifted away as difficult life experiences continued.

It was not until 2016 that I began to have experiences that made me feel as if I was being guided back onto a spiritual path. I also learned about the Afterlife Research Education Institute, which has become an important affiliation for me. I've now attended two AREI symposiums in Scottsdale, where I met some of the people who are making important contributions to the field: Dr. Gary Schwartz, who has been performing scientific research into life after death at the University of Arizona, Tucson for many years. Suzanne Giesemann, a former naval officer who became a phenomenal evidential medium and teacher after her stepdaughter was killed by lightning. Scott Milligan, a young physical medium who makes mediumship training available to anyone who feels called. Sandra Champlain, whose *We Don't Die* YouTube interviews bring fascinating information and comfort to thousands. Dr. Craig Hogan, an author and researcher who leads AREI. And Sonia Rinaldi from Brazil, who made me one of her "Group of 30." To try and explain the scientific process Sonia has developed would take a lot more space than I have here. Suffice it to say, she has been receiving actual photographs of people from the other side, including Jennifer, which are posted on the internet. I could write an entire book about these experiences alone.

I've told you all this to provide a little background. What I really wanted to share is that last year, while writing *Proof of Life,* I was told by several different spiritual mediums that this book was being channeled by my daughter. I wish I could say that Jen just poured ideas and words into my head and the book fell out fully formed, but that would not be true. It was plenty of hard work. What is true, however, is that there were a number of times when I wrote a scene or a sentence and knew it did not come from me.

While I have thought about writing a book about Jennifer, I never contemplated writing about the spirit world. It just occurred to me one day that it was something I needed to do. And while I was cooking up a plot, the idea came to me to bring back Jessica Mack, the young woman with amnesia from *What She Saw.* And while that was coming together, I realized that Sage Boles from *Written Off* needed to be in the book. And my late boyfriend, whose middle name was Jay, decided he needed to be there, too—he just rode up on his bicycle in two different scenes and when I asked what he was doing there, he let me know, and it was perfect. Even after *Proof of Life* was "finished" and I was doing what I thought were final edits, I got what I believe to be an inspired thought that resolved a problem I'd been having with a scene.

I don't know how readers of my *Forensic Handwriting Mysteries* series are going to feel about my veering off course with *Proof of Life*, but I hope they will give it a try. There are some familiar characters in the book—Claudia Rose makes an appearance, as does Annabelle Giordano and Dr. Zebediah Gold.

Finally, many people seem to fear letting others know of their experiences with loved ones who have crossed to the other side of life. They think they'll be seen as "crazy." But me, having a big mouth, well, I mention it to everyone I can. And guess what? People tell me their stories and are happy to have someone to share them with. I've found it is extremely common to have contact with so-called deceased relatives or friends. If you think you've received a message in a dream or some other means, you are not crazy. Welcome those loved ones (including pets) in.

If you have an experience you would like to share with me, I would love to hear from you: sheila@sheilalowe.com.

Resources

If you are bereaved and looking for comfort, here are a few of the many available resources:

Victor and Wendy Zammit probably provide more resources on their website and their Friday newsletter than anyone else: http://www.victorzammit.com/ Wendy hosts numerous free sessions on Zoom covering a wide variety of spiritual topics.

The Afterlife Research Education Institute: https://dev.afterlifeinstitute.org/

Sheri Perl offers free training to record afterlife voices: http://www.sheriperl.com/evpguide

Suzanne Giesemann has published several books and hosts a radio show: https://www.suzannegiesemann.com/radioshow/

Sandra Champlain's YouTube interview show We Don't Die Radio: https://www.youtube.com/channel/UCjfFXqs2gw4q3OMKxF86bwg

I don't have personal experience with them, but this organization has a wonderful reputation: Helping Parents Heal: https://www.helpingparentsheal.org/

ABOUT THE AUTHOR

Like her fictional character Claudia Rose in the Amazon #1 Bestselling *Forensic Handwriting Mysteries* series, Sheila Lowe is a real-life forensic handwriting expert. Author of the acclaimed *The Complete Idiot's Guide to Handwriting Analysis*, *Handwriting of the Famous & Infamous*, and *Handwriting Analyzer* software, she is president of the American Handwriting Analysis Foundation, a nonprofit organization that promotes education in the area of handwriting, and on the board of directors of the Scientific Association of Forensic Examiners. Sheila holds a Master of Science in psychology, teaching and lecturing around the US, Canada, and the UK. Her latest nonfiction book is *Reading Between the Lines, Decoding Handwriting*. She lives in Ventura, California, with Lexie the Very Bad Cat. Despite sharing living space with a feline, however, Sheila does not write cozies. She describes her books as medium-boiled psychological suspense.

POISON PEN
Book 1: *A Forensic Handwriting Mystery*
(#1 Bestseller)

Sheila Lowe "wins readers over with her well-developed heroine and the wealth of fascinating detail" (*Booklist*) in this captivating mystery set in Hollywood, where forensic handwriting expert Claudia Rose knows that despite the words it forms, a pen will always write the truth.

Before her body is discovered floating in her Jacuzzi, publicist to the stars, Lindsey Alexander, had few friends, but plenty of lovers. To her ex-friend Claudia, she was a ruthless, backstabbing manipulator. But even Claudia is shocked by Lindsey's startling final note: *It was fun while it lasted.*

It would be easier on the police—and Claudia—to write off Lindsey's death as suicide, but Claudia's instincts push her to investigate further, and she quickly finds herself entangled in a far darker scenario than she had anticipated. Racing to identify the killer, Claudia soon has a price on her head. Unless she can read the handwriting on the wall, she will become the next victim.

"The well-paced plot develops from uneasy suspicions to tightly wound action."
—*Front Street*

https://amzn.to/2RMhn6f

WRITTEN IN BLOOD
Book 2: *A Forensic Handwriting Mystery*
(Top ten pick of Independent Booksellers and
#1 Bestseller)

Sheila Lowe's Poison Pen was hailed as a "fast-paced, crisp…novel that penetrates the world of celebrity." (*Armchair Interviews*) And Hollywood forensic handwriting expert Claudia Rose is about to prove once more that no matter what words it forms, a pen will always write the truth.

Claudia Rose's latest client is a dime-a-dozen type. The widow of a rich older man, Paige Sorensen is younger than—and hated by—her stepchildren. And they're dead set on proving that Paige forged their father's signature on his Will, which left his entire estate, including the Sorensen Academy, to her.

Intrigued by this real-life soap opera, Claudia soon breaks one of the cardinal rules of business: Never get personally involved. But Claudia has grown attached to a troubled Sorensen student, and when disaster strikes, she'll realize that reading between the lines can mean the difference between life and death.

"[Claudia's] sharper, tougher, and more tenacious than ever."
—*American Chronicle*

https://amzn.to/2E0c3ZD

DEAD WRITE
Book 3: *A Forensic Handwriting Mystery*

Sheila Lowe's mysteries "just keep getting better," (*American Chronicle*) thanks to feisty forensic handwriting expert Claudia Rose, who knows that when it comes to solving a murder, sometimes the pen can be mightier than the sword.

Claudia heads to the Big Apple at the behest of Grusha Olinetsky, the notorious founder of an elite dating service whose members are mysteriously dying. The assignment puts Claudia at odds with her boyfriend, LAPD detective Joel Jovanic, who suspects Grusha is trouble.

Drawn into the feckless lives of the rich and single, Claudia finds herself enmeshed in a twisted world of love and lies fueled by desperation. But desperate enough to kill? Clues in the suspects' handwriting might help Claudia save Grusha's already dubious reputation, before the names of more victims are scribbled into someone's little black book.

"Sheila Lowe is the Kathy Reichs of forensic handwriting—a rip-roaring read."
—Deborah Crombie, National Bestselling
Author of "Necessary as Blood"

https://amzn.to/2ShVuAM

LAST WRITES
Book 4: *A Forensic Handwriting Mystery*

Claudia's friend, Kelly, learns that she's an aunt when her estranged half-sister, Erin, shows up at her home in desperate need of help. Erin and her husband have been living quiet lives in an isolated compound as members of the 'Temple of Brighter Light.' But now her husband and young child have disappeared, leaving behind a cryptic note with a terrifying message.

Seizing an opportunity to use her special skills as a forensic handwriting expert, Claudia becomes one of the few outsiders ever to be invited inside the mysterious compound. She has only a few days to uncover the truth about Kelly's missing niece before the prophecy of a secret ancient parchment can be fulfilled, and an innocent child's life is written off for good.

"A fascinating view into the world of handwriting analysis… captivating."

—Robin Burcell, Author of "The Bone Chamber"

https://amzn.to/2SANIBs

INKSLINGERS BALL
Book 5: *A Forensic Handwriting Mystery*

A body left in a trash dumpster; a tattoo artist killed in a firebombing attack; a soccer mom, shot in the living room of her home; vicious thugs whose job is to protect a suspected criminal. Just another week on rotation for LAPD detective Joel Jovanic... until he uncovers a connection between the disturbing series of vicious crimes and Annabelle Giordano, who is in the temporary custody of his soulmate, Claudia Rose.

Annabelle is a troubled and traumatized teen who suffered the tragic loss of her mother and later witnessed the brutal murder of a beloved mentor. Neglected by a father who scarcely acknowledges her existence, it's little wonder the girl makes some disastrous life choices.

But she has one staunch ally in Claudia, a highly regarded forensic graphologist who digs into the darkest of human secrets through the study of handwriting. When Annabelle involves herself with a questionable tattoo artist, she re-opens a door to the grim side of life and goes down a path that could get her killed. A distraught Claudia will do anything to save her, even if it means jeopardizing her relationship with Jovanic.

" 'Inkslingers Ball' is the perfect novel for an afternoon by the pool. With vivid characters, smooth writing, and a twisty plot, Sheila Lowe has crafted a mystery that will keep you guessing to the very end."

—Boyd Morrison, International Bestselling Author

https://amzn.to/2MSdQ5L

OUTSIDE THE LINES
Book 6: *A Forensic Handwriting Mystery*

What should have been a routine afternoon on the witness stand for Forensic Handwriting Expert Claudia Rose turns into a shocking assault that leaves her bruised and bloodied. Following on the heels of a series of other traumatic events, the attack sends Claudia to the brink of a breakdown.

Her fiancé, L.A.P.D. Homicide Detective Joel Jovanic, learns of the attack while leading a homicide investigation into a mailbox bomb. An innocent housekeeper in the tony Venice neighborhood is dead and the homeowner is the CEO of a major pesticide-producing corporation that has been targeted in the past. When a notebook found in a geocache near the crime scene leads to the protest group People for Safe Food, Jovanic needs Claudia to identify the handwriting of a suspected eco-terrorist.

Though she may have recovered physically from the assault, weeks later Claudia's fears continue to plague her. Desperate to get away, she accepts an invitation to lecture in the UK, but her trip turns into a nightmare when she runs afoul of both the FBI and New Scotland Yard. Jovanic's homicide case has followed her to London where she finds herself unexpectedly allied with the chief suspect.

"Full of thrilling suspense, 'Outside the Lines' by Sheila Lowe is a fascinating story of modern greed, betrayal, and revenge. The stakes rise to an exciting ending that reveals a long-standing injustice—and a twist no reader will see coming. Enormously entertaining, this terrific mystery is one you'll want to linger with."
—Gayle Lynds, *New York Times* Bestselling Author of "The Assassins"

https://amzn.to/2TCde6F

WRITTEN OFF
Book 7: *A Forensic Handwriting Mystery*

When she travels to Maine to interview convicted serial killer Roxanne Becker, handwriting expert Claudia Rose is exposed to a shocking secret about a group of grad students dubbed "Maynard's Maniacs." Was Professor Maynard—herself brutally murdered—conducting unethical research that turned deadly? Swept up in the mystery of Madeleine's life and death, Claudia soon realizes that the professor left behind more questions than answers, and no shortage of suspects at Greystones University. After inspecting a newly produced, handwritten will for the local police chief, a blizzard forces Claudia to seek refuge in the professor's isolated house, where she becomes trapped with a killer.

"A simply riveting read from cover to cover, 'Written Off' by Sheila Lowe is an impressively entertaining and deftly crafted novel of suspense from a novelist with a complete mastery of the genre and a genuine flair for originality."
—*Midwest Book Review*

https://amzn.to/2SdP8Tb

WHAT SHE SAW
Book 1: *Beyond the Veil Mystery (A Prequel)*
(#1 Bestseller)

Imagine waking up on a train and having no recollection of how you got there. The more you think, the more you realize that you don't have any idea who you are…no name, no memories, no life.

This is the situation you're drawn into in "What She Saw."

A woman…no name, no memory, no life…only fear.

By chance or fate, she runs into someone who knows her and gives her a ride home.

At her home she finds two IDs, two sets of keys, one face… hers, but two separate lives!

https://amzn.to/2SuyLRB

READING BETWEEN THE LINES: HANDWRITING DECODED

If you have ever wondered what the squiggles and strokes in a line of ink say about personality, or if you are a handwriting professional who learned the "trait-stroke" method, "Reading Between the Lines, Decoding Handwriting," introduces you to a new way to look at handwriting and understand personality. The gestalt method versus trait-stroke is the difference between viewing an object under a microscope that offers a very small field of vision, and a telescope that shows the bigger picture. One is not better than the other, they simply appeal to different thinking styles. Trait-stroke analysts are more comfortable with an atomistic step-by-step approach, building up a picture of personality one stroke at a time. Gestaltists are more conceptual thinkers who look at space, form, and movement, learning to recognize the whole personality at a glance.

https://www.amazon.com/dp/B07H1KG1C2

ADVANCED STUDIES INHANDWRITING PSYCHOLOGY

The monographs in this volume are the result of a study and practice in the field of handwriting analysis that began in 1967 and continues through today. Their author, Sheila Lowe, earned a Masters in psychology, is a court-qualified forensic handwriting expert, and has taught handwriting examination in the extension programs at UC Riverside and UC Santa Barbara. Topics in this book include: Signs of childhood sexual abuse seen in the handwriting of adults - The addictive personality and its handwriting - The Lower Zone and the Subconscious - Motivations and handwriting - what makes you tick? - Finding personality traits in handwriting with the gestalt method – Abraham Maslow and the Pyramid of Needs - Serial Killers, the Face of Evil.

https://amzn.to/2SdccS2

PERSONALITY & ANXIETY DISORDERS:
How They May Be Reflected in Handwriting, And other important topics

The material in this volume is based on articles and a series of talks presented to members of the American Handwriting Analysis Foundation by the late Israeli psychologist/graphologist, Dr. Ze'ev Bar-Av. Sheila Lowe had co-presented papers with him at several handwriting analysis conferences, and when he asked her to help him with the lecture series, she accepted with pleasure. I provided most of the demonstrative handwriting samples and edited the material. After Dr. Bar-Av's untimely death, Sheila compiled and further edited this important material to preserve and make it available for handwriting professionals and others who are interested.

https://amzn.to/2wGPELO

THE COMPLETE IDIOT'S GUIDE TO HANDWRITING ANALYSIS
Second Edition

Space-Form-Movement: A basic course introducing the gestalt method of handwriting analysis. Using hundreds of famous people's handwritings, the CIG2HWA shows you how to understand the core personality of a writer without having to take dozens of measurements. Learn what spatial arrangement reveals about how you arrange your life and time, what writing style says about your ego, and what writing movement reveals about your energy and how you use it.

https://amzn.to/2DZFwCW

HANDWRITING OF THE FAMOUS & INFAMOUS
Second Edition

Handwriting communicates much more than what is committed to paper. A quick note, a carefully composed letter, an autograph or a scribble also reveals a great deal about the personality of the writer. What are the clues to look for in a person's writing and what do they reveal? What do they tell experts that the writer might prefer to keep hidden? This fascinating book is a collection of handwriting samples of some of the most influential and notorious people of the past and present.

https://amzn.to/2MVlgFd